DOMINOES

He stared at t[illegible]
He saw th[illegible]
two triggers[illegible]
move; the ha[illegible]
the right ham[illegible] the
left. He heard [illegible]nged roar
which seemed [illegible]ver – and then the
spray of shot ca[illegible] from both barrels . . . and he saw that, too. He felt the shot, as it plucked at his clothes; as it penetrated to the skin; as it tore at tiny nerve-ends at his chest, and his neck, and the lower half of his face. Then came the agony; everlasting agony . . . As the breast-bone slowly fractured . . . and the heart and the lungs took up the massive symphony of pain; One gigantic, slow motion orchestration of increasing pain.

And, after forever, as he felt himself being thrown backwards, the last thought to pass through Cooley's pulsating mind was that he was dead . . . and glad to be dead, if only to end the pain.

Also by John Wainwright
in Magnum Books

LANDSCAPE WITH VIOLENCE
THE DAY OF THE PEPPERCORN KILL

JOHN WAINWRIGHT

Dominoes

MAGNUM BOOKS
Methuen Paperbacks Ltd

A Magnum Book

DOMINOES
ISBN 0 417 06100 5

First published in Great Britain 1980
by Macmillan London Ltd
Magnum edition published 1981

Magnum Books are published
by Methuen Paperbacks Ltd
11 New Fetter Lane, London EC4P 4EE

Made and printed in Great Britain by
Richard Clay (The Chaucer Press) Ltd,
Bungay, Suffolk

It is a modest creed, and yet
Pleasant if one considers it,
To own that death itself must be
Like all the rest, a mockery.

The Sensitive Plant
Percy Bysshe Shelley

ONE

I can fix the day and the date. I can even fix the time to within a few minutes. I can certainly fix the place.

A bleak, albeit gentle, slope of the Nidd Valley. The after-Christmas snows of last winter had arrived two days before . . . two days or thereabouts. The hills funnelled the wind, and the wind drove the flakes on near-horizontal waves as they fell from a solid grey sky. The white had already topped the windward side of dry-stone walls, and each exposed stretch of wall had its own plume which threatened to bridge the road with one more drift. Underfoot, the boards were treacherous with wet clay and, despite the makeshift tarpaulin weather-break, the flakes settled on the lid of the coffin and, in some strange way, seemed to make the grave even more final.

In front of me – up the cemetery slope and alongside the road – the severe, puritanical bulk of the chapel wore a top-knot of snow and white bibs on the sills of its windows. The face of the rough stonework was webbed in white where the flakes had found footholds in tiny crevices.

A white world. A dead world; the snow muffled the grinding and gear-changing of ploughs and gritters hauling themselves up the slope of some distant road. A cold world. A dead world. We, the tiny group of mourners, shivered in the biting weather, but none was as cold as my beloved Hannah.

'. . . In the midst of life we are in death: of whom may we seek for succour, but of thee, O Lord, who for our sins art justly displeased? . . .'

The minister was a young man; too young – or so it seemed – to carry the weight of such solemnity. The wind blew his wispy, blond hair in all directions; the flakes seemed to touch it with a scattering of twinkling sequins. The flimsy pages of the open Prayer Book fluttered as he held one hand flat against their surface.

'. . . Yet, O Lord God most holy, O Lord most mighty, O holy and most merciful Saviour, deliver us not into the bitter pains of eternal death . . .'

The undertaker's men took the strain. The gravediggers stooped, reached from behind the knot of mourners and pulled the supporting baulks from beneath the coffin. Slowly the undertaker's men allowed the canvas strips to run through their fingers and the coffin began the last few feet of its journey.

'. . . Thou knowest, Lord, the secrets of our hearts; shut not thy merciful ears to our prayers; but spare us, Lord most holy, O God most mighty, O holy and most merciful Saviour . . .'

The undertaker removed one of his gloves. He bent, picked up a handful of heavy earth and crumbled it in his fingers.

'. . . Forasmuch as it has pleased Almighty God of his great mercy to take unto himself the soul of our dear sister here departed, we therefore commit her body to the ground . . .'

The undertaker tossed some of the crumbled earth into the grave. It rattled gently on the coffin lid.

'. . . earth to earth, ashes to ashes . . .'

The undertaker moved his arm and threw the remaining earth on to the lid of the coffin. It was clayish soil. It scattered only slightly. One piece, larger than the rest, spread and stained the wood.

'. . . dust to dust . . .'

And that was when.

That was the *exact* moment – at a few minutes past half past two on Wednesday, February 1st – when I decided that I must kill Gerald Morley.

*

I spent that night with Hannah's parents. We talked into the small hours; talked, remembered and wept a little.

They were 'dales folk', which meant their emotion was not for public display. In the chapel they had stood silent and stone-faced throughout the short service. At the grave they had watched the coffin dry-eyed, unblinking, unmoving and apparently impervious to the weather. But at their home they allowed their feelings to surface a little more.

Harry was (still is) a local builder. Nothing big – his total work-force, including himself and an apprentice, numbered a mere half-dozen – but, as with many such firms, he refused to cut corners and his work carried its own impeccable 'hallmark'. He was not (to use his own expression) a 'Big-hammer Builder'.

He was a tall man and gaunt to the point of emaciation. His head was skull-like; the run of the jawbone was plainly visible; his sunken eyes were accentuated by hollows at each side of his temple; he was bald, except for a few strands of grey around the ears. The skeletal impression extended to his hands; long-fingered, knuckle-boned and almost fleshless. And yet, at around sixty years old, he was fitter than most men half his age. It was a teak-hard, greyhound fitness; a fitness only acquired by years of hard work in all weathers.

By contrast his wife Sarah carried the typical middle-aged plumpness of most country women. She was not obese. Indeed, she was not even 'fat' in the accepted sense of that word, and she was remarkably agile. Always she reminded me of the women of Rubens' school; the spirits of the sea in his *The Reception of Marie de' Medici at Marseilles*, the two sisters in his *The Rape of the Daughters of Leucippus*, the nymph in Jordaens' *Pan and Syrinx*. There was a smooth rotundity about her which came very near to innocent sexuality. I had often watched this woman – this middle-aged but still basically beautiful woman – when Hannah and I had visited, and always the perfect balance of vivacity and tranquillity had fascinated me.

(In retrospect, had Hannah been more like her mother she might still have been alive.)

But as that awful Wednesday drew to its close – after we'd toyed with food and were sitting around the blazing fire – I realised that some light within Sarah Hinchcliffe had been extinguished and would never shine again.

I recall there was a silence during which she twisted a handkerchief between her fingers – occasionally touching her eyes with it – and then, very suddenly and almost in a whisper, she said, 'Tony. Were you a good husband?'

'Sarah!' rebuked Harry gently.

I ignored his rebuke and tried to answer her as honestly as I was able.

'I don't know. I don't think any man knows.' I spoke slowly and cautiously. 'I've never been unfaithful to her . . . but it's arguable that that's not too important. I loved her. But what does *that* mean? There are so many kinds of love. So many kinds of married love. Did I give her the right kind? The kind she needed? That's what you're asking, Sarah . . . and I don't know. Only she could have answered that question.'

'It wasn't a fair question,' muttered Harry.

'Yes, it was.' I glanced at Sarah and tried to send her a quick smile of comfort. 'In these circumstances – and from her mother – it wasn't an unfair question.'

'Y'see . . .' Sarah hesitated, then stammered, 'I *still* can't understand. To – to do that. To take her own life.'

'I know.' I nodded.

'There has to be a reason.'

I remained silent.

Sarah breathed, 'She wasn't a wicked girl.'

'Lass . . . she wasn't a *girl*,' said Harry gently. 'She was thirty-five. A grown woman. A married woman.'

'She was *my* girl,' said Sarah and her stubbornness was born of heartbreak.

'Look, Sarah lass.' Harry tried to steady their tottering world. His voice held firmness and understanding in exactly the right proportions. 'I've lost a daughter, too. Tony's lost a wife. Rather than *her* . . .' He moved his narrow shoulders expressively. He sighed, then continued, 'We don't know why she did it. We'll never know. It doesn't help, but it has to be accepted. By everybody. Especially by us three.' He reached out and thin fingers closed over a chubby hand. He murmured, 'Hold on, lass. Hold on and don't blame people. Don't blame Tony.'

Sarah tried to speak, failed, then wept.

It was not an easy night. Such nights never are. Beyond the closed window the gale gradually blew itself out, by daylight the drifts would still be there, but would not be impassable when the time arrived for me to leave and return to The Ridings – the ploughs and gritters would have opened the roads.

Meanwhile . . .

It had been one of those mentally brittle days. Tiring almost beyond belief. The mind, the mouth, even the emotions, had all been gyved; every word, every expression, every thought. Over the years Harry had come to accept me as a satisfactory son-in-law. Not, perhaps, the man *he* might have chosen for the husband of his only child; not the deliberate, down-to-earth 'dalesman' he might have had in mind. But if not that . . . satisfactory.

In fairness, I'd met him half-way. On the surface I'd accepted his built-in bigotries as carefully thought-out conclusions. I had rarely argued and, when I had, I'd always refrained from pressing my arguments home. I'd allowed him to 'win' . . . for the sake of Hannah.

Hannah For fifteen years of my life she had *been* my

life. Since we'd first met at university. Had it not been Hannah, I doubt if it would have been any other woman. We received our B.A. degrees on the same day; her main interest was in English literature, mine was in art . . . not as a painter or a sculptor (although I did a little of each), but as an 'appreciator' and a person anxious to pass perception to those eager to receive. Within the year we were man and wife.

For a few years things had been difficult. Bed-sitters do little for the less gregarious and for months at a time we spent evenings and most weekends within sight and sound of each other. Nor had the money been plentiful; a few temporary teaching posts, some private tuition, an occasional job in some gallery or some library; rarely did we both have a job at the same time.

Then, like a gift from the gods (or so it seemed), had come the dual appointment at The Ridings. Hannah as English Lit. mistress, I as art master. Neither of us had been naive enough to think that The Ridings was in the top rank of British private schools; probably not even in the second rank. But compared to what we'd been used to!

The two-bedroomed, self-contained flat on the third floor had clinched everything. Our salaries might have been higher, but we mustn't forget the flat. Our extra duties, extra responsibilities, tended to be staggering, but we must remember the flat.

And, to be fair, it *was* a beautiful little flat. Over the years we furnished it, decorated it and gradually came to look upon it as 'ours'; came to forget that it was part of work which, equally gradually, sapped Hannah's resilience. Its elevation on the third floor gave it a glorious view from every window. We grew to know the Wolds in every weather and all seasons and the Wolds, no less than the Dales, have a splendour beyond description.

Those days – those happy, then those gradually less-happy

days – are what I remembered in the darkness of that bedroom.

And the coffin being lowered into the grave.

And the note she'd left me, propped against the wedding photograph, on the bureau shelf. *My* note, meant for me and, so far, read by nobody else.

Those are the things I remembered throughout that night.

Other than the slight fracas with the stupid horse, the journey back to The Ridings was uneventful. Having left the village and reached the A-class roads my only problem was (as always) with the mud-coloured spray thrown up by heavy vehicles. Lazy flakes of snow still dappled the vision but, without the wind and in temperature a few degrees above freezing, they darkened into slush the moment they touched roads or pavements.

Nevertheless, I drove at a very moderate speed and it was past noon when I turned at Ripon Square and pointed the car east towards the A1 north-south division of the county. Thirsk was its usual cluttered self and, in a cautious second gear, Sutton Bank gave no problems.

I was on the downhill run towards Helmsley when the idiot woman rode her horse directly into my path. I braked hard. The horse whinnied and reared, twisted, then fell sideways into the snow bank. The woman was thrown and ended in an undignified heap with her left foot still in the stirrup. By the time I reached them they were both on their feet unhurt; the horse a little wild-eyed and trembling, the woman dusting snow from her jodhpurs and, obviously, in a raging temper.

'You maniac!' She almost screamed the words. She stooped, retrieved her hat, then grabbed for the reins. 'You blasted lunatic! Don't you know the basic rules of the road? That bloody motor cars give way to a horse and rider?'

Controlling my own indignation, I said, 'Are you hurt?'

'No. But that's no thanks to . . .'

'The wonder is you didn't break your silly neck,' I snapped. 'And if you do – *when* you do – don't blame anybody but yourself.'

She was holding the horse and still calf-deep in snow, otherwise I'm sure she would have rushed at me. She looked a spoiled, ill-tempered and arrogant young woman; I'd seen so many of her kind; I could recognise the type on sight. Leaving her speechless I spun on my heel, returned to the car and drove away. In the rearview mirror I saw her standing straddle-legged in the road, still holding the reins and waving a fist at the rear bumper.

I turned right on to the B1257, and the driving became less easy. Only the worst drifts had been cleared, and then only wide enough for single-line traffic. My left turn into the web of unclassified roads (little more than macadamised cart-tracks), which would eventually lead me to The Ridings, brought even worse conditions but eventually a slithering, skidding journey ended at the gates of the school.

The Fall of the First Domino

Billy Edwards climbed hurriedly from the horse-box as he heard the clip-clop of the mare's shoes on the concrete of the yard. They were slightly uneven; the rhythm wasn't there; it was the first sign that something was wrong. Still carrying the brush with which he'd been scrubbing out the horse-box he hurried to where the woman was swinging herself from the saddle.

The woman was wet and dishevelled. Her volatile temper was obviously on hair-trigger edge as she threw the reins at Billy.

Billy caught the reins and said, 'Has there been . . . ?'

'A blasted motorist,' snapped the woman. 'She reared and

threw me. Get her rubbed down and stabled. I'll be back when I've had a bath.'

'Yes, miss.'

Billy dropped the wet brush on to the concrete and stroked the velvety muzzle of the mare as the woman strode away towards the house.

Less than thirty minutes later the woman was back in the stable yard. She looked what she was: a superbly healthy specimen of female independence; an as yet untamed wildcat who might one day meet her master and thereafter become a splendid breeding animal and the mother of heroes and heroines not yet born. She wore expensive, skin-tight jeans and a polo jersey which allowed her unrestrained breasts to sway and the nipples to prink as she strode towards the stall with the name reading 'Lady' above the door.

'How is she?' she asked curtly.

'She's hurt, miss.' Billy Edwards straightened from where he'd been crouched alongside the mare. 'Left hind, I think.'

'Nonsense. I rode her back easily enough.'

'That's no proof, miss.' Billy jutted his chin a little. 'When she walks. When she dips her head. She favours her left side. It's the left hind . . . I'm sure it is.'

'Here. Let *me* see.'

The woman elbowed past Billy and squatted alongside the mare.

Billy watched and in his teenage mind wished to hell she'd wear more underclothes. The jersey. The slacks. Christ, she might as well be mother-naked for what good *they* were. He tried to concentrate his mind upon the woman's hands as they worked their way up and down the mare's left hind leg. He tried but only partly succeeded and, because the prurience in his loins was something he couldn't control, his outrage against the woman mounted.

She ended her inspection and as she straightened her breasts brushed against his thigh.

She said, 'There's nothing wrong with the leg.'

'Yes, miss.' Billy's voice was low and breathless.

'What?' The woman stared.

'She's hurt,' insisted Billy.

'Don't be such a fool.'

'She needs a vet . . . something.'

'Edwards.' Her lip curled. 'Are you suggesting you know more about horses than I do?'

'About *that* horse,' blurted Billy. 'About Lady.'

'Don't be so damn ridiculous.'

She turned to leave. As she reached the door of the stall the youth exploded; something inside him seemed to burst; his voice was high and his eyes shining with held-back tears of frustration.

He shouted, 'You – you bloody *cow*!'

'What?' She stopped in mid-stride, turned slowly and gazed at the excited teenager with cold, contemptuous loathing. 'What was that you said?' she whispered.

'She's – she's lame.' Billy Edwards pointed at the mare's hind leg. 'She's hurt. I don't care . . .'

'What did you call me?'

'Miss . . .' The outrage had spent itself in that sudden rush. All that remained was fear and pleading. 'Miss, she's hurt. Lady's hurt. I know. If you'd seen her . . .'

'What did you call me?'

'I'm – I'm sorry, miss.' He lowered his chin on to his chest and stared at the straw-strewn floor. 'I – I didn't mean it.'

'Yes . . . I think you meant it.'

'Miss.' He raised his eyes. 'It's Lady. You – you shouldn't have ridden her. Really, you shouldn't. That leg. If you'd . . .'

'Shut up!' She took a backward step into the yard, turned her head and called, 'Preston. Come here a minute.'

A solidly built, middle-aged man joined her at the stall's entrance. He looked a hard man; a hard man to please, a hard man to cross; a man without humour. He wore riding-breeches, a heavy tweed jacket, a stained, plum-coloured waistcoat and a cloth cap. He waited.

The woman flipped a derisive finger in the direction of the quelled teenager and snapped, 'Get rid of him.'

'Eh?' Preston's eyebrows moved fractionally.

'That foul-mouthed little guttersnipe. I want him out of here within the hour. Finished! And if he sets foot on this farm again run him off.'

She elbowed her way past Preston, and stormed towards the house.

Jack Warton was a farmer of the old school. In the parlance of those who know little about husbandry, he might have been described as 'a gentleman farmer' . . . except, of course, that that breed doesn't exist, and never has existed, in the Broad Acre County. In the old days (when his father had owned the farm) he'd soiled his hands. He'd worked until his muscles ached. In his early years he'd followed plough-horses until he was ready to drop from fatigue. Warton knew *exactly* what was meant by the word 'graft'.

He also knew what was meant by the word 'brass'.

Brass. Money. Wealth. The only real base for power; forget all that pap about brotherhood-of-man – only them who had damn-all preached *that* garbage – what you wanted you paid for and, having paid for it, you bloody-well *owned* it. Beasts, land, machinery, crops . . . *and* employees. Each one you paid for a slice of his life; you *owned* that slice; and, because you owned it, you could use it as you damn-well pleased, and if *he* didn't like the arrangement he could pack his bags and for all you cared beg for bread.

A hard man?

Warton would have laughed in your face had you even suggested it. He just wasn't there to be kidded, that's all. He'd have felled you had *you* suggested that he'd killed his wife; that he'd exercised the same right of 'ownership' over *her* and to a degree which had sent her to an early grave. Had you said that to him – had you so much as hinted – he'd have driven you into the ground . . . left-hand thread!

But that wouldn't have made it any less than the truth.

Jack Warton was a man to whom women – any woman and all women – were just fractionally more important than cattle. They could understand what you said. They hadn't to be prodded with a stick. If necessary they could answer back. After that . . . nothing. At times, they were certainly as daft as cattle; as obstinate and as fickle as anything ever to waddle from a byre. But if you kept 'em in their place – y'know, none of this 'equality' crap. Well, you had to have kids, didn't you? You had to have *somebody* to leave it to when they planted you.

Such was the hauteur of Jack Warton.

He stretched out in the parlour of the farmhouse in a green-velvet-covered wing-chair whose arms, wings and back were almost as wide as its seat. A massive chair with its twin facing him across the thick-piled carpet and the immense sofa which made up the 'set' on his right. He drank near-neat whisky from a tumbler and smoked a Churchillian cigar, and he waited for his elder daughter to return home from some Young Farmers' function she'd been attending.

He heard the front door open and close, and bawled, '*Angela!* In here.'

The woman entered. She carried her folded mac over her right arm. Her handbag and headscarf in her left hand. Her eyes shone and she looked a little flushed.

'What was it tonight?' asked Warton.

'A dance. One of the . . .'

'Till *this* time?' Warton glanced at the grandfather clock.

'For God's sake. You're not going to . . .'

'Just so you know, young lady.' Warton inhaled cigar smoke. 'No mid-week dance at that place goes on past midnight . . . and it doesn't take anybody two and a half hours to drive you from *that* bloody place.'

'Look, I'm not going to . . .'

'Just as you're told. Just as *I* tell you whilever you're under this roof.' Warton didn't raise his voice; his authority was absolute . . . he didn't require to raise his voice. He sipped the whisky, inhaled enough to expand his barrel chest a little, then tapped the lapel of his jacket, gently, with the fingers holding the cigar. The ash spilled down his waistcoat as he said, 'I'm just reminding you of summat, girl. Get yourself in the club . . . and you'll get yourself out of it. As long as *that's* understood.'

'Of all the . . .'

'Sit down.' He jerked his head, once, in the direction of the great sofa.

She hesitated. Her own temper was building up but never once in her life had she dared to oppose this pile-driving father of hers.

Warton looked mildly surprised at her hesitation and repeated, 'Sit down, girl.'

She perched herself on the edge of the sofa.

'Now . . .' Warton tasted the whisky. 'You had Lady out today.'

'Yes.' She nodded.

'That was bloody stupid. This weather. You don't ride the best point-to-pointer in the district . . . not the way *you* ride.'

'It was good for her.'

'Oh, aye?'

'She needed the exercise.'

'She also needed a bloody vet.'

'What?'

'This evening. While you were flashing your arse at all the young rams around here. The vet . . . and vets cost money. She'd pulled a tendon on her left hind.'

'Oh!' She swallowed. 'I didn't know. Some crazy motorist . . .'

'Preston told me all about the motorist.'

'In that case . . .'

'The motorist won't pay the bill.'

'Look, you can't blame me . . .'

'The motorist wasn't driving his car in the stable yard.'

She remained silent. Again she moistened her lips.

Warton inhaled cigar smoke, exhaled it, then said, 'You didn't know about the left hind?'

'No. I – er . . .'

'You *should* have known.'

'I'm not a . . .'

'Young Billy told you.'

'Edwards? That little snotnose.'

'Aye.' Warton nodded, sipped whisky, then said, 'That little snotnose. He knows more about horses than you'll ever know. All you know is how to ride the bloody things.'

'You . . .' Her voice trembled slightly. 'You know what he called me?'

'Young Billy?' A slow grin touched Warton's lips.

'He called me a cow. That's what he called me . . . a bloody cow.'

'He must know you.' Again the cigar travelled to and from the mouth. 'Aye. Preston told me that, too. About what Billy called you. All about everything.' He shifted in the huge wing-chair until he was facing directly at her. His voice didn't alter, his expression didn't change, as he said, 'That's why I waited up. To ask you who the hell you think you are? And when the hell did *you* get authority to hire and fire.'

'I'm your daughter.'

'That's what you are, lass,' he agreed.

'That gives me the right . . .'

'None.' It was a single word, quietly spoken, but with

absolute finality. 'You live here. I give you an allowance. You're allowed to bugger about enjoying yourself in your own way. But don't talk about rights. When *you* pay 'em, *you* can sack 'em, but not until.'

'You – you mean you've taken Edwards back.'

'He's never left. Preston had more sense till he'd seen me.'

'In that case . . .' She closed her mouth.

'Aye?' He seemed mildly interested.

'Every time I see him. Every time *he* sees *me*.'

'Aye?' There was a gentle taunting quality about the repeated question.

She took a deep breath, then said, 'If he doesn't go, I *do*.'

He nodded, touched his lips with the whisky, then said, 'Y'know, I thought it might end like this. I told Preston.'

She remained silent.

Warton continued, 'Preston thought it mightn't be a bad idea. You not pushing your tits at the men all day. Might give 'em summat else to think about.'

It was the cigar's turn to travel to and from Warton's mouth.

'What about Edwards?' she asked harshly.

'He stays.'

'In that case, I go.'

'Aye.' It was off-handed, unemotional agreement. 'You've a brother. You've a sister. You'll find a bed somewhere.' There was a nicely timed double-entendre pause, then his lip curled and he added, '*Somewhere*.'

She stood up from the sofa. Walked stiff-legged and straight-backed to the door. At the door she turned.

She said, 'I mean it.'

'Lass.' He sipped at the whisky. 'What *you* mean matters sod-all round here. *I* mean it . . . that's what counts.'

TWO

I climbed from the car at the shallow steps leading to the main entrance. I stood there, gazing up at the snow-etched frontage and, not for the first time, wondered what sort of a mind could design such a monstrosity. A Victorian mind, obviously. A mind cluttered by the hypocrisies of that particular era. A mind to which every addition was an improvement; every piece of unnecessary scrollwork a transfiguration; every architectural gewgaw an enrichment. There was no balance. There was no 'line'. There was only tasteless opulence in brick and stone.

The Ridings had originated as the 'country house' of one of the Victorian railway barons. One of the 'super spivs' to jump on to the tail-gate of the Industrial Revolution. He probably liked the place; the taste of that class during that particular period of English history seems to be grounded in vulgar ostentation. Whatever – and like so many of his kind – he went broke. From what little background one can gather about such places, The Ridings was thereafter used and misused over the years. For some time it was an isolation hospital . . . when such institutions were in vogue. Talk (rightly or wrongly) suggests that the Home Office almost took it over as a staging post between prison and freedom for convicted men almost at the end of their term. But, reading between the lines, for much of its life it remained empty until Morley bought it at a knock-down price.

Morley – Gerald Morley . . . I must tell you about Morley.

The holder of a Redbrick University B.A., he was wise enough to know that his degree (rather like mine) was worth little more than the scroll upon which it was printed. This was the period (you will remember, no doubt) when, for no logical reason, 'The Sciences' surged ahead of 'The Arts' in popularity; the discipline of a university degree – *any* university degree – was ignored and only the degree itself mattered. The teaching profession – that one-time bottomless barrel into which all unwanted arts and science graduates were dumped – was suddenly only interested in the latter; B.A. men and women drew unemployment benefit, while B.Sc. people were almost offered a choice of posts.

Morley was more fortunate than most. A legacy – a considerable legacy – from the estate of some uncle solved his problem. He decided to launch a private school 'for girls and young ladies' – those words are still on the brochure and syllabus – and, having acquired a wife with like ideas, he found The Ridings and set up in business.

God knows how many such schools there are, even today. They cater for a demand; the demand of parents anxious to relinquish as much parental responsibility as possible. They make a mockery of genuine public schools. Their discipline compares with that of any Borstal institution; discipline which is, supposedly, 'character forming', but which in fact is little short of subtle cruelty. Their educational standard is deplorable; throughout my whole period at The Ridings I never knew one pupil who might, by any stretch of the imagination, have earned entrance to university. In the main they are an expensive pound, wherein children might be held in custody during their formative years.

Morley (*and* Mrs Morley) showed wisdom and good self-assessment.

He sought out and joined every official body willing to accept him; he was a 'licentiate' of this, a 'fellow' of that, an 'associate' of the other; by the time he'd finished 'B.A.' headed a list of letters which stretched half-way across the official notepaper. It looked very impressive and it helped bring in the pupils.

His wife, too. She was a qualified nurse when they married. By the time she took upon herself the matronship of The Ridings her 'paper qualifications' were such as to make her second only to Florence Nightingale.

But Morley's genius – his real genius – was in his understanding of human nature and, particularly, the nature of the parents for which The Ridings catered. I recall one year at the end of the minor lunacies of the annual Fathers' Day when the visiting parents had left and the girls were all in their dormitories. Morley had, perhaps, imbibed more than usual, and the liquor had loosened his tongue a little. We were alone in the main hall amid the clutter of the remains of the running buffet.

He smiled expansively and said, 'Hemingway, old man, whilever people like that walk the earth, people like you and I need never starve. The *nouveau riche*. The good schools are barred to them, but they don't realise it. Therefore, they sniff out the more *expensive* schools. The two words "expensive" and "excellent" – as far as *they're* concerned the two words are interchangeable. The best, you see, costs the earth. Ergo, if it costs the earth it *must* be the best. Hence the fees. Outrageous? Of course, Hemingway, I'd be a liar if I denied it. But if we lowered the fees we'd lose the pupils. Some other equally grotty educational establishment would become so much the richer.

'We provide a service, Hemingway. A service to the parents. We provide a balm to what little conscience they possess. They make out their cheques – money they don't miss anyway – and in return we give them the right in later life to round on their offsprings and remind them of the *expensive* education they provided. This lot upstairs, asleep in their uncomfortable little cots. They, too, will talk of their 'schooldays' with mock nostalgia. Because they don't know better. They'll forget that the only thing we *really* did was loosen their bowels when they were constipated, give them an aspirin when they had headache and explain the mysteries of the menstrual cycle, that plus the dates of a few unimportant battles and the utterly irrelevant fact that, for some peculiar reason, Southampton enjoys more high tides than anywhere else in the United Kingdom.

'What they'll remember is that we – the male staff – were their first knights in shining armour. And that's *all* they'll remember. Education? They don't *need* education. They have rich parents. In time they, too, will be rich parents. Our duty is to perpetuate the breed, old boy . . . perpetuate the breed and make damn sure all that money isn't wasted.'

I returned to the car, took my suitcase from the rear seat, then mounted the steps, pushed open the glass-fronted door and entered the tiled-floored entrance hall. From one of the doors, set in the gloom of the mahogany surround, a maid appeared.

She said, 'Oh, good afternoon, Mr Hemingway.'

'Muriel,' I nodded.

'Shall I take your case up to your room, sir?'

'Please.' I handed over the case. 'I'll garage the car. Leave the case on the bed. I'll be up later.'

'Yes, sir.'

As I left the row of garages at the rear of the school I met Johnny. It was nice. Comforting, in a strange sort of way. He was the science master – known naturally enough as 'Stinks' by the pupils. He was a few years younger than I, nevertheless we'd each recognised a fellow-believer (or, if you like, *dis*believer) within days of his arrival just over a year ago.

We fell into step and, as he pushed his ill-fitting pebble-lensed spectacles back into place, he said, 'Rough?'

It was a gently asked question; a single-word question asked in the tone of a man who knows what it's like to be hurt.

'Rough,' I agreed shortly.

'You were apprehensive about her parents.'

'Her father took it okay.'

'And her mother?'

'I don't know. I think she hates me.'

'Oh, come on, Tony.' He pushed his spectacles back into position again. It was almost a reflex action. 'Why should she hate *you*?'

'My fault.' I moved my shoulders.

'Oh, come *on*!'

'She's Hannah's mother.' I remember I got the tense wrong. It should have been 'She *was* Hannah's mother'. The realisation hit me like a blow in the stomach. We turned a corner of the building and I said, 'Sarah – her mother . . . she has a strong man for a husband. A successful man. She'd be less than human if she didn't make the comparison.'

'Strong?' We stopped at a side entrance and Johnny held the door open for me.

As I stepped inside I said, 'Stronger than me.'

'That's so much balls, Tony.' He allowed the door to close upon its own spring. Once more he pushed his spectacles back to the bridge of his nose. 'So much balls, and you know it.'

I tried to smile my appreciation of his friendship, but the effort was too great.

He said, 'I'll have to leave you. I have a class.'

'That's okay.'

'Keep your fingers crossed, mate, with any luck we might blow up this whole bloody school.'

He hurried ahead and I followed at a slower pace. I climbed the stairs to the first floor to where some of the classrooms were situated. I walked along the corridor and from one room I heard the unmistakable voice of Miss Lowther.

'. . . the doctrine which is known as "The Real Presence".

It relates to the Eucharist. To Holy Communion. It was first used in the eleventh century, in the great controversy between Berengarious and Lanfranc. Basically, what it means is . . .'

I walked on out of earshot and thought, 'It means faith, Miss Lowther. Faith in something I can't accept. I can accept beauty. I can accept the concept of abstract beauty. But I can't accept the concept of an abstract God. I wish I could . . . it might help.'

Can an agnostic believe in blasphemy? I was no philosopher; I was unable to carry an answer to that question to its logical conclusion. Nevertheless, it seemed somehow blasphemous that a woman with a voice like Miss Lowther – a woman with a harsh, penetrating, neigh-like voice – should be engaged to guide young minds along the intricacies of religious education. Occasionally I'd heard her holding forth in the staff room; being teased, perhaps, and hammering home some basic theological argument. The phrase 'militant humility' sprang to mind whenever I heard Miss Lowther voicing her creed. Nevertheless, she was a good woman; to her credit she lived what she taught. Assuming there is such a thing as a soul hers was a fine soul, imprisoned in a body incapable of doing it justice.

I climbed the stairs to the flat on the third floor.

Souls and bodies. I sat there on the edge of the chair, before the quietly hissing gas fire and, for the first time in my life, almost believed. Possibly it was the flat; a continuum of memories of what the flat had come to mean. Equally, it may have been some convoluted form of delayed shock; the mind's first acceptance of the truth. For whatever reason, I suddenly felt incomplete; incomplete to the point of deformity. Something was missing. Something more than Hannah; Hannah . . . plus. A soul, perhaps? Part of *my* soul? Yes, at that moment I was even prepared to accept *that*.

Because Hannah had gone. Again I think that was the first time I faced the truth. Gone! Not 'gone away'. Not 'missing'. Not merely 'no longer there' but no longer *anywhere*. Hannah – my beloved Hannah – had ceased to exist. This awful thing was no simple parting. It wasn't even a prolonged separation. Not even a divorce. In any other circumstances it might have been possible – however remote the possibility – that I would, at least, *see* her again.

But now . . .

I began to tremble. It was as if I had contracted some tropical disease; malaria, perhaps. Some form of shivering fit. I tried, but I couldn't control it; I clasped my fingers together, then held my clasped hands tight between the lower part of my thighs, but it did no good. The trembling continued. I seemed to lose body-heat; the fire no longer gave any warmth.

No tears came. (There is, it would seem, a depth of grief beyond the reach of conventional tears.) I simply sat there on the edge of the chair, holding myself as tightly as my muscles would allow . . . and trembled. Unable to control myself. Unable even to think.

It lasted perhaps half an hour. Perhaps a little longer.

Eventually – and gradually – the trembling eased enough for me to reach into my pockets and light a cigarette. But it was a poor attempt at smoking; the cigarette suffered because of the twitching of my fingers and it became stained from the perspiration which dripped from my upper lip. I squashed what was left of the cigarette into an ashtray, took a few deep, lung-stretching breaths of air, then pushed myself upright. I walked to the window; I moved unsteadily, like a person leaving bed after a long energy-sapping illness. I held on to the side of the window in a posture of high-armed crucifixion, and stared out beyond the grounds of the school and to where the landscape rose to faraway ridges before it dipped to the unseen coast.

A wild and white landscape. *My* landscape. Yorkshire; where men were supposed to be hard-headed and practical; where dourness and lack of emotion prevailed; where only women – and only weak women – wept.

So be it . . . I wept.

The moistened eyes at the grave had been little more than a required token. The low-toned, sad conversation with Harry and Sarah had been an expected façade. But this was sorrow, this was heartbreak, this was despair as I'd never before thought possible. It was an explosion of grief which tore my mind and body to shreds.

It ended. It took almost an hour to run its course, but it ended. I walked slowly to the bathroom, splashed my face with cold water, returned to the living room, unlocked the bureau cupboard and reached for the half-empty bottle of brandy and a wineglass. At the same time I took the note from its hiding place.

I drank the brandy in gulps; not really tasting it but feeling its warmth thaw me back to near-normality. I stared at the envelope for a moment . . . at the one word '*Tony*'. Then, quite calmly, I took out the note and re-read the scrawled words.

Tony, darling,

I'm sorry. The sixth form, and Morley. I really can't take any more. Forgive me, darling.

She hadn't signed it. The 'g' and the 'i' in 'forgive' were smudged and ran together; a tear – it *had* to be a tear – had dripped on to the paper before she'd folded it, prior to putting it into the envelope.

Staff discipline required that I be present at dinner in the refectory at seven o'clock that evening. I was there. I bathed, changed into a less crumpled suit, slipped into my academic gown (a nicety insisted upon by Morley) and was with the other masters and mistresses on the top table when Miss Lowther intoned grace. I was, I knew, an object of some curiosity by teachers and pupils alike.

I was beyond caring. I kept my head lowered, concentrated upon the food and discouraged any conversation from other members of the staff within speaking distance. It was, I suppose, an awkward meal for those on the top table; an embarrassing meal in some respects. Again I didn't care. From left and right I caught snatches of murmured small-talk. From the tables in front of me I heard the rattle and chatter of the pupils as they enjoyed the one substantial meal of the day. It was all so unimportant; so trivial; so empty. An expensive sausage-machine, geared to produce hollow but perfectly rounded links. An immaculately contrived joke in deplorable taste.

The meal ended and as usual everybody remained seated until Morley rose to his feet to leave.

As he passed behind me he paused and said, 'If it's convenient, Mr Hemingway, might I see you in my office?'

I nodded.

When he'd left the hall the rest of the staff pushed back their chairs. Miss Quanty, the French mistress, was on duty; she stepped down in order to control the pupils as they left. The others eased their way towards the staff entrance.

As he passed Johnny paused and asked, 'A date with Morley?'

'Yes.'

'See you in the staff lounge.'

'Probably.'

'Please.'

I shrugged and nodded.

From the refectory I went straight to Morley's office. I tapped on the door and entered at his invitation. And, not for the first time, I felt grudging admiration for what can only be called 'academic showmanship'.

His diplomas and the certificates of registration from the many societies and organisations of which he was a part were all carefully framed and, with equal care, positioned around the wall. These in turn were punctuated by group photographs taken of the pupils and staff at the end of each summer term. Every cup, plate, shield or trophy presented to the school – and for whatever reason – sparkled behind polished glass on the shelves of a truly handsome cabinet. Wing-chairs, and not the usual straight-backed chairs, were placed around the room for the comfort of visitors. The desk was a massive piece – almost the size of a ping-pong table – with a veneered surround encompassing a surface of rich green leather. Floor-to-ceiling windows looked out on to a wide stretch of lawn beyond which was a belt of trees.

These were the obvious and more impressive gimcracks, but the overall impression conveyed exactly what it was meant to convey; that any man deserving of such an office *must*, almost by definition, control a veritable powerhouse of learning and scholastic accomplishment.

Morley was on his throne; seated in the high-backed, swivel-armchair behind the huge desk. He was reading – or, more likely, *pretending* to read – the contents of a leather-backed folder. He was smoking his pipe and, above and behind his left shoulder, the extractor fan set into a pane of the high windows coaxed the tobacco smoke clear before it could fog up the room.

He looked up as I entered, flicked a smile with the precision of an Aldis lamp opening and closing its shutters and without lifting the wrist from the surface of the desk, moved a hand in the direction of one of the wing-chairs.

I sat down and waited. I compressed my lips a little, allowed a frown to crease my forehead slightly; it was a deliberate ploy; the mild distortion of my face muscles removed the mixture of contempt and hatred which, I feared, might show in my eyes.

He closed the folder, placed the pipe carefully into the ashtray on his desk, flicked the on/off smile at me again and said, 'Your journey?'

'Moderately easy considering the weather.'

'Good. The wreaths arrived?'

'Yes.'

'One from the staff? One from the pupils?'

'They both arrived.'

'Good.' He paused, leaned back in the chair slightly, then said, 'Advice from an older man, Mr Hemingway. Would you take it?'

I waited and he took my silence as an affirmative answer.

'Work,' said firmly. 'One of the best antidotes of all to mental hurt.'

'Advice from an older man?' I said gently.

'What?' He raised his eyebrows in surprise, then smiled a rather forced smile and said, 'Point taken, Mr Hemingway. Not *so* much older. But, shall we say, with infinitely more experience.'

'Of mental hurt?'

'I, too, have known the death of a loved one,' he said stiffly.

'Really?'

'Of a sister. Of a brother.'

'But not,' I said quietly, 'of a wife.'

'Degree only, Hemingway. Degree only.'

'Did they take their own lives?' I asked innocently.

He stared at me; lips compressed and breathing a little more heavily through his nostrils.

'Work?' I murmured.

'I'm here to help, old boy.' The bonhomie was so blatantly false as to be farcical.

'I'm sure.'

'Your friend. Not merely your headmaster.'

'I'm very appreciative.'

'You've had a shock. We all take that into consideration.'

'Work?' I repeated.

'Quite.' He leaned forward, rested his elbows on the desk and picked a slim ballpoint from the pen-rack. He fiddled with the pen – watched the pen – as he spoke. He said, 'English literature is a vital part of the syllabus. Since – er – since your wife died, Miss Lowther has done her best to fill the gap.'

'Along with religious education?'

'It hasn't been easy for her.' He looked at me for a moment, then emphasised, 'She's worked very hard.'

'I'm sure.'

'It has meant a complete re-shuffle of the timetable.'

'I'll thank her,' I promised.

He stared at me for a moment, then returned his attention to the ballpoint.

'My task,' he said smoothly, 'is to find a balance. A balance between my duty to the pupils and my duty to the staff. You . . . for example. Forgive me, if I sound unsympathetic. That is not the case. But – of necessity – my natural sympathy must be tempered with the requirements of the school.'

'You're asking me to vacate the flat,' I said bluntly.

'No.' He twiddled the pen for a moment, then, in a slightly heartier tone, said, 'No. Good heavens, no. Not at such short notice.'

'But you'll be advertising for a new English Lit. teacher?'

Softly – almost teasingly – he said, 'Not immediately. Not – that is – unless you insist.'

'I?'

'What I had in mind . . .' His tone remained soft. Gentle. 'Miss Lowther agrees. If the two of you – Miss Lowther and yourself – were prepared to share the English literature classes. If only until end of term.'

'But I don't know enough *about* English literature.'

'As much as Miss Lowther . . . surely?' He lowered the ballpoint on to the desk surface, raised his head and smiled at me. He repeated, 'Surely?'

'Is it fair to the pupils?' I asked.

'The balance I've already mentioned. Pupils and staff.' He paused, then added, 'Unless, of course, you prefer to seek bachelor accommodation in the village. In which case . . .' He moved his hands.

'I'd – I'd like to stay in the flat,' I muttered. 'At least for the present.'

'In which case . . .' He repeated the obvious ultimatum and, again, moved his hands.

'And the pupils?' I argued weakly.

'Hemingway.' The tone changed. We were no longer master and headmaster . . . that was the impression meant to be conveyed. We were friends; men of the world; companions in a mild duplicity of which we were both aware. He almost chuckled as he said, 'Hemingway, old man. Face facts. These girls are not academics, indeed they've no *desire* to be academics. A working knowledge of as many subjects as possible. A mere working knowledge . . . nothing more. Enough to form the basis for cocktail chatter. Wouldn't you agree?'

I said nothing and my silence was taken as unspoken agreement.

'We groom them,' he continued. 'We prepare them for a niche already waiting. None of them will ever be required to *earn*. Always remember that.' Again the near-chuckle as he continued, 'Few of them will be even required to *think*. Their parents have money. They, in turn, will marry more money. They lack nothing . . . and will never lack anything. Their future is assured. Therefore . . .' For a third time the near-chuckle. 'Augment the Brontë sisters with whatever authors you feel suitable. That, I think, is the limit of Miss Lowther's efforts. It suffices . . . at least until term-end.'

I accepted. Of course I accepted . . . Judas (if you recall) also accepted. And, strangely, my acceptance did not seem to be a form of treachery to Hannah until I'd left the office. Then it did.

I walked slowly – sadly – away from Morley's office, and gradually what I'd agreed to became more apparent. I'd assisted in making Hannah superfluous; she'd been the English literature mistress . . . and The Ridings didn't *need* an English literature mistress. Hannah had driven herself – literally driven herself – to death for a cause which was dismissed as unnecessary. What she'd done was worthless. The hours of preparation she'd worked at wasn't worth a snap of the fingers.

'A basis for cocktail chatter . . .'

My God! What an epitaph. What a summing-up of a life's work.

The Fall of the Second Domino

Julie Warton sloshed her way towards the ramshackle pig-pens. Her heavy gumboots made tiny bow-waves in the thin gruel mush of melted snow and mud. In the barn the four Jerseys moved restlessly and one of them gave voice to a half-hearted bellow, as if to attract her attention. Geronimo, the rooster, strutted on top of a battered mudguard of the tractor; a minor monarch exercising flat-footed, head-bobbing arrogance over his tiny harem of assorted mates who scrambled for perches on lower parts of the ancient David Brown.

Julie wore work-stained dungarees, a heavy lumberjack shirt open at the neck and, as a slight acknowledgement to her sex and the desire to keep her hands free of callouses, stout rubber gloves. She carried two buckets each full almost to the brim, and the khaki-coloured goo spilled over the sides as the black and white cross-bred collie cavorted ahead and around her.

Less than a quarter of an hour later the girl and the dog returned to the farmhouse kitchen. Julie padded across the stone-flagged room. Her feet looked ridiculously large in seaboot stockings. Tiny splashes of mash speckled her face.

As she stripped off her gloves she said, 'Those pigs. They don't come to breakfast . . . they power-dive the trough.'

'And this is self-sufficiency?'

The question was asked by her elder sister, Angela, and nothing was done to hide the disgust.

'It's healthy.'

'It's *filthy*.'

'Honest farmyard muck, Angie. You should try it sometime.' She struck a match, turned a tap, then lighted a burner on the bottled-gas cooker. As she stretched to take a king-sized frying pan from a shelf, she asked, 'One egg or two?'

Angela Warton huddled herself deeper into the borrowed dressing-gown of blanket material and muttered, 'Kippers . . . if I had a choice.'

'One egg or two?' repeated Julie.

'Two.'

'Rashers?'

'The same home-cured stuff?'

'The same. Oodles of fat . . . crisp if you like it that way. Any thickness you want.'

'One rasher,' sighed Angela. 'And, *please*, cut some of the fat off.' She turned her head, glanced at her sister, and said, 'God only knows how you keep so slim. The stuff you eat . . . you should look like something from a seaside postcard.'

Julie busied herself at the cooker; frying the bacon, frying the eggs, frying the bread. She boiled the water and brewed the tea. She warmed the plates, unhooked the beakers, took the cutlery from the drawer and set two places at the plain, deal table.

Meanwhile Angela pulled her sister's dressing-gown tighter and eased the wooden armchair a fraction nearer to the spluttering fire; a fire which gave off surprising heat from its cunning mix of split logs and small coal.

They were in the main room of the tiny farmstead; a room which might have been described as 'cosy' or 'gloomy'; a functional room which originally had been meant to keep out the weather, but not necessarily to provide comfort. The two-foot-thick stone walls could shrug off gales and storms alike, but the small tiny-paned window could equally refuse entry to sunlight. Above their heads the beams showed adze-marks and, above the beams, the underside of the planks which formed the floor of the bedrooms were of the same seasoned oak as the beams themselves. The walls were rough-plastered over the stonework; as a gesture to modernity their present owner had painted the plasterwork with enough coats to give a white, easily-washed-down sheen, but the shelves and 'built-in' cupboards followed the gentle rise and fall of the plaster and any do-it-yourself attempt at 'improvement' would have looked scrappy and out of place.

The flagged floor was scrubbed clean and held a scattering of rugs; the dog was house-trained and, when not being spoken to, sat on an old clip-rag rug in one corner of the room. The furniture consisted of the plain deal table, a sideboard which had seen better days, a settee which had either come from, or belonged to, a jumble sale and a variety of kitchen chairs . . . these plus the wooden 'grandfather's' armchair which had been claimed by the older woman.

Taken item at a time they should have spelled austerity. They didn't. Instead they spelled contentment; they represented achievement and modest pride in that achievement; as with so many rooms this one reflected the character of its owner.

When it was prepared and laid they ate their meal in silence. On the part of the elder woman it was a silence born of petulance and an anger with nobody to whom she might direct it. The younger woman's silence was a more natural thing; a silence born of habit; a silence born of chosen solitude.

When they'd eaten, the younger woman eased her plate aside, moved a cheap tin ashtray nearer and lighted a cigarette. She tossed the packet across the table and Angela Warton joined her in an after-breakfast cigarette.

Quite suddenly the younger woman said, 'I think you've made your point, Angie, don't you?'

'Point?' Angela Warton stared.

'With Father. You've left home. Been away since Wednesday . . . four days. He'll have got the message.'

'For God's sake! I wasn't . . .'

'It's time you thought of going back.'

Julie Warton knew exactly what she was doing; she was deliberately setting herself up as Aunt Sally for her sister's frustrated fury; she was giving the elder woman a ready-made target at which she could aim the accumulated spite which had built up over the last few days. She was laying the basis for an almighty row.

Okay, so be it. It was one of those inevitabilities. They *always* fought. They always *had* fought. All this sisterly-love stuff had never been part of their relationship. And anyway – if Angie *was* planning a prolonged stay – certain home truths had to be aired.

From behind tightened jaw muscles the elder woman said, 'Are you telling me to go?'

'Not necessarily.'

'The hell you aren't. You're as good as . . .'

'Stay,' said Julie coolly. 'Stay as long as you like. Stay forever. Just understand the rules . . . that's all.'

'What rules?'

'This place.' Julie inhaled cigarette smoke. 'Five acres . . . not *quite* five acres. Four cows that give good milk. Milk that makes good cream. Three pigs . . . plus a week-old litter. A few chickens and a rooster. Some clapped-out farm machinery. That's all the place boils down to.'

'You mentioned rules.'

'Plus work – lots of work – *that's* the main rule.'

'Aah!' The elder woman's eyes glinted.

'I've shared everything else since you arrived,' said Julie calmly. 'Stay – I'm not saying you can't stay but if you *do* stay I share that.'

'If you seriously think . . .'

'No!' Julie Warton snapped the interruption and silenced her sister's outburst. In a calmer, more controlled voice she continued, 'I still remember why I'm here, sister dear. I still remember the reason. The *real* reason.'

'You wanted independence. You wanted . . .'

'I wanted to get married.'

'Oh! That?'

'That,' echoed the younger woman. 'Everything fixed. Everything arranged. Then you took a hand . . . and dragged him into bed.'

'He'd still have married you.' The lips curled contemptuously. 'You're the one he wanted.'

'You're the one he *got*, and where men are concerned I don't wear cast-offs.'

Angela Warton drew on her cigarette, then waved the hand, and said, 'Who'd have known?'

'You. Me. Him. Two too many.'

'Oh, for God's sake.'

'You were lucky.' The memory made her voice hard and brittle. 'If father had even suspected he'd have killed him, and probably have crippled *you* for good measure.'

'Father's darling,' mocked the older woman.

'No. We understood each other, that's all.'

'And so . . .' Angela moved her head to survey the room mockingly. 'This is the self-imposed penance? This hovel?'

'Not a penance.'

'No?'

'Clean air,' said Julie softly. 'At that time I couldn't bear to breathe the same air as you.'

'Oh, boy!' The elder woman's eyes widened. 'You can really hate.'

'I learned.'

'And now?'

'I can tolerate you.'

'Just that?' The inbred arrogance and mockery were both there in the question.

Julie Warton nodded, then tasted cigarette smoke.

Angela said, 'All this crummy pride of yours. I have pride, too, or doesn't that count?'

'You have pride,' said Julie flatly.

'I don't "obey orders" if that's what you have in mind.'

'Accept conditions?' Julie raised a questioning eyebrow.

'Much the same thing.'

'No.'

'You think not? Even when *you* lay down the conditions?'

'I don't run a guest house.'

'You'd be pushed for customers.' Again the mouth twisted.

Julie ignored the taunt and said, 'If you stay here, we share. The past is just that . . . past. But the future needs planning.'

'For example?'

'More livestock. A little more land . . . assuming there's any for sale. More work – shared work – for any degree of self-sufficiency.'

Angela said, 'I can pay for my keep.'

'I've told you. I don't run a guest house.'

'And that's the deal? The "conditions", as you call them?'

Julie nodded.

'You need money,' said Angela.

'Maybe.'

'Don't be such a damn fool. You need money.'

'For two of us I need muscle more than money.'

Angela stared for a moment, then, realising that Julie wasn't bluffing, she squashed what was left of her cigarette on to the edge of her plate and snapped, 'Get stuffed.'

'It's a pleasure.' Julie smiled without humour and added, 'Get packed.'

That day being Sunday it was the next morning when Angela and Julie Warton parted company. Something of a slender bridge of communication had been built since the breakfast conversation of the previous day. A poor thing, but strong enough to allow them to shake hands as they stood on the cobbles of the market-town square.

Angela said, 'Get your bus back home. Don't wait around here for two hours. I'll catch the service connection to Harrogate.'

Julie nodded and said, 'Give my love to Andrew.'

'Sure.'

Julie hesitated, then said, 'I *still* think you should go home.'

'Not while Edwards is there.'

'He's little more than a child. He'll apologise.'

'He *goes*,' said Angela harshly. 'No employed hand calls me *that* and gets away with it.'

'Okay.' Julie shrugged. 'Anyway . . . good luck.'

Angela nodded and Julie turned away and hurried towards where the local single-decker was waiting for the last of its few passengers.

On the way back to her home, as the rural bus zigzagged its way along the lanes, catching villages and hamlets much as an entomologist nets moths and butterflies, Julie sat in the comfortless seat and thought of her sister.

With charity to be pitied rather than disliked. Capable of

moments of real cruelty, but incapable of recognising that cruelty. Unless she changed – and changed drastically – her whole life would be built upon hurt; the hurt which she inflicted and the hurt which was returned to her as payment. The poor bitch . . . she didn't even know. And if she was told she wouldn't believe.

Andrew? Andrew wouldn't tolerate her for more than a week. He wasn't the 'protective brother' type. In a lot of ways he was like Angela herself; a neat cross between Angela and Father. Well, maybe chartered accountants had to be a little bit bloodless. There wasn't much scope for sensitivity in the handling of other people's money. A man who walked through life, with his head lowered and the hint of a frown on his face. That was Andrew. That just about summed him up. Always looking for the catch. Always vaguely worried. Always ready to pour scorn on anything he couldn't add up and bring to a nice, round total.

Poor old Andrew.

Poor old Angela.

THREE

The staff lounge. Living quarters apart it was, I suppose, the most comfortable room in The Ridings. It was, I think, two rooms knocked into one; whether or not it was certainly a large enough room with a sufficiency of armchairs and small tables; with fitted carpet, wall-lighting, stand-lamps and a restful décor. In one corner there was a tiny television set for those who wished to use it. Newspapers, magazines and periodicals were there for the reading. For its size, it was a remarkably warm and comfortable room; much used by the staff when they were not required for duty elsewhere. Other than when we slept, the staff lounge was rarely unoccupied.

As I entered there was the expected hush of embarrassment. Just for a moment – for no longer than about three seconds – the tiny groups of masters and mistresses fell silent in their low-toned talk and every face turned towards me. Then they looked away, and the hum of conversation continued, but to me it sounded contrived conversation.

Johnny heaved himself from an armchair, raised a hand to readjust his spectacles, then walked across the room to join me.

'Name it,' he smiled.

'Not here.'

'A few quick jars?'

I nodded.

'Okay.' He touched my arm. 'I'll get Bertha . . . meet you out front.'

I said, 'Thanks,' and I meant it.

I settled myself into the not-too-comfortable seat and for

the first time – for the first time it seemed since I was born – I felt a smile ease the tension of my facial muscles. The combination of Johnny and Bertha would have made Job smile. How on earth he coaxed that two-seater M.G. sports through its annual Ministry of Transport test remains one of the lesser mysteries of the universe. His boast was that the car had 'character', and indeed it had, if by 'character' you mean a perversity which almost amounted to a mind of its own. In America I suspect it would have been called a 'hot rod'. In this country where less flamboyant expressions are the rule it was an old and somewhat battered open sports car, with all the unnecessary fripperies removed; with good tyres and an engine tuned to concert pitch; with certain additions to its working parts which made it go faster, and noisier, than had been originally intended.

Johnny knew how to handle it. He – and, at an educated guess, he alone – could bring the beast thundering into life with a master's touch on the choke and a first flick of the ignition; in a stranger's hands (and I'd seen it too often to have any remaining doubts) Bertha demonstrated her independence by immediately 'flooding' . . . and, moreover, by repeatedly 'flooding' until she once more felt the backside of the man who loved her in the driving seat.

Johnny accompanied by Bertha was, perhaps, what I needed most at that moment.

We were both scarfed and duffle-coated against the weather and, as the M.G. snarled its way between headlight-slashed hedges, the mix of snow and sleet raced towards us, swooped up to clear the windscreen, then caught our flying hair and, literally, forced us to accept the fact that we were alive.

The village was about six miles away. The public house was one of those country hostelries which, despite token acknowledgements of a modern way of life, retain the basic and genuine 'olde worlde' atmosphere beyond the scope of craftsmen who try to re-create the past. The beer was from the wood, 'real ale', and without artificial fizz; strong stuff which quenched the thirst and, within the first two pints, loosened the tongue. Heat was provided by a huge, old-fashioned grate, which held at least half a hundredweight of 'nutty slack', fanned it into a white and orange furnace and sent warmth, like an all-embracing blanket, throughout the taproom and included in the black-leaded ironwork of the range which surrounded this grate was a large oven in which (we knew) pies and sausage rolls were being made piping hot for customers wanting a snack with their late-evening drinks.

Only a handful of drinkers were in the taproom. The weather was keeping all but the hardy indoors, and moreover 'country drinking' doesn't start in earnest until after nine o'clock.

We found a quiet table out of earshot of the few customers chatting at the bar and after Johnny had placed the first glasses on the beer mats we tasted then talked.

'Better?' asked Johnny gently.

'There's only one way,' I sighed.

'Up.' He nodded understandingly.

We sipped beer in silence for a few minutes, then Johnny said, 'The big bwana. Anything serious?'

'English Lit.'

'What?'

'Cut-price schooling, Johnny.' I tried to keep the contempt from my words, but failed. 'Miss Lowther and I. We share English Lit. from now on.'

'How the hell . . . ?'

'I know. But, "You will . . . or I'll need the flat." Not in as many words. But that's what he meant.'

'The cold-blooded bastard.'

I tasted beer again, then said, 'He can't get away with it forever.'

Johnny didn't say anything.

'That animal,' I said, 'is an updated version of Squeers.'

Very quietly – very deliberately – Johnny said, 'Does it bother you, Tony?' He pushed his spectacles back into place, then added, 'I mean, *really* bother you?'

I was on the point of being mildly outraged at the question when the truth seemed to stand up and stare me in the face.

I compressed my lips, scowled at my beer glass for a moment, then muttered, 'No. Dammit . . . *no*! It used to, but it doesn't any more.'

'Usage,' murmured Johnny.

'Usage,' I agreed. I raised my head and looked at him. 'Okay, you're right. Of course you are. Art. Art, be damned. I've been encouraging them to daub. Little more than *daub*. For God knows how long.' I shook my head in slow perplexity. In a puzzled voice I asked, 'When? When did the rot set in? And why the devil didn't I realise it?'

From behind the pebble lenses the eyes looked sad and sympathetic. 'All of us, mate,' he said gently. 'Me? I perform indoor fireworks . . . that's all.'

'And the rest?'

'All of us,' he repeated. He hesitated, then added, 'Except Hannah. She wouldn't buckle . . . didn't you know?'

I heard a soft, croaking voice echo, 'Except Hannah,' and for the moment I didn't realise it was I who had spoken. I tasted my beer, took out cigarettes, held the open packet out towards Johnny, then, when I'd lighted both cigarettes, I said, 'Tell me. Squeers. Morley. You seem to know these things, Johnny. Seem to be able to . . . understand. I'm – I'm still vague. Still not quite in focus. You've obviously given it some thought.'

'A lot of thought.'

'So . . . tell me.'

The way Johnny told it . . .

Dickens's Squeers and Morley. The difference was only a difference of façade; a top-dressing difference. The same motive-power applied. Greed. The cruelties were, perhaps, more subtle in the case of Morley; more refined and less obvious. But the contempt for his charges, the lack of any real interest in their education, and the fawning towards the parents and guardians – the people from whom he milked money – was a perfect parallel.

This I already knew. Indeed, it was I who had made the comparison, 'an updated version of Squeers'. But the truth is I'd meant it to be an exaggeration; an over-statement concerning a man whom I disliked. Disliked? A man whom I *hated*.

At the grave the previous day I'd promised myself that I'd kill him. Nor had it been melodrama. I'd meant it. I *still* meant it . . . even though the cold fury of that moment had passed. I still meant it, or I *think* I still meant it.

Who knows? Who can ever swear to such a thing? Emotions like that are as impermanent as dust motes. Therefore, who ever *really* knows?

But even at the grave I hadn't known why. I could not have given a reason; an excuse; a motive. Just that his name had been in the suicide note. That Morley was one reason why Hannah had gassed herself . . . one of two reasons.

Beyond that? Nothing.

God forgive me, I'd toyed with concrete – more disgusting – reasons. That behind my back he'd tried to force his attentions upon her. That he might have succeeded. That shame might have driven her to . . .

But even with a mind numb with misery I'd dismissed such a possibility. In the first place I knew Hannah – had *known* Hannah – too well. She'd have rejected him and, furthermore, she'd have told me; the very notion of us having secrets was ludicrous. And in addition – and with all his faults – Morley was not a philanderer. His greed for wealth, and his silly pride in The Ridings, would have prevented him from taking even a tentative step which might have led to scandal and the withdrawal of pupils.

Therefore . . .

That she'd *named* him . . . that had been enough.

And now Johnny told me *why* she'd named him.

Corruption, incompetence, cheeseparing – call it what you will – starts at the top. The truth really was as simple as that. A school holding itself to be as excellent as The Ridings presupposed over-staffing rather than under-staffing. And, moreover, the masters and mistresses could be expected to hold more than bare *baccalaureus* degrees. The pretence of Morley went much farther than his study. It riddled the whole school; it made the tutor/pupil ratio a sick joke . . . or, to be more accurate, the *truth* of it made it a sick joke. On paper that ratio was satisfactory, and indeed more than satisfactory. But the required 'doubling up' – the extra duties demanded from each master and each mistress – made that 'on paper ratio' little more than a deliberate confidence trick.

I'd been something of a fool. I'd accepted this 'doubling up' system; our previous life style, and the dangled carrot of the flat, had brought on a form of desperation, therefore I'd accepted everything without question. And having accepted it – and having had no previous experience upon which I might base an assessment – I'd acted accordingly. I'd done what I'd had to do . . . what Morley must have *known* I must do.

I'd ceased to keep abreast of my subject and I'd cut 'lesson preparation' to an absolute minimum.

Not consciously, you understand. But of necessity . . . because a day holds only a limited number of hours. And in time this pushing aside of vital, out-of-classroom work had become first a habit, then the norm upon which I based my chosen profession.

It had happened to me and, as Johnny told it, it had

happened to him and to every other master and mistress at The Ridings. All, that is, except Hannah . . .

'Hannah wouldn't lower her standards,' said Johnny sadly. 'I don't know why she did what she did, but . . .'

'Over-work,' I interrupted flatly. 'She worked herself into a state of collapse, saw no way out . . . and found a way out.'

'You sound sure.'

'I am now.'

'Look . . .'

'No.' I drained my glass, squashed out my cigarette and stood up. I waited until Johnny had finished what was left of his drink, took the glasses to the bar for re-fills, then returned to the table. I sat down again, having touched my lips with the freshly drawn beer, I said, 'She – er – she left a note.'

Poor Johnny. His eyes rounded, his mouth became slack and, almost as a gesture of self-reassurance, his hand went up and his finger touched the bridge of his spectacles.

In a gentle but firmer voice I repeated, 'She left a note.'

'I – I didn't know. The report of the inquest didn't . . .'

'Nobody *does* know. Just us two.'

'Oh!'

'She blamed Morley . . . and the sixth form.'

'God, I'm sorry.' He seemed to be on the point of tears.

'Why the sixth form?' I asked, quietly.

'I – I don't know. I . . .'

'You've explained why Morley. Now, tell me, why the sixth form?'

'It's – it's guesswork, Tony.'

'More than guesswork.'

'Guesswork,' he insisted.

'Okay. But *good* guesswork. Guess the rest.'

He tasted his beer, touched his moistened lips with the back of his hand, then nodded.

'They – they know,' he muttered.

'The sixth formers?'

'Look . . .' He moved a hand in a gentle, hopeless gesture. 'They aren't kids any more. Seventeen. Some of 'em eighteen. They aren't *children*. By that time they've fluffed. Dammit, Tony, they've *lived* with it. The con. They don't mind. It's too late for them to mind, but they *know*. They're at the end. They're going to leave the damn place. And they know they haven't been educated. They have, at least, that much gumption.'

Again he tasted the beer, then, in a less hesitant voice, continued, 'The parents? Hell, they don't know what parental love means. Neither the kids nor the parents. That's the strength of these places. The kids don't know until it's too late and if they did know they aren't close enough to their parents to blow the gaff. The *parents* are too thick – too pre-occupied with their own petty little lives – to notice what isn't paraded in front of their eyes, they're sold the pup. The kids – the sixth formers especially – they couldn't care less. They know they haven't been educated. They know they aren't going to *be* educated. Most of 'em don't *want* education anyway. They want entertaining, that's all. Me? I do peculiar things with chemicals. A sort of water-into-wine routine. It means damn-all. It teaches them nothing. But they like it. Miss Lowther? Have you ever listened outside her classroom? The controversial bits. The bits they can trot out in small-talk, and not know what the hell they're on about.'

'Cocktail chatter,' I murmured.

'Just that. Exactly that.' Johnny nodded. 'Okay – who knows? – some of 'em might be bitten by the religious bug sometime in the future. But at this moment in their young lives they don't want to know. Just – say – the Spanish Inquisition, because that's not too far removed from historical romance. That sort of junk. But no depth, mate. No depth

. . . in anything. They bite back if you try anything in depth.'

'Hannah,' I breathed.

'She wouldn't join the club. She was too honest. She was going to *teach* the little bitches if it . . .'

He stopped, closed his mouth and looked acutely embarrassed.

'If it killed her.' I ended the sentence for him.

'I'm sorry, Tony,' he muttered. 'This mouth of mine. I . . .'

There was a few moments of silence. I felt sorry for this friend of mine; this very observant, very honest friend who had answered so many questions. I felt sorry and at the same time grateful.

For myself? I, too, could now answer some questions . . . having been shown the way.

I spoke my thoughts aloud. That, in essence, is what they were. Spoken thoughts to be shared with this very honest friend.

I murmured, 'Like Picasso. Like his *Guernica*. Stand up close – near enough to see the minutiae – and it doesn't make too much sense. Straight lines and curves. Blocks of dark colour. Nothing obvious . . . not what Picasso is saying. But stand away. See the whole canvas from the right distance. *Then* it becomes obvious. The horror of war. The jagged waste of beauty. Everything! And so obvious. So bloody *obvious*.'

I stopped speaking.

Johnny said, 'You,' in a gentle understanding tone.

'I was too close,' I said sadly. 'Too close to see. You saw. Her mother, too, I think *she* saw. Maybe her father. Perhaps *he* saw. Perhaps . . . I can't be sure. But her mother. Women know these things. Instinctively. And *you*, Johnny.'

'Yeah. And me,' he murmured.

'But not me. Her husband. I was too damn close. Just the lines – just the shapes – but not once the truth.'

Angela Warton watched the local bus ease its way over the cobbles, pause with trafficators blinking until the road alongside the square was clear, then heave itself gingerly across the pavement, down the kerb and on to the carriageway. It gathered speed, turned a corner and was gone.

And so much for sister Julie . . .

She was a silly little cow. Kinky. Kinky? She was completely devoid of marbles. *That's* how kinky. Up to the kneecaps in mud and cow shit and calling *that* 'independence'.

These last few days had been a stop-gap, a breathing space in which to formulate some sort of plan. That pig-headed old sod of a father of hers could get knotted. Sheep-shank, reef and bowline. The lot! If he seriously thought she was going to hang around while that mouthy little jerk Edwards slung insults around he, too, had lost his marbles. Any crawling wasn't going to be done by *her*, that for sure!

Meanwhile . . .

Jesus Christ, not Andrew. Not *Andrew*. Okay, they'd taken it for granted . . . next stop Andrew. Like a blasted railway wagon being shunted from siding to siding. First siding sister Julie, second siding brother Andrew, third siding . . . back home to Daddy. Like hell she was a railway wagon. And 'Daddy' could go screw himself. *And* Andrew.

Andrew's thought-process bordered upon the prehistoric. It always had done. He wasn't just square . . . he was *cubic*. It followed; anybody capable of going ga-ga about figures had to have square edges. The thought – just the thought of Andrew and that whey-faced wife of his – brought on the heebie-jeebies. The lectures. The pontifications. The 'thou shalts' and the 'thou shalt nots'.

No way, my friend, no bloody *way*!

She scowled at her thoughts, nibbled at her lower lip for

a moment, then hefted the suitcase from its resting place alongside her foot and stepped from the bus shelter. She glanced around the square, noticed the supermarkets, the banks, the cafés, the scattering of pubs and shops and the three hotels. Outwardly the hotels all looked much the same; moderately inviting, but at the same time moderately *un*-inviting; fairly old but with bits and pieces of modernity added here and there; porch-entranced and gloomy windowed.

She stared at each hotel in turn.

Then she muttered, 'Bloody hell!' and walked towards the Beechwood Brook Arms.

The receptionist smoothed the page of the impressive guest-register and asked, 'May I have your name, please?'

'Warton. Angela Warton.'

The receptionist recorded the name.

'And your address, Mrs Warton?'

'*Miss* Warton.'

'I'm sorry . . . Miss Warton.'

Angela gave her father's address.

'And today is – er – what?' The receptionist turned her wrist, consulted her expensive digital watch, then answered her own question. 'Monday, February 6th. And you'll require the room until . . . when?'

'Further notice.'

'Oh!' The receptionist's surprise reached near-shock proportions.

'Days, rather than years,' added Angela sarcastically.

'A – er – an indefinite stay?' suggested the receptionist.

'Unless it's illegal.'

'Oh, no, ma'am – *miss* – it's just that . . .'

'I'll meet the bill week at a time,' said Angela wearily.

'Thank you, miss.' The receptionist looked relieved.

'A single bedroom with bathroom attached.'

'Ah!' The receptionist looked worried and sucked the end of her ballpoint.

'More problems?' mocked Angela.

'The – er – the rooms with baths, miss. They're all doubles.'

'All occupied?'

'Well, no. As a matter of fact, none of them are occ . . .'

'All double beds?'

'No, miss. Two of them have twin beds, but they're . . .'

'These two with twin beds. Where are they?'

'First floor, miss.'

'And the outlook?'

'I – er – I beg your pardon.'

'You look out of the window. What do you see? Dustbins?'

'Oh no, miss. They look out on to the grounds at the rear. The park. It runs down to the river. It's a very nice . . .'

'Which one can I have?' asked Angela brusquely.

'Well, y'see, miss . . .' The receptionist hesitated. 'They're both *doubles*. As I've already explained we . . .'

'Take a good look at me, woman,' sighed Angela dangerously. 'I'm not a circus freak. I can only sleep in one bed at once. To ease your conscience, you can move the bedclothes from the bed I'm *not* going to use. And if you get a sudden influx of visitors and want the room I'll move out . . . to another hotel.'

'I'll – er – I'll see what the manager says,' stammered the receptionist.

'Do that small but obvious thing.'

The chances were that Egon Ronay had never even *heard* of the Beechwood Brook Arms. It was one of those places: not a dump, not a doss-house, but by no stretch of the imagination a five-star hostelry. In the main it catered for farmers of both sexes and all ages. It ran a Morning Coffee

Room for the benefit of weary housewives from outlying districts visiting the town to stock up their pantries and deep-freezers. On market days brown boots with half-inch-thick soles stumped a path between its entrance and the public bar. On a *wet* market day the air of the hotel was heavy with the smell of damp tweed. Its 'all in' lunch and dinner menus were displayed on typewritten sheets of hotel notepaper in a brass-rimmed, glass-fronted rectangle alongside the main entrance; the menus never varied and the original black typing was becoming sun-bleached.

Years before some enterprising manager had invested in a brochure and the brochure boasted 'Accommodation (11 bedrooms); Historic interest; Luncheons and dinners; Car park (20)'. What the brochure left out was the fact that never, in its whole history, had all eleven bedrooms been occupied at the same time, and that the citizens of Beechwood Brook had long since claimed the right to leave their cars, Land-Rovers, and sometimes even tractors, on the hotel car park at any hour of the twenty-four.

The interior was armchaired and gloomy; a left-over from the Edwardian/Victorian eras of comfort, nebulosity and half-hidden alcoves. In the main rooms dusty chandeliers hung from the high ceilings, but they were rarely lit; for all except special occasions the lighting came from low-wattage wall-lights, interspersed with stand- and table-lamps. If there was a 'colour scheme' upon which the décor was based it was of dark autumn tints with a background of de-oxygenised blood.

'When,' asked Angela Warton sourly, 'does the cortège arrive?'

'Miss?'

The waiter was a young man, little more than a youth. His wine-coloured, Eton-style jacket showed cleaned-up stain marks on the left breast and was a size too small. He stood, pencil poised, waiting for the dinner order.

Angela Warton said, 'This place. You could rent it out as a cemetery.'

The waiter grinned his agreement, then said, 'The second sitting, miss. It's a little livelier.'

'Livelier?'

'More people,' amplified the waiter.

Angela Warton moved her head to stare at the other occupants of the dining room. An elderly couple; the man's elbow-crutches leaning against a nearby empty chair, the woman sipping cheap sherry with the timidity associated with hemlock. A young couple – at a guess honeymooners or out for an illicit series of bed-romps – sharing giggled jokes and oblivious to all except themselves . . . serve *them* bird-droppings garnished with sphagnum moss and they wouldn't have tasted the difference.

Angela Warton breathed, 'My God!'

'It does liven up, miss,' promised the waiter.

'I believe you.' She consulted her copy of the menu. 'All right – you're a very honest man – what do you recommend, shrimp cocktail for starters?'

'Frozen shrimps,' warned the waiter. 'And this time of the year the lettuce isn't what it might be.'

'Soup?'

'Canned,' said the waiter flatly.

'Okay. You say.'

'The melons are fresh,' he said.

'Thanks. I'll have melon.'

He jotted the order on to his order book and said, 'Main course?'

'You tell *me*.'

'The chops aren't bad,' he said carefully. 'But if you order a mixed grill you might be disappointed with the other things. The mischievous grin touched his lips for a moment. 'The sausages for example.'

'Okay, no grill.' She glanced at the menu again. 'Fish? Trout?'

'Frozen trout.'

'My God!'

'But,' said the waiter, 'the sole was swimming around in the North Sea yesterday.'

'Thank you. Make it sole.'

'Yes, miss.' He added more jottings to his order book.

'Trimmings?' she asked.

'French fries. Sprouts. Peas. Carrots.'

'A little of everything. And tartar sauce.'

He nodded and made some more jottings.

As he turned to leave, she said, 'Before you go – while you're in a truthful mood – what about the sweet?'

'If I was ordering?'

'If you were ordering.'

'I'd play safe. Ice cream.'

'This weather?'

'There's a gateau trolley, miss. I'll bring it round when you've had the main course. Good stuff, large helpings and real cream.'

She nodded and the waiter hurried towards the kitchens.

As she waited, she tried to be philosophical. Okay, this was no Hotel Intercontinental, but what the hell? It was a few strides ahead of Julie's dump and it had the advantage of being well beyond the earshot of darling Andrew and his wife. Nor was Beechwood Brook a hot-spot of late-night high-life, but maybe she needed a few days of quiet relaxation. There was a bar; she could get stoned if she felt so disposed. The bed was comfortable enough, there was a nice view from the window and the private bathroom squirted hot water through the taps and shower whenever she needed it.

So, relax, honey. Let those who don't know where you are do the worrying.

*

The truth was – and thanks in no small part to the helpful young waiter – it hadn't been such a bad meal. The sole had, indeed, been fresh; succulently fresh. The gateau had been rich and fluffy; a fruit-filled confection swimming with cool, thick cream. And now she was in the lounge, sipping black coffee – surprisingly *good* black coffee – and smoking a cigarette.

She watched the small traffic of diners and customers drift into the hotel foyer. Couples and groups out on an evening's quiet enjoyment. Some headed straight for the dining room, others peeled off towards the bar. She sought (and, because she sought, she found) a basic boredom in their exaggerated sauntering. This dump – this place, Beechwood Brook – really was a morgue peopled with zombies. A couple of days – three at the most – and that would be her limit. The sheer, slow-paced 'rusticity' would drive her up the wall.

She finished her coffee and, still holding her cigarette, she stood up and strolled to the hotel entrance. She had no intention of leaving the hotel – there was nowhere to go – but she needed a few breaths of air.

As she reached the porch she saw the car.

It was carefully parked to one side of the hotel entrance, and it was as readily recognisable as a well-known signature; this despite personalised number plates. The Mercedes-Benz people knew how to build cars, and their larger more expensive models had that stamp of racing luxury reserved for only the best vehicles in the world. This one had it . . . plus. The low-slung elegance; the sheen of the cream-coloured bodywork; the mirror-finish of the chrome; the black leather of the upholstery; the sheer size and latent power of the car. She'd seen it before at point-to-point meetings. Maybe half a dozen times. She knew its owner, Nick Page. Knew him but not well. Knew him as a man with money . . . lots of money. And with a wife who, under her maiden name, was one of the top experts in the interior decorating world.

And Nick . . . oh boy! That slim figure, that bronzed skin, that carefully trimmed moustache, that infectious gaiety. His age? Well, who cared? Forty. Maybe closing up to fifty. He had that charisma which comes only with years of good living. That immaculate, rarely achieved magic which *must* have wealth for its basis but which, even with wealth, is only granted to a favoured few.

She turned and returned to the foyer of the hotel.

A porter was passing and she attracted his attention, and asked, 'Mr Page. That's his car outside. The Merc.'

'Yes, miss.'

'Is he at the bar?'

'No, miss. He's having dinner.'

'Is he?' The information surprised her.

'Just occasionally,' smiled the porter. 'It puts the chef on his mettle.'

'I'll bet.' She paused, then said, 'Coffee in the lounge? Like lesser mortals?'

'Coffee in the lounge,' murmured the porter.

She nodded slowly, then said, 'I'd like more coffee if I may. In the lounge.'

'Certainly, miss. I'll arrange it immediately.'

She settled herself into a strategically placed armchair, lighted another cigarette and, when it arrived, sipped coffee while she waited.

It was almost an hour later when he strolled from the dining room. The complete self-assurance of the man was that he was wearing a dinner suit complete with cummerbund; the only guest in the hotel who'd dressed for the meal . . . and yet this man, if he *hadn't* dressed, would have looked strangely incomplete. He was accompanied by a young woman – an evening-dressed, brittle female who (maybe!) gave subtle promise of things to come, but a female who was too slim to be *really* voluptuous – who smiled a possessive smile before leaving him for the ladies' room.

Angela Warton waited until he was well within earshot then said, 'Nick, how nice to see you.'

'Angie!' He turned, smiled, then strolled across and lowered himself into the neighbouring armchair. 'What the hell are *you* doing in this mausoleum?'

'I could ask the same question?'

'My local. I live about ten miles out.'

'I didn't know.'

'But not *your* local,' he smiled.

'I'm staying a few days. A short break.'

'Nice.' He inclined his head. 'Comfortable?'

'Moderately. Room seven . . . complete with bath. Very restful.'

'I must remember.' His eyes twinkled.

'Please,' she invited gently. She glanced to where the woman had rounded a corner on her way to the ladies' room and said, 'Not your wife I notice.'

'She's away. In Ireland for a month. Some stately home she has to make look comfortable.'

'Your wife?'

'Yes.' He nodded cheerfully.

'And while the cat's away . . .. Not that I'm calling your dear wife a cat, of course.'

'My wife . . .' He chuckled; a deep-throated sound of genuine glee. 'I didn't check, but I doubt if she'll have included a chastity belt among her undies.'

'Meanwhile . . .'

'Female companionship. A little local talent.'

'I'm not criticising,' she smiled.

'Envious?' he suggested.

'I wouldn't know.' She matched meaning for meaning.

He stood up from the chair, smiled down at her and murmured, 'Say tomorrow evening. Seven o'clock?'

'Female companionship?' she mocked.

'Who knows? You might end up finding out whether you should be envious or not.'

He turned, strolled away and turned the corner in search of his escort.

And, okay, it had been a pick-up; a blatant, no fencing-around-the-edges pick-up. Less than five minutes; less time than it had taken to finish a partly smoked cigarette; much less than five minutes. While his girl-friend-for-the-night had been away in the ladies' room.

Nor had it been a teasing session. They'd both known. *Known*. Tomorrow night they were going to hoist the flag . . . complete with bugles and brass band accompaniment. From the moment she'd voiced his name – from the moment he'd turned and seen her – they'd both *known*!

The needle jets of the shower pounded at her skin, the steam rose then condensed and ran down the tiles in tiny rivulets, her whole body glowed with warmth and yet, from somewhere inside, a tiny explosion of emotion made her tremble with excited anticipation.

FOUR

The beer, the heat from the huge fire and, perhaps, the backlash from days of pent-up emotion. We were, I think (indeed I'm sure), a little drunk; not bereft of our senses, but nevertheless approaching that maudlin state where friendship assumes titanic proportions to be measured only by confidences.

And, to be fair, Johnny *was* my friend; with Hannah gone he seemed to be the only friend I had in the world . . . and perhaps he was.

Certain it is that, in some perverse way, I enjoyed telling him of the details. A masochistic pleasure, perhaps. Who knows? Who knows what complex twistings and turnings the human mind travels in an attempt to purge itself of near-intolerable hurt.

For almost an hour I re-lived that Saturday . . . Saturday, January 28th.

I kissed Hannah goodbye before herding the handful of senior pupils into the mini-bus which was to take us to Leeds. I explained to them en route that this exhibition we were about to see consisted of paintings (and prints of paintings) by Jan van Eyck; I emphasised that they must remember that what they were about to see belonged to the fifteenth century; that to give a true assessment it was necessary to compare like with like, and era with era. That (for example) *The Marriage of Giovanni Arnolfini and Giovanna Cenami* might, at first sight, seem almost caricature-like; that the faces of the two figures might seem devoid of real expression. But (I advised) examine the drapes of the bed, the folds of the gowns, the intricacies of the hanging candle-holder and, above all else, the beautiful detail of the whole scene, reflected in the convex mirror on the wall between and beyond the two standing figures. I enthused all the way to Leeds. I wanted them – I almost *willed* them – to see true art. The *St Barbara* monochrome. *The Virgin and Child with Chancellor Rolin.*

I had a catalogue and I went through it, item at a time, and worked – God, how I worked! – to instill some tiny grain of enthusiasm into them.

In the event, they gazed with bored eyes at the masterpieces, but enjoyed the café meal arranged for them after the visit to the gallery.

On the journey back to The Ridings I was morose and disappointed. I should not have been; had I realised then what Johnny had pointed out to me, I would have been neither surprised nor concerned . . . art, like all beauty, demands an effort before it can be understood.

We arrived back at the school at about seven o'clock. It was dark and the girls had a certain amount of evening study awaiting them before bedtime. For myself, I was tired and ready for a couple of hours of relaxation with Hannah before we, too, retired.

As I approached the door to the flat I smelled gas. It wasn't overpowering; Hannah had done much with cloths and folded rugs and the gas was contained in the main room. Nevertheless, I sensed that something was wrong.

The door was locked and, even before I called for assistance, I kicked in one of the panels, reached inside and turned the key. I saw Hannah on the hearthrug . . . and immediately knew the worst. The gas caught at my throat – made my head swim and brought a suffocating tightness to my chest – nevertheless, I staggered across the room, turned off the tap, then threw a chair through the window.

Then I saw the envelope containing the suicide note and,

acting almost instinctively, I took it and slipped it into my inside pocket.

After which came what can only be described as incomprehension. A confusion of masters, mistresses and pupils, pushing and jostling at the broken door of the flat; of Johnny, elbowing his way through, until he was by my side; of the pupils being ushered back to their dormitories; of the arrival of uniformed policemen; of the staff lounge and Johnny feeding me black coffee; of an elderly police sergeant, looking strangely naked without his helmet, asking unanswerable questions in a sombre and kindly voice; of these and a thousand other shards of memory which at the time – and even later – seemed not to make sense.

Then followed a post mortem, an inquest, a verdict and a funeral.

But there were other things. Personal things; important things; things which almost broke my heart to recall.

How she'd bathed, before taking her life. How she'd clothed herself in a clean nightdress. How she'd placed the pillow on the hearthrug within a foot of the gas jets. How she'd even crossed her arms high on her breasts . . . as if to cause as little 'trouble' as possible.

Those were the things I told that night. The little things, but the *important* things. The things that, even in death, combined to make her Hannah.

And Johnny listened and he, too, became a little more sad and (perhaps) a little more drunk.

'The meek shall inherit the earth' . . . ah, yes, but not while louts are around. And the louts proliferate; they spread like scum on stagnant water, until they reach out beyond the cities, beyond the towns, and touch even village pubs with their uncleanliness.

They were a quartet, and they had already visited other drinking places before they arrived. We – Johnny, I and the other customers – heard the car stop, heard the shouting and swearing, before they burst into the taproom. They charged through the door and seemed to hurl themselves at the bar. They pushed Johnny aside and demanded service before he had a chance to place our own empty glasses on the bar-counter.

The transformation in the taproom was immediate and absolute. From a warm, womb-like niche, in which conversation had been relaxed but subdued and almost hushed, to a ranting, shouting, argumentative madhouse. The leading culprit was a not-so-large, not-so-heavy mischief-maker who bawled foul-mouthed observations to the other three. Having tasted his drink, he placed the glass on a table, swaggered to the until-then-silent juke-box, chose a record, then fed money into the machine. As the amplified stridency spewed itself from the contraption, the leader jerked his head and one of his companions rose from his seat and together they performed a lunatic morisco; shouting, stamping in tempo to the ear-splitting (and to me quite tuneless) 'pop music'.

Johnny was still at the bar waiting to be served.

The other customers were frowning their disapproval or turning their heads in embarrassment.

The expression 'something snapped' is, perhaps, a little melodramatic. Melodramatic, but nevertheless quite apt. It was, I think, the sudden switch from the gentle exchange of confidences to this noisy, moronic atmosphere.

I said, 'For God's sake,' but my words were lost in the din.

At the top of my voice, in a near-hysterical tone, I shouted, '*For God's sake!*' . . . and this time they heard me.

The leader pushed his partner aside, sauntered to my table and leaned stiff-armed towards me until our faces were little more than a foot apart.

'Something worrying you, mac?' he sneered.

In a very tight, slightly trembling voice I said, 'Take your hooliganism elsewhere.'

'Hooliganism?' he taunted.

'What else is it?'

'You calling us hooligans, mac?'

It was far too late to back down, therefore I nodded and said, 'That's exactly what I'm calling you.'

'We're quiet.' The alcohol fumes hit me as he spoke; I could smell them despite the drink I had taken. 'What we *can* be like, mac. This is nothing. Nothing!'

I felt the anger rise in me and knew the lout had to be answered in his own vernacular.

I stared at him, eye for eye for a moment, then, very deliberately and very calmly I said, 'Piss off.'

He jerked his head slightly; almost as if the words had been a slap across the face. Then he transferred his weight on to one arm and moved a hand to the back pocket of his jeans. As the knife came out of the pocket – before the blade had time to leave its housing – I heard the smash. Then Johnny appeared behind the lout, his left arm hooked itself across his throat and the terrible teeth of the smashed glass came round to hover almost on the skin of the lout's face.

Johnny said, 'You heard what the man said.' Two of the lout's friends made a movement as if to make some attempt at rescue. Johnny glanced at them, then warned, 'If anybody – *anybody* – comes within reaching distance he'll need a white stick.'

The lout breathed, 'You haven't the bottle, mac. You couldn't . . .'

He stopped as the longest shard of shattered glass touched the skin, about an inch beneath the eye, pressed the flesh inwards and, finally, sank home and drew a thin trickle of blood.

'You,' warned Johnny softly, 'are in no position to place bets.'

Henry, the landlord, moved from behind the bar. He stooped as he passed the juke-box, and the noise stopped. He jerked a thumb and the three louts hesitated, then lounged towards the door. Four customers – hefty 'young farmer' types – followed them from the taproom. Henry reached out and took the knife from the leader's fingers.

Then he growled, 'You, too, Mr Stirk.'

Johnny held the glass at the lout's face for a moment longer, then gradually released the pressure of his arm and lowered the glass. Henry took the broken tumbler and both he and Johnny stepped away from the injured hooligan.

'Just go,' said Henry flatly. 'Your pals are waiting. Don't try anything . . . the lads outside are itching to knock hell out of you.'

Just for a moment the lout seemed undecided.

Henry repeated, 'Just go, son. And don't come back. That's good advice . . . take it.'

The lout shrugged, then left.

Henry pocketed the knife and placed the broken tumbler on to the bar counter. From outside we heard a car start up, then drive away. The four customers who had acted as escort returned to the taproom and they and the other customers eyed Johnny and me with hard-eyed disapproval.

Johnny was pale and shaking a little. At a guess I, too, had lost a little colour.

Henry said, 'Mr Hemingway. Mr Stirk. The same applies to you. I won't make fish and fowl.'

'I need a drink.' Johnny's voice was a dry-throated croak.

I could see Henry's point of view, nevertheless I argued, 'They were yobs.'

'Mr Hemingway,' said Henry, '*you* don't order people from this house. Anybody. And the knife or the broken glass? Which is worse?'

I nodded. As I say, I could appreciate Henry's viewpoint.

'I need a drink,' repeated Johnny.

Henry seemed to make a decision. Without a word, he returned behind the bar, measured out a single whisky into a clean glass, added about an equal amount of water, then placed the drink on the counter.

He said, 'On the house, Mr Stirk. Drink it, then go. . . both of you.'

It was (at least) a new experience . . . for both of us. To be debarred from a public house; two respectable schoolmasters who were now refused re-admission into a village pub. Oddly enough, I found the thought mildly amusing; we were now both as near sober as to make no difference and, as Bertha's slip-stream ruffled my hair, I chuckled at the ludicrousness of the situation.

By contrast Johnny was livid.

'I don't think it's funny,' he snapped.

'We aren't heavy drinkers. Neither of us. It's no hardship.'

'There's a principle involved.'

'Not a matter of life and death.'

'A *principle*.'

'Johnny,' I smiled, 'Henry, the landlord, was right. A knife or a broken glass? They're both evil weapons.'

'Damn it, if I hadn't . . .'

'I know, I know,' I soothed. 'And I'm grateful. At this moment I could be in an ambulance, and I'm grateful. But I had no authority to order anybody from the pub.'

'Bloody excuses.'

'No . . . facts.'

'Those four,' he rasped. 'They were *bastards*.'

'Johnny . . .'

'No!' He raised a hand from the wheel and swatted me into silence. 'No more, Tony. I don't want to know. I don't want to listen to empty excuses. They're scum. Scum. Don't compare *us* with *them*. For Christ's sake, don't insult yourself and me by doing that. Don't insult Hannah . . . she would never have married *that* type. They're bloody animals, Tony. Worse than animals. We're not. We can think. We can feel compassion. We can try to understand how other people feel. But not them, mate. Not *them*. Whatever they can't understand they destroy. That's their creed. Destruction for the sake of destruction. They're evil, Tony. They don't belong to the same species as decent people.'

I glanced at him and in the combined glow from the dashboard and the backwash from the headlights it was possible to see the signs of the furious passion which was boiling up inside him. He was truly upset; the muscles of his face were stiff with emotion; his eyes – hard and hate-filled – stared ahead.

I left it at that; silently agreeing to *dis*agree. When we arrived back at The Ridings he dropped me at the front entrance and his grunted 'Good night' suggested a desire for solitude in which he might re-establish a more moderate outlook. I therefore watched the M.G. turn the corner towards the garages then climbed the stairs to the empty flat.

Strange – strange indeed and, in a disconcerting way, conducive of a feeling of guilt – but the double bed felt roomy and more comfortable that first night back at The Ridings. It took me almost two hours to find sleep, but they were not as I had expected hours of black misery within a darkened bedroom. I could allow myself to remember and without pain. I could view the canvas of our marriage, perhaps for the first time. Objectively. Without my near-worship of Hannah or the crippling pain of her death blinding me.

It had been a good marriage. A fine marriage. Its carnality had been secondary to the union of something more ethereal; we had, over and above the man-and-wife relationship, been friends . . . *good* friends. This, I think, had been the true strength of our marriage. That as *friends* we had each been considerate of the other.

And yet . . .

In this almost-perfect marriage there had been a blind spot. A corner around which I had not been able to see; a dark corner in which Hannah had crouched alone with her torment. And Johnny had seen what I had not seen, but should have seen. To that small extent he had known Hannah better than I had known her, and for a moment that realisation brought a stab of envy which might even have been jealousy.

My silent oath at the open grave?

Perhaps. Perhaps not. It is a peculiar hatred which can be nursed and kept blazing for great lengths of time; a peculiar hatred reserved for an unusual type of man. Not my type, perhaps. I wasn't 'physical' enough. The veneer of learning – of education – had burned out much of my so-called 'animal passion' . . . perhaps.

But on the other hand perhaps not. In the village pub earlier I had felt no inhibition when faced by the young tearaway and the momentary threat of his knife had caused me no qualms. Therefore . . .

The truth, I suppose, is that we all know ourselves, but not well.

Eventually, I slept. Deeply and without dreams. It was, I suspect, the sleep of the physically and mentally exhausted.

The Fall of the Fourth Domino

By the third night – by Thursday, February 9th – she'd moved out of the Beechwood Brook Arms and (in effect) into his bedroom. Such had been the speed of their acceptance of each other. It had been a form of madness; a form of nymphomania and a form of satyriasis . . . as blatant and as uncontrollable as *that*.

That first night – that Tuesday evening – he'd called for her and taken her to Harrogate. To one of the fine eating houses of the north; to a restaurant where good food was well prepared and washed down with best wine. They'd dawdled over the meal. Murmuring their thoughts via small-talk innuendo. Speaking to each other with their eyes. Each of them sure, but not *quite* sure – *almost* sure.

In a way, it had been a sort of courtship; a ritual similar to the love-play of exotic birds prior to their choice of a mate. And part of that courtship had been a wild drive in the Merc. West and high until they'd reached the savage solitude of the Pennine Moors. Moors still white under a covering of unmelted snow, with the few roads snaking across their whiteness like dark umbilical cords.

Nick Page had steered the car off the road and into the part-shelter of a high-banked layby. He'd switched off the engine and turned off the lights. High on the windscreen a moon had silk-lined a scattering of cloud and, beyond the moon's brilliance, stars beyond number had pin-pricked the sky in a profusion unknown except in clean cool air. In the distance beyond the rise and fall of the black skyline a glow, like the first hint of sunrise, had touched the blue-black bowl from the streets of distant Skipton.

Page had lighted a cigarette, smoked in contemplative silence for a few moments, and had then murmured, 'Yorkshire.'

'We have that in common,' she agreed.

'Nowhere quite like it.'

'This part.'

Page had grunted.

'South Yorkshire. Parts of West Yorkshire.'

He'd said, 'Muck and money.'

'Exactly.'

'Don't knock it. It has its own beauty.'

'You sound like my father.'

'I don't know him too well.'

'Greedy. Possessive.'

He'd chuckled as if at some secret joke. Then he'd smoked his cigarette in silence, before lowering the window and tossing the glowing end into the darkness. The red tip had hissed as it had hit the wet ground; hissed and then died. He'd raised the window then easily – nonchalantly – he'd rested his left arm across her shoulders.

'Possessive,' he'd murmured. 'You buy a thing. It's yours. You possess it . . . who else should possess it?'

'Like father,' she'd repeated.

'The right idea.'

'In some things.'

'In *all* things.'

'Very masculine,' she'd teased gently.

'What else?'

They'd both felt the attraction stir inside them; that indefinable, biochemical energy which sparks and fires and, if not controlled, becomes a wild emotion.

He'd leaned a little closer; tightened his hand at her left shoulder, then released the pressure and dropped the hand until it cradled the roundness of her left breast.

He'd asked, 'Enjoy tonight?'

'Nice.'

'Only "nice"?'

'So far.'

'Only *so* far?' he'd mocked quietly.

She'd smiled and said, 'Who knows?'

He'd leaned forward and sideways to kiss her, and her mouth had reached out to meet his lips . . . and the kiss had been a calculated release of the fire. Slow and open-mouthed; probing, exploring and indelicate in its naked sexuality. Then (as the passion had rocketed) hard and almost savage; as if each had wished to devour the other. Her hand had closed around his neck and strained their mouths closer. His hand, in turn, had moved until the palm and fingers had cupped and squeezed her breast, while his right hand had dropped to her knee, to begin its journey along the smooth surface of her tights.

She'd deliberately bitten him on the lower lip and he'd jerked his head back.

'What the . . .'

'No!' Her voice had trembled slightly.

He'd touched the bleeding mouth with the back of his hand.

'What the hell sort of . . .'

'Not that, Nick. Not *that*.'

'Angie,' he'd said dangerously, 'if you're some sort of tease . . .'

'Shhh.' She'd smiled and raised a hand to finger the bleeding lip. Her voice had lost its tremor as she'd said, 'Any yokel, Nick. A front-seat groping session. A back-seat rumble. Any yokel I care to encourage.'

He'd waited and she'd stroked his lip with the tip of her finger.

Then she'd smiled and said, 'If you want to bed me, Nick, bed me . . . but *bed* me. Properly.'

He'd breathed, 'Christ!'

'Properly,' she'd repeated softly.

He'd taken a handkerchief from his pocket, dabbed the blood from his lips, then driven the Merc back from the moors towards Beechwood Brook and his home.

She'd been stunned when he'd guided her through the hall and had switched on the lights of the main room. The combination of wealth and interior-décor expertise was something she'd never seen before; something she'd never imagined.

Externally the place had looked like a farmhouse; a large farmhouse and a solidly built farmhouse, but nevertheless a farmhouse. The hall had been something of a surprise – indeed the heavy iron-studded door had raised a sardonic eyebrow – but the mild shock of the hall, with its floor of mosaic tiles, its shoulder-high panelling of seasoned oak and its near-museum-pieces of heavy furniture, beeswaxed to a dull rich sheen, had been a mere curtain-raiser to the main room.

As she'd entered the main room a phrase – a title from Grieg's *Incidental Music to Peer Gynt* – had flashed into her mind. *In the Hall of the Mountain King*. It was huge, high and raftered; magnificent but at the same time brutal in its sheer weight of mediaeval masculinity. The walls towered, dark-panelled, and above the panels dark-balked between the cream-coloured plasterwork until they married with the great beams overhead. The four symmetrically placed windows were narrow, but almost the height of three men and, as Page had sauntered to each window, heavy velvet drapes had closed and overlapped . . . the Middle Ages complete with electrical gadgetry! The massive table, the chairs, the chests, the sideboards. They were all of a kind. Their colour was the colour of age and usage, and their shine was the shine of beeswax; no stain and no silicone-based polish had touched *those* surfaces. And the room-lighting – more than twenty torch-shaped wall-lights – had reflected the smooth-surfaced age of the furniture and the buffed steel of dozens of ancient weapons which decorated the walls.

Page had grinned at her astonishment and said, 'Like it?'

'It's . . . unusual,' she'd gasped.

'Like a bloody armoury,' he'd chuckled. 'She had a ball doing this.'

'Your wife?'

'She had an absolute ball,' he'd repeated. He'd waved a hand and said, 'My father collected all this garbage. His hobby. When he snuffed it I got the lot, and it was too good a chance for her to miss.'

He'd taken her on a quick tour of the weapons; sometimes lifting them from their place on the wall and allowing her to handle them. To feel their weight. To estimate their killing power.

'A flail. Nice . . . eh?' He'd hefted it in his hand. 'No long-distance slaughter for those boys. On horseback, of course, and a belt across the skull with one of these things needed more than an aspirin to cure. Assuming, of course, he didn't slash *your* guts out first . . .

'A war hammer. Very early, round about the mid-fifteenth century. Always the head, you see. All that plate armour. Anywhere else but the head – specifically the face – and the damn thing bounced off . . .

'A halberd. This one is a *real* halberd. This one – shorter hafted – is *called* a halberd by those who don't know. Actually, it's a form of poleaxe. The cavalry, okay? A charge and of course some horses go down. That's what these were for. To finish off the wounded horses after the battle. Very humane. Next time you watch Trooping the Colour – the cavalry: watch for the halberdiers at the rear. They still parade. They don't *use* the damn things these days, of course. But that's what they are. They're not battle-axes . . .'

She'd suppressed a shiver as visions of horses, mad with pain, had invaded her mind.

The small tour had continued. Partisans and tridents; guisarmes and linstocks. Then the swords; the hand-and-a-half and the two-handed slashing weapons; the more modern swords with their cross-guards, their shell-guards and their basket-guards.

'And this.' He'd stopped at a beautifully chased scimitar. He'd lifted it from its brackets and stroked the flat of the curved blade. He'd said, 'The old man's pride and joy. One-handed. Perfectly balanced. He went to his grave believing it was Saladin's sword. *The* scimitar . . . you know the story, of course?'

'No,' she'd breathed.

'No?' He'd looked surprised. 'I thought everybody knew it. Part of every school's history of the Crusades.'

'I – I don't know it.'

Still holding the scimitar easily in one hand he'd drawled, 'The Third Crusade. Saladin – Sultan of Egypt – boss man of the Moslems. War was more civilised in those days. When they weren't actually chopping each other up, the leaders of both sides entertained each other. Cœur de Lion was entertaining Saladin. Big drinks – one presumes – and Cœur de Lion was something of a show-off. His favourite sword was a two-handed job. A bloody great thing . . . like that one over there. Something of a bet – so the story goes – and Richard hefted this damn great sword and cleaved a piece of furniture into two pieces.

'Saladin picked up a silk scarf, then his scimitar . . . *this* scimitar if the old man is to be believed. Threw the scarf in the air, held the scimitar steady and allowed the scarf to fall across the blade. Just the weight of the silk scarf . . . and the scarf hit the ground in two halves.' He'd smiled and ended, 'Let me show you something, the old man's party piece.'

He'd taken a cigarette from his case, then, very carefully, balanced it across the blade of the scimitar. He'd said, 'Watch,' and moved the weapon no more than six inches – a short thrust, against the weight of the cigarette . . . and the cigarette had been sliced neatly into two perfect halves.

She'd whispered, 'My God!'

He'd smiled at the sight of her awe, then, as he'd replaced the scimitar to its place, he'd mused, 'Could be the old man was right after all. Who knows? Maybe it *is* Saladin's neck-cropper.'

That had been three days ago – on the Tuesday – but by now, the Thursday (or to be accurate the small hours of

Friday morning), she knew more of the house than that main-room-cum-armoury. The bathrooms – three of them – each with bath, shower, bidet and 'all mod cons'; each with a cork-tiled floor, ankle-deep mats, huge tinted mirrors and a central-heating warmth which made personal ablution more than a pleasure . . . almost an esoteric luxury. The lesser bedrooms; beautifully proportioned and superbly decorated; each with its own 'scheme'; each with its own individuality. The dining room with its 'breakfast alcove', complete with draught-proofed French windows giving the sort of view rarely seen except in glossy-magazine adverts.

It was a house in which the word 'millionaire' sprang easily to mind. A house in which wealth – great wealth – was accepted as naturally as was the water whenever a tap was turned. Equally, it was a house in which the normal mores of conduct could be disregarded should they ever threaten to become boring.

Witness the last three days . . .

They had both been invaded by a form of concupiscent insanity. They'd lusted, slept, bathed, eaten, then returned to the master bedroom for more fornication. A treadmill of uninhibited lechery; a tiny world, the centre of which was this magnificent bedroom and this king-sized bed.

God, the things they'd done . . . the things they'd said . . . the experiments they'd tried . . .

Angela Warton lay awake in the semi-darkness – a darkness washed by the light of that same moon which had stared through the windscreen while the Merc had been parked on the moor tops – and, as she stared at the sleeping figure of Nick Page, she knew she would never be the same woman again. A reversion to real normality was impossible. A husband? . . . and what husband wouldn't *know* within days of their marriage? Even accepting present-day promiscuity, what man would honour a wife whose knowledge of the secret backwaters of debauchery was as complete as hers;

as complete as hers had become within three ever-to-be-remembered days and nights? A man like Page, perhaps? Perhaps, but where, within the circle from which she might select a husband, *was* there another man like Page?

In the gloom of the bedroom she watched him as he slept; on his back, mouth slack and slightly open, teeth peeping from behind the lips, a tiny almost inaudible snore accompanying each exhalation of breath.

A whore, she thought. A complete and accomplished whore . . . and that's all I'll ever be, and all I'll ever want to be. You've given me a trade, Nick Page. You've given me a profession and with less than a hundred hours of apprenticeship you've turned out an expert. You've ridden me and broken me – as savagely and as ruthlessly as any horse *I* ever broke – and the end product can be relied upon to answer the rein of any other rider.

I asked for it. I begged for it. Therefore . . .

And then she heard the noise. Such a slight noise – such a small noise – and yet *different*. Not one of the noises of the night. Not one of the tiny creaks of timber or metal as the night frost squeezed minor contractions upon various parts of the house.

A noise which – for vague, womanly reasons – frightened her.

She glanced at the illuminated dial of the bedside clock. It showed 2.18 a.m. on Friday, February 10th.

Watch the box, read the books or sit in the darkness of the cinemas. Use fiction as a ground-base for supposed fact and the conclusion is that a 'professional criminal' can be bumped into at every street corner. And what criminals! What crimes! What superbly planned, smoothly executed *coups de maître* of gay lawlessness! The police are baffled, the private eyes are made to look dumb-bells and the laughing, debonair villain strolls into the sunset with the heroine clinging to his arm.

Thus the fairy tale.

Ben 'Poxy' Cooley could, had he wished, have put the record straight. Cooley *was* a professional criminal . . . a *rara avis*, but complete in every detail. On the wrong side of his fortieth birthday, he'd spent almost half his life in establishments of official detention – the last being an eight stretch for an abortive attempt to make himself rich via a short cut through a Bradford jeweller's shop – and could, therefore, have signed a sworn affidavit to the effect that, whereas private eyes could be ignored in the United Kingdom, the police were very rarely baffled. Pressed, he might even have admitted that being bent was not the Robin Hood life-style it was sometimes cracked out to be. Sometimes it was okay, but in the main it stank to the high heaven.

So, why *be* bent? Specifically, why be *professionally* bent?

Had he thought about it, he might have pointed out that the question could be paralleled with football coupons. Why fill in the pools? Why make an organisation bulging with loot that little bit better off every week from your own meagre pittance? For the big win . . . what else? For the promise of happy-ever-after and bank-notes to burn.

Hence, this night's escapade.

It was his work. His trade. His profession. And like all professionals he'd gone about things in the right way. The 'professional' way. Mugs – amateurs – lifted things first . . . *then* looked around for a market. They held on to the hot stuff too long. Forever sometimes. Mugs. The rozz liked that; that was just what the rozz wanted. Lift something, stick it up your jumper, shove it under the floorboards, bury it in the back garden, then start asking around about possible markets . . . that was *just* what the rozz wanted. By the time you'd found a buyer – by the time you'd fixed a price – all the size twelves in the world were standing around admiring the stuff you'd nicked . . . and waiting to nick *you*!

Cooley didn't work that way. He was a professional. He had the market ready and waiting before he even planned a break.

And Hall, the receiver, had said, 'Okay, Cooley, maybe we can do business. But with the right stuff. Only with the right stuff.'

'So what's the right stuff?' Cooley had asked.

'Well, not clocks. Not watches.' Hall had raised his hands in despair. 'Clocks – watches – I need never ask the time again as long as I live. I can't *give* 'em away.'

'Not clocks. Not watches.'

'Not transistors. Not television sets.'

'Okay, that's what's "not". Now tell me what *is*.'

'Well now . . .' Hall had rubbed his stubbled jowl reflectively.

'And don't,' Cooley had warned, 'get too ambitious. Forget fancy things like gold bars. Anybody buys them.'

'Not *anybody*, Cooley.'

'Hey, Hall. I can find other buyers.'

'So, why give *me* problems?'

'Because I can trust you.'

'That's an important thing to . . .'

'I can trust you,' Cooley had interrupted, 'because I have you over a barrel.'

'Uh?'

'Anything *too* stupid . . .' Cooley had smiled a particularly non-humorous smile. 'We see each other in court.'

'Is that nice?' Hall had waved his arms a little.

'No. Not particularly.'

'Is that friendly?'

'This isn't a social call.'

'So, you're asking what I'll buy?'

'When you get round to telling me.'

'And you're holding a gun to my head?'

'I'm reminding you, that's all.'

'Okay. I'm reminded.' Receivers are, of necessity, philosophical creatures; their business interests ensure that they do not insult too easily. Hall had shrugged and said, 'Stones. But forget the settings . . . right? Settings don't interest me. Settings are dangerous until they're melted down.'

'Okay, stones. What else?'

'Silver.' Mild enthusiasm had entered Hall's tone. 'Good silver. Georgian stuff, but nothing with some family name inscribed. Just good solid Georgian silver. The collectors aren't too fussy.'

Cooley had pondered for a moment and had then said, 'Have the cash handy.'

'How much?'

'Up to five grand.'

Hall's eyes had widened and he'd remarked, '*You'll* be lucky.'

'Yeah, I feel lucky.'

And, indeed, he had felt lucky . . . and *still* felt lucky.

As he worked on the window he felt very lucky; lucky that a few weeks before he'd leaned against the bar of a local pub, listening to the chat of a stranger talking to another stranger; lucky that the first stranger had happened to be a gardener employed by Nick Page; lucky that, among the baked beans of general conversation, certain pearls of information had been dropped.

That, for example, Mrs Page was packed and ready for a trip to Ireland for a spell of interior-decoration advice.

That, for example, the Pages were in the middle of 'servant problems'; that 'living-in' staff were hard to come by and that for the moment various 'little women' were employed on a daily basis, therefore at night Nick Page slept alone in his castle.

That, for example, the word 'sleep' was an understatement when applied to Nick Page. He didn't sleep . . . he took a short course on death.

Hence Cooley's visit to Hall.

And now he *still* felt lucky. The moon gave enough light for him to see what his gloved hands were doing; the pencil-torch in his breast pocket wasn't needed. More luck, hell, a man couldn't *wish* for more luck! He licked the concave surface of the tiny rubber sucker and pushed it firmly into place on the chosen surface of the pane. The sucker was fixed to one leg of a cheap set of dividers. On the other leg was soldered the head of a diamond glass-cutter. With his left hand, he steadied the sucker. With his right hand, he experimented with the diamond head until he felt the point bite into the glass then, using steady pressure, he cut a perfect circle. To be on the safe side – to be doubly sure – he cut round the scribed circle a second time.

He took out his pocket-knife, opened the blade and eased the point under the rim of the rubber. At the ingress of air, the sucker released its hold on the glass and Cooley slipped the home-made breaking-and-entering tool into his jacket pocket.

He worked systematically and without haste, gloved fingers as sure as those of any surgeon. But (as always) the pains hit him. They always did, somewhere at the beginning of a job, before his nervous system had properly adjusted itself to an acceptance of the calculated risk. They hit him now and he paused to screw up his face in pain. He massaged his stomach then broke wind, but the pains remained.

From another pocket he took out a length of tape tacked to a tiny square of wood. Another home-made gadget. Next, he fished from the same pocket a tiny tube of glue. Despite the pains he grinned, God bless the commercial chemists; God bless contact adhesive, it made the old treacle-birdlime-

and-brown-paper routine look like something from a kid's conjuring outfit.

He untopped the tube and smeared a thin layer of adhesive on to the glass in the centre of the circle, then smeared a similar layer on to the surface of the square of wood. He replaced the top on the tube, returned the tube to his pocket, then placed the square of wood and his pocket-knife carefully on the sill.

From an inside pocket he took some folded sheets of toilet paper. He walked away from the window, found a corner shaded from the moon's light, then lowered his trousers and emptied his bowels. As he squatted there he marvelled at the function (or perhaps malfunction) of the human body. In particular, his own body. Castor oil wasn't in it. Every job . . . every bloody job! That's why he worked alone. A companion would have been nice. A look-out, maybe. Somebody to give a hand searching the place once he was inside. A companion *would* have been nice – nice and handy – except for this crapping business. Okay, he visited the bog, he always visited the bog before coming out on a job. He needn't have bothered. Ever! What the hell he did . . . first the pains then his whole inside seemed to turn to slop. And with somebody else along that would have been embarrassing. Very embarrassing. They might get a wrong idea. They might not understand.

He finished, zipped and belted his trousers, then returned to the window.

He examined the square of wood; tilting it, to catch the glow from the moon. Then he squinted at the circle of glass from one side, closing one eye in order to achieve the same angle of sight. On both the wood and the glass the sheen of the adhesive had been replaced by a dullness; a little like the opaque condition of a cataracted eye. Just to be on the safe side he blew on to the wood, then blew on to the glass.

Slowly – gently but firmly – he brought the two treated

surfaces together. He held the wood against the glass until he counted fifty . . . slowly. Then he released the wood, stared at it for a moment, then tested it for strength. It was firm – so, God bless contact adhesive.

He folded a handkerchief, then, with the haft of the pocket-knife, he tapped the circle cut by the diamond through four thicknesses of cotton. Sharp, carefully aimed taps, delivered at the stretched material. Taps which, because of the muffling effect of the cloth, could hardly be heard more than a few feet away. Periodically he lowered the handkerchief, held the knife in his teeth and took the pencil torch from his pocket to check that the break in the glass was following the diamond cut and that the break was continuous and all the way through the pane.

He replaced the knife and the handkerchief in his pocket. He took the tape and, allowing no more than two inches of slack, gripped the tape with his teeth. Then, carefully and methodically, he put pressure on the disc of glass with his two thumbs. He started at the top and worked down the circle on both sides and, as he pressed, soft gratings of powdering glass preluded the pushing inwards of the piece he had cut away. It took him all of five minutes before he was satisfied that the disc was separated from the pane, then he took the tape from his teeth, held it in one hand and with the other hand pushed inwards.

The disc left its parent pane and he fed the tape through the hole and lowered the disc silently on to the carpet of the room.

He took time off – about two minutes – in which to quieten his nerves. Then he hoisted himself on to the sill, removed the glove from his left hand and threaded his arm through the hole. It was a sash window and lightly – too lightly ever to leave prints – his fingers moved along the inside of the sash, feeling for telltale signs of an alarm. He found none. He eased out his arm, replaced the glove then once more threaded the arm through the hole, unscrewed the fastener and slipped the catch.

Then came the actual opening of the window.

The amateur rarely takes into account the accumulative coats of paint, but the professional knows. He knows that paint can hold a window (and especially a sash window) as tightly as any catch. The grip of the paint must be overcome unless the window is in constant use . . . and that is a possibility which the professional deliberately ignores.

Again the amateur delights in using a 'jemmy': that leverage tool which in the building trade is known as a 'ripper'. The professional wants no jemmies. He wants no rippers. What tool he is unable to carry lightly in his pocket he finds at the scene. Any tool . . . including a leverage tool.

Cooley had found a garden spade. He'd carried the spade to his point of entry, leaned it against the wall and was now ready to use it. One pressure, that's what he was after, a single, paint-breaking pressure. A certain amount of noise, but for only a split second. Just the one crack, as all resistance was overcome.

He fed the blade of the spade into the crack between the frame and the lower bar of the window; easing it home as far as it would go; leaning against the spade handle in order to drive it in as far as possible. Using his pencil torch he hunted around until he found a flat stone and two bricks. He placed the flat stone with one of the bricks on top of it on the sill . . . directly under the blade of the spade. Gently, he eased the haft of the spade up slightly, in order that he could wedge the second brick on top of the first. Then he tested the spade handle for firmness and strength.

Again there was a moment's respite as he sucked in night air to steady his nerves.

Then with his left shoulder turned partly away from the window, with his left hand clasped around the spade's shaft and with his right hand gripping the handle of the spade, he stiff-armed himself almost clear of the ground in a single, downwards push.

There was a crack – the loudest sound he'd made until that moment – and the window opened at the lower sash.

Angela Warton shook Page by the shoulder and whispered, 'Nick!'

Page grunted in his sleep and tried to turn away.

'Nick!'

'Not now, sweetheart. Later. When I've . . .'

'For God's sake, Nick. Wake up.' She shook him harder.

'What the hell . . .'

'*Nick!* For God's sake.' She curled a fist and punched him on the back of his shoulder. 'Wake up. There's somebody downstairs.'

'Eh?' He awakened with a rush and pushed himself on to his elbows.

'There's somebody downstairs,' she whispered urgently.

They listened for a moment, then he said, 'There's nobody. It's the . . .'

'I *heard* them.'

'No. It must have been . . .'

Then they both heard the muted protest of a sash window being eased open.

'Stay there.'

Page threw the bedclothes clear of his legs and swung his feet on to the carpet. He took a silk dressing-gown from the back of a chair and draped it over his nakedness. As he tied the cord he walked to the dressing-table. He opened one of the drawers and took out a .45 revolver encased in a stiff leather army holster. He drew the gun from the holster, lifted a box of cartridges from the drawer and began to load the revolver's chambers.

Meanwhile the woman had also scrambled from the bed and clothed herself in a terry-cloth bathrobe.

As he clicked the cylinder of the revolver back into position, he repeated, 'Stay here.'

'No . . . I'm coming with you.'

'Please yourself. But keep out of the way.'

She followed him from the bedroom, along the passage to the landing, and down the stairs. They walked slowly; barefooted and silent. Page held the revolver levelled and with his finger through the finger-guard.

They reached the ground floor . . . and now they could hear the sound of careful movement from the main room.

Still holding the revolver, Page placed the back of his hand against the partly open door. With his left hand he felt for the light switches.

In a single movement he pushed open the door, switched on the lights and stepped into the room.

He snapped, 'Stay right there' . . . and they were met by the terrified stare of a pock-faced stranger.

Cooley *was* terrified. Not merely frightened. Not merely scared. *Terrified.*

The big thing – the awful thing, the most awful thing of all – had happened and was still happening. He'd been caught half-way through a break, and by an angry householder, and that householder had a gun and was obviously prepared to shoot.

Last time it had been an eight stretch. This time? Christ only knew. They'd throw the book; double figures for sure. Back inside with all the landing bosses and the block bosses; with the handful of sadistic screws found in every nick; with the stench of slops and carbolic which seemed to penetrate every stone and every pore; with the jealous queers and their nancy-boy 'wives'. Day at a time – hour at a time – that was supposed to be the hidden secret. Forget the end. Forget the stretch. Live it, day at a time. One hour at a time . . . that was the secret of prison sanity.

But how many hours in (say) ten years? How many tiny slivers of sanity? Of so-*called* sanity?

Christ . . . *No!*

He dived towards the open window and as he did so the .45 roared its explosive warning and the sound seemed to fill the whole room. Seemed to make the walls tremble. The woman screamed, but Page missed his aim by more than a yard and the slug split one of the wall panels before burying itself deep into the plaster.

Page was firing with a one-handed grip and few people (and they only real experts) can hit a target with a .45 revolver other than with a two-fisted grip.

Had he known it Cooley was comparatively safe, in so far as being shot was concerned. But he didn't know it, and the rubber soles of his lightweight canvas shoes made a squeaking sound as he swerved and raced for the shelter of the massive sideboard.

Again the revolver roared its anger. Again every piece of furniture seemed to vibrate as the explosion hammered the eardrums in that confined room. And again the bullet missed Cooley by a country mile.

But Cooley didn't know this. Cooley thought he was virtually dodging bullets. He threw himself sideways, hit the wall and collided with a fanned-out display of pikes, bills and spetums, with a noise like somebody bumping into a rack of billiards cues. One of the pikes fell away from its holdings and Cooley grabbed, instinctively, and caught it by the shaft.

What followed was not premeditated. It was a force of circumstances. It was a by-product of blind panic. It was genuine, albeit mistaken self-preservation.

Nevertheless . . .

Cooley swung to face Page and the revolver. He yelled – a howl of terror-ridden rage – then, with the pike at a levelled position, he hurled himself at Page and the revolver.

The leaf-shaped blade took Page low in the chest. The force

bowled him over and, as the blade tilted and tore into his heart, the dying twitch of his forefinger sent a third bullet high into the rafters.

What followed was pure madness.

There was a witness . . . and Cooley had enough sense left to know that there *mustn't* be a witness. He grabbed Angela Warton by the terry-cloth of her robe and dragged her from the doorway. Maces, flails and war hammers were at hand and, having killed one, Cooley knew he *had* to kill the other.

She was screaming: climbing, sobbing shrieks of terror.

Silence came as the mace smashed its way into her skull. Silence other than Cooley's whispered, 'I'm sorry! I'm sorry! I'm sorry!'

FIVE

The next day – Friday, February 3rd – I began what in honesty can only be described as a personal vendetta. The sixth form – that handful of teenage shrews – had been partly responsible for the death of my wife. Hannah had said so. She had accused them in her suicide note; accused them and in effect demanded retribution. Justice, equity, fair play – call it any name you wish – insisted that her unspoken wish be honoured.

The second period was art, for those who professed interest in that subject and as I entered the art room they were ready, seven of them each at an easel, each wearing a stained smock, each with palette and brushes at hand.

I slammed the door, strode to the front, eyed them with open contempt for a moment, then snapped, 'Right. Take off the smocks. Put away the easels and settle down.'

The head girl (an oversized, bumptious bitch called Leah Sykes) put up token resistance.

'Mr Hemingway, this is an art session. We'll need . . .'

'You'll do as you're told, Sykes. In the interest of accuracy, I will remind you that these are art and art *appreciation* lessons. Today, and for the rest of this term, we will concentrate upon the latter.'

It quietened them for the moment. Indeed it stunned them; I doubt if they'd ever been spoken to like that in their lives before. Nevertheless, they removed those ridiculous smocks and folded those useless easels while I, in turn, cleared the model table of its junk of vases, bowls, twigs and similar trivialities which in the past had been used in various pathetic attempts at 'still life'.

I strolled to the main easel and pinned up a copy of Van Gogh's third *Self-Portrait*. Then I returned to the front of the class and waited with the backs of my thighs resting comfortably against the edge of the model table and my hands in my trouser pockets.

When they were settled I stared at them, then said, 'Last Saturday you – you and others – travelled to Leeds to view an exhibition of the work of Jan van Eyck. I doubt if ever a journey was more wasted. For what good it did – for the educational value of that journey – you might just as well have watched a Mickey Mouse cartoon. Before we arrived – on our way to Leeds – you were briefed. You were told what to look for. That, too, was a waste of time. You closed your eyes. You were deliberately blind. You chose not to see. As far as *you* are concerned, Jan van Eyck need never have lived. He need never have painted. His masterpieces need never have been created. You are, in other words, artistic morons.'

I paused and Sykes moved her hand in a gesture which indicated that she wished to say something.

'Yes?' I raised a sarcastic eyebrow.

'Sir, I object to that remark.'

'Do you?' I deliberately pitched my tone to show a complete non-interest.

'I object – I object on behalf of the class – to being called a moron.'

'I note your objection, Sykes,' I said gently. 'You have that right. I, too, have rights. The right to hold an opinion and the right to express that opinion.' I nodded towards the copy pinned to the main easel and continued, 'If, then, you are not a moron what do you see there?'

She hesitated, then said, 'A – a face.'

'A face,' I scoffed. I half-turned, picked a foolscap pad from the table, took a charcoal pencil from my pocket and drew a circle. In that circle I placed two dots, between and below the two dots I drew a perpendicular line, below the perpendicular line I drew a horizontal line. I held the pad to face Sykes and said, 'And *there*, what do you see?'

'A face,' she choked . . . and had the grace to blush as she spoke.

'Two faces,' I sneered. 'That's what you see. That's *all* you see. That's what you *all* see. And you have the impudence – all of you – to claim to have an appreciation of art.'

It silenced them. It hurt them. It was meant to hurt them.

I placed the pad and the charcoal pencil on the table, strolled to the easel and, in a voice which held the contempt I felt, I threw the facts at them much as a man might toss a dog a bone.

I said, 'Vincent van Gogh. Even *you* may have heard the name. Born 1853. Died 1890. He shot himself, he too committed suicide. Why? Because he had too much charity and was subjected to too much sorrow. Because he too was surrounded by morons.

'Rembrandt – hopefully, you've heard of Rembrandt – Rembrandt used his canvas as a means of ensnaring shadows. Van Gogh, on the other hand, tried to capture sunlight. Consider that fact, please. All the man wanted to do was capture sunlight – happiness, joy, beauty – and share it with his fellow-men. Nothing more. Not riches. Not fame. He was one of the most humble men ever to live. But he loved brightness . . . and he yearned to share his love with the less fortunate. And for this they drove him insane. They scoffed. Eventually they enjoyed their perverted victory . . . they drove him to the point where he no longer wanted to live.'

It was absurdly simple. They were teenage girls; moving unsteadily through the emotional trauma of puberty; cosseted against the hurts and hammerings of everyday life. They were vulnerable. Ridiculously vulnerable, but I didn't give a damn, *they* had been partly responsible for Hannah's death.

For a moment I felt something not too far removed from

sympathy. Then the ball of hatred inside me swelled and re-heated itself and I turned to the print and continued my tirade.

'Your attention, ladies. Look at this self-portrait in more detail. Start with the eyes. The windows of the soul . . . so-called. Van Gogh knew more about the eyes – more about the soul – than most men. All of you . . . he's looking at you. Personally. Hang that portrait in any room. Stand anywhere you wish in that room . . . and the eyes remain fixed upon *you*. They move – or seem to move – you can never rid yourself of their accusation. The eyes of a madman, perhaps. The eyes of a man *driven* mad. Certainly the eyes of a man unable to understand the cruelty of his fellow-men.

'Now, the mouth. The curve – the hint of contempt – is perfect. The slightly protruding lower lip, resultant upon a thrust-out jaw. Van Gogh wasn't a *weak* man. Never forget that. He was a man with a self-imposed mission. The mission to give the world beauty, and that the world refused to accept that beauty embittered him. And yet, to the end, he blamed himself as much as he blamed others. It's all there in the face. Disgust and self-disgust. Anger and self-anger. The eyes. The mouth. The hint of a scowl. And yet the magic of the man – the humanity of the man – was such that he could convey all this on canvas, and at the same time show the underlying love. His love of life. His love of beauty. His love of people undeserving of that love. His love of dolts. Dolts who in the end drove him to his death.

'Examine the face, ladies. Examine the expression. Do not merely "look". *See*. And having seen, remember this. Van Gogh was not alone. Other men – other women – had and still have this monumental compassion and they, too, are often ridiculed. Their faces – like this face – reflect that norm of inhumanity which today is taken for granted. They do not understand. Their nature is such that they can *never* understand. This – here in the outside world – is their true madhouse. Far from being insane, they are the only sane persons alive. Understand that and you will be part-way towards understanding what this self-portrait is trying to say.'

I paused. I stared at each face in turn and as I stared some had the grace to lower their eyes. Seven spoiled brats. Seven females . . . too old to be called 'girls', but not yet old enough to be called 'women'. Some were blushing. Some had lost all facial colour. Some, while not yet openly weeping, had the glint of moisture in their eyes.

This 'art appreciation' class was something they would never forget; something which for the rest of their lives would haunt them. They would know. They would remember; they would remember Van Gogh – and they would remember Hannah and what they had done to Hannah – forever.

I nodded gently, as if satisfied.

'You are,' I said coldly, 'beginning to understand. One must be thankful for small mercies. You are, at least, *beginning* to understand. It is no longer . . .' I glanced at Sykes. 'It is no longer merely "a face". It is a message. A message of hopelessness. A message of despair. A message with nuances of misery which mere words can never convey.

'Now look at the picture . . . the whole of the picture of which the self-portrait is only a part. It is a "green" picture. Its overall colour is that sickly green which artists – and stage technicians – recognise as the colour of madness. The colour of hell. Hell is not red, ladies. Hell is a very personal thing. If it *has* a colour, that colour is green. A sickly, bilious green. That . . .' I tapped the print with the knuckle of my forefinger. '*That* green. Striated with streaks of off-white and pale blue. And note, ladies. That colour – the colour of madness – not only fills the background. It continues all over the jacket. All over the waistcoat. The right side of the face. The left cheek, above the beard. It grips the throat below the beard. It touches the lips and the eyes. It speckles the hair.

Van Gogh was telling the world something when he painted this self-portrait. Not merely what he *looked* like . . . he'd done that twice before. But what he had become. What the world had *made* him.'

Once more I paused, but this time only for a moment. What I had yet to say had to be said quickly. Quickly, before I lost control of my voice and my message became little more than broken-hearted ranting. Quickly . . . before the message of the portrait caught *me* by the throat and choked me.

I said, 'And, finally, ladies . . . the brushwork. The brushwork, too, has much to say. It augments all other things. It underlines everything the colour and the portrait itself has already said.

'Madness. Consider madness, ladies. Consider the proposition that madness – true madness – comes in two general forms. The passive madness of those who opt out of the world. Who opt out of a world which has crushed all life from them . . . and yet they continue to live. The "cabbage people". The unfortunates who refuse to think. Those whose bodies remain alive – *just*, but whose lives have become nothing because their minds have ceased to function.

'But there is another form of madness. Van Gogh's madness. The madness of those who fight . . . and are defeated. Their minds run riot. Their skulls pound and echo with hurt and humiliation. Theirs is the madness of movement. Wild movement. Frenzied movement. A movement of the mind beyond their control, but not beyond their comprehension.

'The movement depicted by the brushwork on this painting. Examine it . . . it is deserving of careful scrutiny. Van Gogh illustrates perfectly the tortures of his own mind through the medium of frenzied brushwork. Whirls. Countless snaking lines where in a normal portrait we would expect to find something restful. A scrawl of windings. A maze of contorted brush strokes . . . everywhere!

'The . . .' I cleared my throat. 'The self-portrait then of a man. "A face" if you wish to put it at its lowest level. The face of Van Gogh. But more than that . . . *much* more than that. The portrait of a personal agony. He painted it in 1890. That same year in which he took a borrowed pistol, walked into the deserted countryside and shot himself.'

I allowed myself the luxury of a deep breath in order to steady my nerves before I concluded, 'The original is in the Louvre. Should the opportunity arise, see it. Study it. Remember what it represents. Remember what I have told you this morning. And when some self-styled expert talks of "perspective" remember that this portrait, too, has a perspective. A relationship . . . which is all that "perspective" means. *This* relationship is the relationship between a good man – a fine and sensitive man – surrounded by morons . . . who eventually could carry that burden no farther.'

I thrust my hands deep into my pockets, then strode from the room. I looked at nobody as I left. The time allocated for the lesson was not yet half over but that was of no importance, the lesson *I* had intended to teach was complete.

By seven o'clock that 'art appreciation' lesson had become the talking point throughout the school. As he edged a way towards his place on the top table, Johnny grinned quick approval and allowed one eyelid to droop in the ghost of a conspiratorial wink. The other members of the staff politely ignored me. Come to that, they almost ignored each other. It was, I suppose, a form of self-preservation, there was only one real topic of conversation and that, it would seem, was *verboten*.

Even the pupils were less noisy than usual. The older girls – especially those in the sixth form – were silent and sullen. They fed the food into their mouths, chewed and swallowed, but if they enjoyed it – if they even *tasted* it – they gave no visible sign. I tried to read their expressions; tried to open up their petty little minds and see what impression my morning's indirect accusation had had upon the seven who had heard it and the others who had heard *of* it.

Sorrow? Perhaps, but if sorrow the shallow sorrow of an over-indulged child deprived of some undeserved treat. A sorrow which sprang from self-pity. Anger? Oh, yes, there was anger there. A pent-up, sullen anger. An anger which might demand some form of retribution. An anger which might have to be watched. But most of all there was outrage. A silent, brooding outrage; the brand of outrage common to a deposed tyrant . . . a very dangerous and unforgiving outrage.

It was an awkward meal. A meal in which the undertow of hatred made even surface politeness portentous. And when the meal ended – when Morley had vacated his chair and was leaving the hall – the summons was only what I expected.

'My office as soon as it's convenient, Mr Hemingway.'

I nodded, without turning my head.

I finished my coffee at leisure and, as I strolled along the corridor, Johnny moved into step alongside me.

'Don't apologise, mate,' he said gently.

'I won't.'

'From what I hear, you gave them hell this morning.'

'Perhaps.'

'Wet handkerchiefs all round.'

I smiled.

'It's what the bitches need.' I was shocked at the savagery of his tone. 'It's what they've needed for a long time.'

'Cool down, Johnny,' I advised. 'This is my fight.'

'*Our* fight. The others haven't the guts.'

I moved my shoulders.

He said, 'He can't sack you, Tony. He can't get a replacement at short notice . . . not at this time of the year.'

'Perhaps not.'

'Don't let him steam-roller you, mate, that's all.'

'I won't,' I promised.

'He'll try.'

I nodded.

We'd reached the end of the short corridor leading to Morley's office. We stopped and Johnny grasped my arm above the elbow in a token of allegiance.

He said, 'Remember . . . eh? Remember Hannah. This place breeds little cows capable of killing decent people. What the hell he says – what the hell he calls you – remember *that*.'

As I walked the few steps leading to Morley's office a thought struck me. Johnny. Specifically, Johnny's hatred.

All my life I'd lived in what might be called 'academic circles' . . . including, of course, pseudo-academic, near academic and would-be academic. The subdivisions made no difference to my basic premise. Circles in which Johnny would have been accepted without question. Circles in which petty annoyances, spite masquerading as wit and even open dislike, were virtually the life-blood of the members. Little genuine love can ever be found within the orbit of such circles, but at the same time little deep-rooted *hatred*.

Johnny's brand of hatred.

Accepting the fact that Morley was a smooth-tongued scoundrel – accepting the fact that basically he was a self-opinionated confidence trickster – even accepting the fact that, however indirectly, he had been partly responsible for Hannah's suicide . . . even accepting all these things, the depth of Johnny's hatred was beyond my understanding.

For myself and in the graveyard I, too, had hated Morley. Hated him enough to want to kill him. But since that surge of emotional abhorrence . . . The truth was I didn't know. The hatred was still there but, with the passing even of two days, it had been tempered by contempt. I disliked him. I disliked him intensely, but was that *hatred*? I thought not. As a man capable of controlling his thoughts – as a man capable of *thinking* – I knew hatred to be a very destructive emotion. Primitive. Blind. Lacking in reason. Indeed not merely destructive, but *self*-destructive.

And that left Johnny . . . where?

Or come to that . . . *why*?

I arrived at the door of Morley's office, tapped, was bidden to enter and composed myself for what I knew was going to be more than a mere skirmish.

Morley watched me all the way from the door to the desk; watched me as if I was a convicted man coming before him for sentence. I reached the desk and he stared up at me.

In a very moderate voice I said, 'Would it spoil the effect if I sat down?'

His mouth tightened for a moment, then he said, 'Sit down, Mr Hemingway.'

It was, I think, first blood to me. That being so I turned my back on him, chose one of the wing-chairs and, with equal deliberation, pulled it across the carpet to a position directly opposite him across the desk. I settled myself comfortably, then waited.

'This morning's art class,' he said in a controlled tone.

'Art *appreciation*,' I corrected him.

'You cut it short.'

'I cut it very short.'

'You had a reason, presumably?'

'I had,' I said, 'explained all that needed to be explained.'

'Indeed?'

'I doubt if the pupils could have absorbed any more.'

'You think not?'

'I'm quite sure.'

'There have,' he said, 'been complaints.'

'About the length of the lesson?'

'About the *content* of the lesson, and other things.'

'From the pupils?' I asked politely.

'From one specific pupil.'

'The complaint of *one* pupil,' I murmured.

'She claims to speak for the rest.'

'Of course, otherwise she'd feel a little foolish.'

'She assures me she *does* speak for the rest.'

'Am I allowed to know the nature of this pupil's complaint?'

'That you called the members of the class morons.'

'Ah, yes!' I smiled as if in sudden recollection. 'Miss Sykes?'

'Miss Sykes,' he agreed.

'My observation seemed to annoy her.'

'It *did* annoy her, and the others.'

'She implied that she *would* complain.'

'And?' He raised a sardonic eyebrow.

'She has that right, of course.'

'Of course.'

'I too of course claim the right to hold an opinion . . .'

'Mr Hemingway, you . . .'

'. . . as I explained to Miss Sykes.'

'Mr Hemingway.' He raised his eyes and stared at the ceiling. He seemed to be seeking approval from the Almighty for what he was saying. 'You are not on the staff of this establishment in order that you might insult the pupils.'

'Life would be much easier,' I murmured.

'Your work entails . . .'

'My work,' I interrupted flatly, 'entails an explanation of what is meant by the word "art".'

'Quite.'

'Also what is meant by the expression "art appreciation".'

'That also.'

'May we take Miss Sykes as a typical example?'

'By all means.'

I said, 'She's in her – what is it? – eighteenth year.'

'She is, indeed, seventeen years of age.'

'She's been here – correct me if I'm wrong – since she was eleven years of age. Six years.'

'Approximately six years.'

'Six years of "art and art appreciation". And yet I very much doubt if she yet knows the primary colours. She certainly does not have *any* appreciation of those colours when mixed and used by a genius.'

'That also is an opinion.'

'No.' I smiled. 'A fact. Last week's jaunt to Leeds to view the work of Jan van Eyck proved to be a complete waste . . . viewed from any angle you wish. A waste of their time. A waste of my time. A waste of school funds. A complete waste.'

'If you say so.'

'I *do* say so.'

He lowered his eyes and purred, 'Which means?'

'It means this,' I said bluntly. 'That after all the years in which I and whoever worked at the task before me – after six years of wasted effort trying to teach Miss Sykes and others the fundamentals of art – I claim the right to call her, and all those like her, moronic in their ignorance.'

'You have the right to hold that opinion,' he agreed smoothly.

'Thank you.'

'You do *not* have the right to voice that opinion.'

'I'm sorry, Headmaster.' I smiled. 'I disagree.'

'Mr Hemingway, you are in no position . . .'

'Unless, of course, part of my duty is to deliberately lie.'

'Lying . . . and not telling the unnecessary truth.' He smirked. 'There is a difference.'

'A very subtle difference.'

'Subtle, but there.'

'Headmaster.' I kept my voice controlled and reasonable. 'Nobody can fill a saucepan with water while the lid is firmly in place.'

'An analogy, I presume.'

'This morning I blew the lid off.'

'Did you?' His voice was hard. Flat. Mildly offensive.

'For the first time they *learned* something. For the first time they saw a *meaning* in a work of art.'

'Van Gogh's *Self-Portrait*?'

'Van Gogh's *Self-Portrait*,' I echoed.

'Forgive me . . .' His fingers touched his mouth, as if to check that the words about to be spoken were appropriate. 'Forgive me, Hemingway, but the girls considered that too analogous.'

'Analogous?' I tried to inject the exact amount of surprise into the word.

'Van Gogh committed suicide,' he said softly.

'Indeed.' I nodded. 'As I explained to the class . . .'

'Your wife also took her own life, Mr Hemingway.'

I waited. He was the one treading on eggshells, not I.

'Another analogy, you see,' he said.

'My wife's name was not mentioned.'

'I'm sure.' His lips curved into a quick, tight smile. 'Neither were saucepans.'

'No,' I agreed. 'Neither were saucepans.'

'You – er – you see what I'm getting at?'

'No,' I lied.

'The – er . . . The suggestion that in some way these girls were responsible for your wife's death.'

'An accusation?' I said quietly.

'No, merely a suggestion.'

'From them? From Sykes?'

'No, Mr Hemingway, from *you*.'

'I see.' I paused, then said, 'Van Gogh shot himself. I told them when. I told them why. That's *all* I told them.'

'Nevertheless . . .'

'Headmaster, I am not responsible for the curious twists and turns of a teenager's mind. Especially the mind of a girl like Sykes. You must ask *her* why a detailed reason for

Vincent van Gogh's suicide brings on a sense of guilt. You must . . .'

'Did I mention anything about a sense of guilt?'

'Why otherwise would she lodge a complaint?'

He moved his shoulders, then drawled, 'As you so rightly remark. Who can follow the twists and turns of a teenager's mind?'

'Or the cause for her complaints.'

'Or the cause for her complaints,' he agreed.

'Or,' I said, deliberately, 'why *you* should place so much credence upon such complaints.'

It stopped him . . . and I knew I'd won. For little more than a second his eyes gleamed resentment. Then he composed his expression into one of long-suffering patience.

'The position,' he sighed. He smiled, then said, 'Forgive me, Mr Hemingway. I sometimes take the responsibilities of headship a little too seriously. If I have – er – angered you . . .'

'No. You haven't angered me,' I taunted gently.

'Or embarrassed you . . .'

'*Or* embarrassed me.'

'I'm glad. I'm very glad.'

'You see,' I mocked, 'I *know* why my wife killed herself.'

'Really!' He frowned. 'In that case . . .'

'Private knowledge, of course.'

'Oh – er – of course. Of course.'

'Is that all?' I asked.

'Oh, yes, yes. And – er – thank you for your time, Mr Hemingway. Thank you for your time. I – er – I like to get these small matters cleared up as soon as possible.'

They were waiting in the staff lounge. The mistresses and the handful of masters; women who were in varying degrees terrified of Morley; men who expected to see a dejected colleague slink, tail-between-his-legs, to some isolated armchair. Other than those on duty supervising evening prep they were all there and my somewhat jaunty entrance surprised them.

'Okay?' asked Johnny.

'Fine.'

'A carpeting?'

'If there was,' I smiled, 'he was at the receiving end.'

And they all heard me and Johnny grinned vast approval, but as for me it was a hollow victory. It had no substance and, if it had a taste, the taste was sour where it should have been sweet.

Johnny seemed to sense my mood. He was curious – knowing Johnny I knew he was bursting with questions – but he didn't press for details and I sat in an armchair and made believe I was engrossed in an article in a month-old edition of *Teachers World*.

And oddly enough, at that moment, Hannah seemed very near. In the lounge surrounded by men and women who had been *her* colleagues too I somehow felt her presence.

Mentally, I sought her approval for what I'd done to Morley; in my mind I took her through the wording of the suicide note. Morley and the pupils of the sixth form. The reason why she was no longer here. The *cause* of it all. Why shouldn't they, too, suffer? Why shouldn't they, too, feel humiliation?

And if she answered – if she reached beyond the grave and tried to comfort me – I was too deaf to hear.

I made it an early night. By ten-thirty I was in my bedroom. On an impulse I swallowed a mild sleeping pill in an effort to quieten my brain. And it worked. I was asleep within minutes of my head touching my pillow.

I awakened to a darkened bedroom with somebody pounding at the door. I climbed from bed, switched on the light, draped a dressing-gown over my shoulders and still bleary-eyed opened the door. Johnny was there and the look on his face brought me fully awake.

One of the sixth formers – Daisy Arkwright – was missing from her dormitory. Everything pointed to her having dressed before running away from The Ridings and outside the temperature was well below freezing, with wind and more snow blowing up to another blizzard.

I glanced at my watch. The hands showed just after 2 a.m.

The Fall of the Fifth Domino

Lennox. Full style and title, Detective Chief Superintendent Lennox, Head of C.I.D., Bordfield Region of the Lessford Metropolitan Police Area. Quite a mouthful, but known to his friends as 'Lenny'. (Oddly enough none of them knew his first name.)

Respected – indeed in some cases almost deified – but these days worried over. And with reason. A man can't lose five stone in as many months and not look haggard. He may look heavy and indeed Lennox *was* still heavy – even portly – but he was no longer the near-obese, Billy-Bunter-like creature of half a year previously. Like a Christmas balloon left too long the life seemed to have leaked slowly from his rotund frame, leaving the skin wrinkled and slack. He was still Lennox – still 'Lenny' to his friends – but such a changed Lennox!

For a man to have to watch his wife die is a terrible experience. For him to have to watch her die, virtually hour at a time for more than three months; being strangled to death by throat cancer; having the simple choice of continual agony or an increasing dosage of heroin-based drugs . . . for a man to have to watch *that* beggars description. It is an experience which must be lived before it can be understood.

Lennox understood it and, in the understanding thereof, he had suffered something akin to ordeal by fire.

The Victorian monstrosity they'd called 'home' was up for sale. The cats – the Russian Blues – she'd bred and loved had already been sold or given as gifts to friends. Every stick of furniture was in storage. There was nothing left to remind him and he wanted it that way.

He deliberately overworked; driving himself to the point of exhaustion, before snatching a few hours of sleep in the tiny night room at Bordfield Headquarters. Officially, he lived in a small guest house on the outskirts of the city, but he never took a meal there and he rarely slept there more than a couple of nights each week. It was somewhere to keep his clothes. Somewhere to which his private mail might be addressed. He had to live *somewhere* . . . he 'lived' there.

And yet he was still Lennox; the man-hunter; the thief-taker; one of that very rare breed of men who are born coppers.

He kept his hands in the pockets of his loose-fitting mac, swung his head to take in the gloomy loftiness of the main room and its array of ancient weapons and grunted, 'Very imposing.'

'Blunt instruments galore,' observed Tallboy.

Chris Tallboy was the Beechwood Brook divisional chief inspector. Maybe young for the rank, but wise in the ways of crime detection, despite his lack of years he had that world-weary look of the working jack who'd seen everything, heard everything and was prepared to believe nothing (but *nothing*) without corroborative evidence. Lennox and Tallboy made up two of a trio of officers and the third was Chief Superintendent Blayde; Beechwood Brook divisional chief superintendent and the man within .whose bailiwick the double murder had been committed. Blayde was not amused and he made no secret of that fact.

'The bloody maniac,' he growled. 'Is there an inventory of these damn things?'

'The insurance people,' suggested Tallboy. 'They should have 'em listed.'

'Let's hope so. If Cooley's tooling around with one of them things in his fist, somebody's likely to be hurt.'

'Sure it's Cooley?' asked Lennox.

'Chances,' said Tallboy shortly. 'The Evostick-and-tape trick. That's his M.O. *And* he messed a pile before he came inside . . . that's another of his trade marks.'

'Cooley's a breaker . . . not a killer.'

Blayde said, 'That should make Page and his girl friend *very* happy.'

'If it's him he killed this time,' murmured Tallboy.

'Pity.' Lennox sounded genuinely sorry that Cooley had on the face of things turned killer.

By this time all the ritualistic 'initial action' had been taken. The two bodies had been found by a daily cleaning-woman when she'd arrived at eight o'clock that morning. Having screamed the place down she'd dialled 999, and before 8.15 the three-ring circus of a murder enquiry had been on the road. Fingerprint-finders, photographers, plan-drawers, scene-of-crime experts, forensic scientists . . . the whole shooting match. Blayde and Tallboy had arrived in Blayde's Rover at a few minutes past nine. By that time the place had seemed to be running wild with coppers, both plain clothes and uniformed . . . and more were sprouting like mushrooms by the minute.

The media people had also had the tip-off and they too were tramping all over the flower beds. Fortunately, a uniformed sergeant had been among the first at the scene and he'd dropped the boom on any idle chit-chat which might, eventually, be elevated to the mock authority of 'a police statement'. The required medic had been and gone, having verified what everybody else knew . . . that the bodies *were* bodies.

And now, with the arrival of Lennox, the double murder might be said to have received the stamp of authenticity.

'Next-of-kin?' asked Lennox.

'Mrs Page is in Ireland,' said Tallboy. 'We're trying to find the exact address, then we'll ask the Irish lads to notify her.'

'The woman?'

'Angela Warton. She'd a kidney-donor card in her handbag.'

'Thoughtful of her.'

'The North Yorks lads have contacted the father. She isn't married. He's on his way.'

Lennox frowned at the two lifeless bundles of bloodstained flesh and said, 'Keep him away from here.'

Blayde said, 'They'll be shifting 'em before long. I'll get 'em cleaned up at the morgue for identification purposes.'

Lennox grunted his approval, then said, 'And Cooley?'

Blayde said, 'We're waiting for news from his home.'

'Detective Sergeant Jackson and a squad-car team,' added Tallboy. 'If he's there, they'll pick him up. If not, they'll put a watch on the house.'

Poor old Cooley. He'd done it this time . . . *and* he knew it. The 'feel' of that pike as it had driven its way through the breastbone – of that mace as it had punched the skull into the brain tissue – was still there at the nerve ends of his hands. It was like an invisible stain; like a tiny everlasting electric shock. It made his fingers tremble as they gripped the steering wheel. It made him fumble the lever at every gear change.

And it made him sweat. His pock-marked face shone with the stuff. His hands were slippery on the wheel. It had soaked into his underclothes and had made them damp and clammy against his skin.

Sweet Jesus!

He wasn't a violent man. Ever! Ask anybody . . . ask the rozz themselves. Ben Cooley was *not* a violent man. He'd been caught. Sure, he'd been caught, everybody gets caught sometimes, but no aggro. No hardship. He'd coughed what he'd known they could prove and he'd done cell time as quietly as the next con. No prison riots for Cooley. No arm-chancing. A third off for good behaviour . . . and don't be a born mug. That had been his motto. Still *was* his motto.

So why the hell . . . ?

Because that mad bastard had been trying to shoot holes in him, that was why. It had been a strictly life-or-death set-up. No messing. No bull. That crazy bastard had been trigger-happy.

Nevertheless . . .

He pulled into a layby, switched off the engine and wiped his sweating palms against the knees of his trousers. A single tear of monumental self-pity spilled from the corner of one eye and trickled down his pock-marked face.

He didn't know where to go.

He didn't know what to do.

He didn't know *anything* any more.

It was closing up to noon on Friday, February 10th, when Lennox, flanked by Tallboy, questioned Madge Cooley. It was a strange interview. Not really an interview at all, more of a gentle question-and-answer session between a frightened, no-longer-young woman and an older, favourite uncle-type man who himself wore the scars of mental hurt. There was no hatred. No bullying. No 'leaning'. Instead, there was near-panic on the one side and understanding and consideration on the other.

The conversation took place in the living room of Cooley's

home. A small, comfortable room, heated by the gas fire which was part of the central-heating system; a room cluttered with rather too much chain-store furniture; a room carpeted and wallpapered like half a million similar 'working-class' homes . . . and that Cooley's 'work' was of a peculiar nature made not a scrap of difference to the clean 'respectability' reflected in every item within that room.

Madge Cooley had once been almost beautiful. It was still there despite the sagging shoulders and the permanent worry lines around the mouth and eyes . . . the remaining shadow of that pride which all good-looking women carry like a second skin. Her clothes and hair were cared for. Her speech was restrained, controlled despite the present emotion which was tearing her apart. This one was no criminal's 'moll'; this one was a decent, sensitive woman who at one time had fallen in love with, then married, a man with a criminal kink in his make-up.

She said, 'You can't be sure it's him, Mr Lennox.'

'Madge, luv . . .' The use of her first name was not first-time familiarity. Lennox had gone through this before; by this time they knew each other and respected each other. He said, 'It was Ben. We're pretty sure it was Ben.'

'But not *quite* sure.'

'Sure enough,' contributed Tallboy bluntly.

Lennox said, 'Look, if you know where he is . . .'

'I don't know where he is.'

'If you know where he is,' insisted Lennox gently, 'you'll be doing him a favour.'

'He's my husband.' She smiled sadly. 'Mr Lennox, you've asked that question before. I've never answered it.'

'I know.' Lennox nodded his understanding. 'This time it's a bit different.'

'Murder?'

'He'll be charged with murder,' agreed Lennox.

'And you expect me to . . .'

'But not necessarily *convicted* of murder.'

She watched his face, and her expression mixed non-understanding with suspicion.

Lennox said, 'Manslaughter, perhaps. Self-defence.'

'Why? Why should he . . .'

'Page had a gun in his hand.'

'Oh!'

'We can prove – we *will* prove – that he fired three shots.'

'Oh, my God!'

Her hand flew to her mouth and fear for the safety of her husband widened her eyes; a new sort of fear . . . fear for his physical well-being. Tallboy watched, listened and marvelled. The old fox had not lost his cunning. Not a lie – not a single untruth – but by playing what few trump cards he possessed, and by playing them at *exactly* the right moment, Lennox was easing the woman away from her natural defence of her husband.

'Is he – is he hurt?' she whispered.

'That we don't know, luv.' (No . . . strictly speaking it wasn't a lie. They knew he hadn't been *shot* – the forensic boys had established that by matching the various bloodstains – but that wasn't the question she'd asked.) Lennox moved his hands and murmured, 'We'll know whether he's in one piece when we find him.'

'He might be dead,' she groaned.

Lennox didn't answer. Nor was the sympathy which showed on his face entirely false.

'What if he *is* dead?' she asked.

'I – er – I doubt if he's dead.'

'But he *could* be.'

'It's not impossible,' agreed Lennox, again without lying.

'Then – then why don't you find him? Why don't you *do* something.'

'Easy, Madge, luv. Easy,' soothed Lennox. 'That's why we're here. We *want* to find him. We'd like your help.'

'What?' She moved her hand helplessly. 'What can I do? What is it you want to know?'

'Names. Places.'

'I keep telling you. I don't know where . ...'

'And I believe you,' interrupted Lennox gravely. 'But he has to be *somewhere*. We don't even know where to start looking. So . . . Put yourself in our shoes. Where would *you* look? Who would *you* visit?'

It was such a reasonable request. And, moreover, it was made to a normal but distraught woman, to a wife who loved her husband. The purists might have argued that the tactics used by Lennox were 'suspect'; that, while not actually telling lies, he had *implied* lies. That to a woman less innocent of the wiles of crime detection this gentle, softly-softly-catchee-monkey approach would have been wasted.

The truth is that to some hard-shelled, run-of-the-mill wife of the average law-breaker, the approach would have been far more aggressive. The so-called 'frighteners' would have been put on. Had she insisted that the sun rose each morning and set each evening she'd *still* have been called a liar. Coppers work that way. They adapt their manner to suit the occasion. They are the finest practical psychologists in the world. Nor do they make excuses. Or need to. Their job is to detect crime . . . period.

Lennox and Tallboy left the home of Cooley complete with a list of possible hiding places and a list of names. One of those names was Archibald Hall.

Cooley parked the car on the prom; on the North Promenade . . . the stretch known as 'The Zone of Ozone'. He wound down the nearside window and allowed the cold wind from the sea to freshen up the interior of the Ford Capri. The gunmetal sea beyond the expanse of deserted sand; the grey, unfriendly sea with its never-ending succession of white-rimmed waves crawling in towards the gentle slope of the shore.

Christ! Even the *sea* seemed wrong. Even the *sea* seemed to scowl its disapproval.

And that niff with all the knowledge; that fellow-con with all the know-how; that prize berk who knew all the bloody answers.

'Mush, if you're ever on the run. Blackpool. No sweat, mush. All the mugs in the world busy enjoying themselves. Lose yourself? Jesus, you could lose this whole bloody nick. All the pigs busy directing traffic. All the bananas on holiday shoving and pushing. If you're ever on the run, mush. Blackpool!'

Well, that prize niff should be here *now*. Out of season. All the way north from Lytham up to here. Busy? As busy as a closed-down cemetery, that's how busy. Crowds? Three stray dogs and a couple of old biddies nattering to each other in a shelter . . . that was about the size of the crowds. Every stinking stall was closed and shuttered. More than half the blinding hotels with locked doors. And trams? Okay, trams, one of Blackpool's big gimmicks, and he'd visited the place a couple of times in high season and you couldn't cross the bloody prom without dodging trams, but today . . . two flaming trams, one going north one going south, in the last six miles or so from Squires Gate.

Cooley felt very exposed. He'd seen a couple of flatfeet strolling along the deserted prom, but as sure as hell they weren't directing traffic. They were bored. They were itching to spot something with which to relieve their boredom. And if he wasn't careful *he* was going to be that 'something'.

He sighed, leaned across the front passenger seat and wound up the window. The hell with it . . . Blackpool was *out*. He started the engine and drove north, watching for the first sign pointing to Preston and back to the east side of the Pennines.

*

Archibald Hall did not like interview rooms. As far as he was concerned, they brought on the shakes. Despite their clinical cleanliness – despite their functional but comfortable enough furniture – they were the twentieth-century substitute for the old-fashioned torture chamber.

To be dumped in a police interview room was to be taken out of circulation. It was the initial step towards being surrounded by granite and he *knew*, because it had happened to him once before.

When, therefore, Detective Chief Inspector Tallboy opened the door and joined Archibald Hall in the interview room, Archibald Hall took a deep breath in order to raise as many objections as possible in one wallop, then closed his mouth without saying anything, because Tallboy looked very contented and when a jack like Tallboy looked contented that was the time to start *really* worrying.

'Now then, Archie.' Tallboy straddled a chair and rested his forearms across its back. 'Let's have a little chinwag, shall we?'

Hall moistened his lips and said, 'Nobody's told me why.'

'Why what?'

'Why I'm *here*.'

'Oh, *that*?' Tallboy grinned. 'You're being a good citizen for a change.'

'Eh?'

'Assisting the police in their enquiries . . . that sort of thing.'

'What – what sort of enquiries?'

'You've a fair old choice.' Tallboy fished in his pocket and tossed a tiny square of wood with a length of tape attached on to the surface of the table. He said, 'That for starters.'

'What is it?' Hall looked puzzled.

'Oh, come *on*.' Tallboy's eyebrows shot up.

'What the hell *is* it?' Hall picked up the square of wood

and examined it suspiciously. As he replaced it on the table he said, 'I dunno what you're getting at. I've never seen that before in my life. I don't know what the hell it *is*.'

'Guess,' suggested Tallboy.

'A piece of wood. Some cheap tape. What else?'

'Breaking and entering?' suggested Tallboy.

'Who?' Hall blinked.

'Not Father Christmas,' Tallboy assured him.

'Look . . .' Hall moistened his lips again. 'I want a lawyer.'

'Why?'

'This thing.' Hall picked up the square of wood again. Then dropped it back on the table. 'Maybe I should know what it is?'

'Don't you?'

'Breaking and entering. That's what you said.'

'Those were my exact words,' agreed Tallboy.

'It don't make sense.'

'No?'

'I ain't no breaker.'

'That's what *you* say.'

'Look, Mr Tallboy, you know me. All I do . . .'

'All you've *done* so far is handle stolen property.'

'I did my stretch for it. I learned my . . .'

'Archie,' sighed Tallboy, 'sticky-fingered little buggers like you *never* learn.'

'You've no right . . .'

'They get ambitious.'

'You've no bloody right . . .'

'Breaking and entering.' Tallboy reached out and lifted the square of wood by its tape. He dangled it just beyond Hall's reach. 'That's what this proves.'

'I don't know what the hell it *is*.'

'Part of a nifty way of opening locked windows.'

'Oh! I didn't . . .'

'Used last night.'

'That's nothing to do . . .'

'With your dabs all over it,' smiled Tallboy.

Hall seemed to shrink inside his skin. His jaw dropped, his eyes widened and he seemed to have difficulty in breathing.

'You're fixed, Archie,' said Tallboy pleasantly. 'Fixed. Tied up in pink ribbon and delivered.'

'Why?' groaned Hall. 'For Christ's sake, *why*? Why *me*?'

There was a tap on the door, Tallboy called for the tapper to enter and a uniformed constable opened the door, handed Tallboy a typed sheet of paper, then left.

As he read the paper, Tallboy murmured, 'Why not?'

'Eh?'

'People like you are a pain in the arse, Archie.' Tallboy spoke softly – almost, it seemed, absent-mindedly – as he continued to read the typewritten sheet. He seemed to be talking to himself. 'The only valid reason for shithouses like you crawling the face of the earth is that you provide hard-working cops with a pension.' He raised his head, smiled at Hall, then said, 'Now, shall we go on?'

'I – I dunno what . . .'

'Fine. I'll tell you. Last night Page's place was done . . . you know Page's place?'

'Sure I know Page's place. But . . .'

'It was bust.' Tallboy held up the piece of wood attached to the tape. 'This little gadget was used.'

'Look, you know bloody well . . .'

'Page was murdered.'

'Oh, my God!'

'Page's lady friend was also murdered.'

'No. You – you *can't*.'

'That's wishful thinking, Archie. I can and I will.'

'Please! Mr Tallboy, *please*.'

'These things.' Tallboy moved the sheet of paper. 'This

list. Nicked property. All found tucked away in a back room of that dump you call an antique shop.'

'Not – not from Page's place, I swear.'

'No?'

'Not from Page's place,' pleaded Hall.

'You haven't read the list yet,' said Tallboy reasonably.

'I know. But – but . . .'

'Nicked property,' insisted Tallboy.

'Yeah. Yeah.' Hall nodded his head vigorously. 'I know.'

'You *know*?'

'Yeah, I know.'

Tallboy leaned forward across the back of the chair and said, 'Okay. Let's hear what you *do* know.'

A different copper, a different technique; Lennox might not have handled the interview in quite the same way. But there again the interviewee wasn't the same sort of person. Hall was as bent as a country lane, ergo, as far as Hall was concerned, cops were all bastards and capable of anything. Anything! Not for the first time that belief had been used as a weapon against somebody holding that belief. Moreover Madge Cooley had been genuinely concerned about the safety of her husband. The only person whose safety interested Archibald Hall was Archibald Hall. And finally – and not least important – Hall had a conscience (or something passing as a conscience) and he knew he was as guilty as hell about *some* things.

In police parlance it was known as a 'cough' – or if you like an 'aria' – and whilever Tallboy expressed scornful disbelief the 'cough' became stronger, the 'aria' was notched up a few notes.

Sure – sure he was a fence. Jesus, the cops *knew* that, didn't they? They'd nicked him for it once. He dealt in hot stuff, didn't he? That was – y'know – that was his *thing*. Antique shops – schmantique shops – who the hell made real bread selling the brand of antiques *he* handled? Some yo-yo found a Turner behind the logs in the woodshed. Would they bring it to him? Would they? Would they hell as like. And supposing they did, y'know, just supposing, he wouldn't know a Turner from a chalk drawing on a paving stone.

The stuff on the list? The stuff they'd found at the back of his place? Well, okay, maybe it *had* been lifted. Okay, okay it *had* been lifted. Who was arguing? Was he in any position to make a big production job out of it? It had been lifted, okay. Yeah, he'd *known* it had been lifted, that too. Poor old Archie Hall. Always left sucking the hammer. Always left with his thumb up his bum. He wasn't complaining, though. Maybe a warrant should have been sworn out. Maybe – he wasn't beefing, you understand – what was a lousy warrant between friends? It was hot stuff and he was handling it, and the cops had to do their jobs, and the cops found it on his premises . . . end of argument. He wasn't complaining.

He'd plead 'guilty', sure he'd plead 'guilty'. What else? Just – y'know – ease off on the Page thing, eh? Don't keep talking about murder. As a favour. Please! Don't keep saying that word. Just give him time. Just give him elbow room and he'd talk. He'd name names, sure he'd name names. Why not? He wasn't a complete mug. Just – y'know – don't keep saying that word 'murder'.

Page's place. Well, now, guessing, you understand? Just guessing. But in his business a man got a gut feeling sometimes. Just a gut feeling, that's all. No proof. For Christ's sake, don't ask for *proof*. Just this – y'know – this gut feeling.

Cooley, right? Poxy Cooley might be the right man. Just *might*, you understand. No proof. Cooley hadn't brought anything hot for weeks. Months. But – y'know – something was on the board. Something just *might* have been coming his way. The word was on the street that Cooley had something lined up.

Cooley? How in hell did *he* know where Cooley was? Cooley was Cooley. Cooley didn't work tandem, did he? From what he'd heard, Cooley never worked tandem. The cops should know, shouldn't they? If the cops didn't know, how the hell could a poor guy like Archie Hall . . .

Okay, okay, please don't keep using that terrible word 'murder'. He was a fence. That's all he was. He was *not* a murderer. He wasn't even a breaker. He handled tailboard stuff, that's all. Off-of-a-lorry stuff. And – okay – he'd handled stuff from Cooley before now. But where Cooley might *be*? Ask his wife, eh? Cooley was a funny guy. He was soft on his missus, right? Didn't the cops know that? Cooley was . . .

Archibald Hall went into great detail about what Cooley was and what Cooley wasn't, but not a hint about *where* Cooley was. The threat of 'fixing' – even the threat of being charged with double murder – brought only what Tallboy recognised as wild and sometimes fanciful guesses.

At last Tallboy stood up from the chair.

As he wound the tape around the square of wood and dropped it back into his pocket, he said, 'That's it, then, Archie. I hope for your sake you've held nothing back.'

'Would you . . .' Hall gave a tiny nod in the direction of the pocket into which Tallboy had dropped the square of wood. He hesitated, then said, '*Would* you?'

'You've saved your bacon, Archie. Handling stolen property, that'll do as far as you're concerned.'

'You *wouldn't*, though, would you?' Hall was almost pleading for reassurance.

Very solemnly Tallboy said, 'With a man like you – with a man like me – be advised, don't place a bet on it.'

Cooley drove into Leeds from the north on the A660 Otley Road, past Adel, past the Ring Road roundabout and south into Headingley. At Headingley he turned off the main road, parked the Capri in a side street, then walked to where he'd spotted a newsagent's.

For about three minutes he waited, then, as the newsagent's became suddenly busy with home-going workpeople, he hurried into the shop, picked up a copy of the *Yorkshire Evening Post*, handed the girl behind the counter the correct money, then returned to the lamplit gloom of the street. He returned to the Capri, climbed inside and eased the car forward until it was under a street lamp.

Cooley was hungry for knowledge. Anything. Some hint as to how close on his heels the police might be, if indeed they *were* on his heels.

Since he'd killed Page and Warton he'd been on the run. Aimlessly. Like a headless chicken. Blackpool? That had been stupid. Stupid! Part of the initial panic. First he'd belted for the A1 and south, south for the Big City and the anonymity of crowds. He'd switched from the A1 to the A1(M), to the M18 and from there to the M1. Then the thought of London – the thought of the London coppers, the thought of New Scotland Yard – had brought about a change of mind. He was a Northerner. He carried an inbuilt distrust of Southerners. He didn't *know* anybody down there. Only that the Big Place was run by 'firms'; terrible men with whom it was suicidal to tangle; tightly knit groups of criminals who'd shop anybody – *anybody* – not in their clique . . . that's what he'd heard and he'd no reason to doubt it. But crowds? The bean-in-a-barrel-of-beans argument still sounded good. He wanted crowds. He wanted a mass within which he was an invisible unit.

He'd left the M1 at the fourteenth interchange and driven west – from Newport Pagnell to Buckingham to Banbury to Stratford-on-Avon – to the fourth interchange on the M5. Somewhere between the M1 and the M5 he'd filled the tank at some tiny filling station east of Buckingham, where he'd been able to stay in the car and hand the money to the attendant without showing his face. Once on the M5 he'd raced north again; north on the M5 to the M6 then on the thirty-first interchange west to the coast . . . and Blackpool.

But Blackpool out of season. That had been his big error. That had been something which with his mind still in a turmoil he hadn't remembered. He *should* have remembered, and by *not* remembering he'd almost lost his nerve.

Then back east along the A59, the A65 and the A660 to Leeds. To crowds; to a multitude which didn't depend on sunshine . . . and to somewhere he *knew*.

And now it was evening, and God only knew how many miles he'd driven – driven with no destination in mind – and he was exhausted and he was hungry and he wanted to *know*.

The report of the killing was on the front page of the *Yorkshire Evening Post*. The usual journalistic background; who the man was, who the woman was; Lennox's name as the officer heading the enquiry . . . and then that last sentence.

'A man is in custody helping the police in their enquiries.'

Holy Mother of God!

They'd boobed. They'd lifted the wrong man. 'Helping in their enquiries' . . . that was copper's jargon for being nicked. The wrong man.

He was safe!

He began to laugh. He tried to control himself, but some of the laughter came nevertheless. Hysterical laughter. Like the sudden release of elastic which for hours had been stretched to near breaking-point. Laughter which lasted all of three uncontrollable minutes. Which streamed his eyes with relief.

Then the tears changed; the emotion changed; like the slow 'dissolve' of one motion picture scene into another, the relief became false, the joy became a mockery and he gripped the wheel, lowered his forehead on to the rim and the sobs ripped their way through his whole body.

SIX

An open M.G. sports car was no car in which to ride out in search of a missing schoolgirl; not even an open M.G. sports with the personal character of Bertha. We used my car and with the headlights on I drove while Johnny leaned forward in the front passenger seat and peered into the weather.

It could have been worse, I suppose. The snow carried sleet with it and the whiteness wasn't thickening. Nevertheless, it was some degrees below freezing and the wind was driving the near-blizzard at too many knots for comfort . . . too many knots for *survival* without the proper clothes.

Johnny grunted, 'The silly young bitch.'

He was right, too, and yet not *completely* right.

Daisy Arkwright fitted uncomfortably into the general pattern of the other scholars housed at The Ridings. As I recalled she was an only child. Her father held some important post within one of the multi-national oil giants; some technical post which required him to spend most of his life in the oil fields of the Middle East. His wife travelled with him and they left their daughter here in England – at The Ridings – in the pious hope that she'd enjoy a 'good education'.

There was (or so I believed) a grandparent somewhere. A grandfather, an elderly man spritely for his years, who visited the school occasionally at weekends. I'd met him a couple of times – I recalled that *his* name was Arkwright, therefore if he *was* her grandfather, his son was *her* father – and each time I'd met him I'd had the feeling that inside he was seething. At a guess the old man had measured The

Ridings for what it was. At a further guess, he thought more about the girl than did her own parents.

'Try there.' Johnny pointed through the mixture of snow and sleet which threatened to prove too much for the wipers. 'Up there. That cart-track.'

I fought the wheel and skidded the car right and on to a road which seemed to lead to nowhere. An unsurfaced road where the tyres threatened to lose traction. It was one hell of a way to spend the early hours of a Saturday morning. God knows where we were. We were merely 'looking' – 'searching' – and the truth was we didn't know where to 'look'.

'What time did she go missing?' I gasped.

'Sometime after midnight . . . we think.'

'How come?'

'Eh?'

'Who found she'd gone?'

'One of the other girls in the dormitory. She got up for a pee, found Arkwright's bed empty. She apparently waited a while – probably thought Arkwright was on a similar mission – then raised the roof.'

'The spice of life,' I remarked bitterly.

'Yeah.' Johnny leaned even more forward in an attempt to see through the weather. 'Where the hell *does* this road go to anyway?'

'Road? You must be joking.'

But it wasn't a joke and we both knew that.

Daisy Arkwright was a girl old for her years. She lived inside herself; refused to become involved with the stupidities indulged in by the other sixth formers. She was the one 'loner' in the pack and because she was different the others could never understand her.

I understood her . . . or thought I did.

She had a loyalty almost beyond belief. A loyalty and an intelligence. The intelligence told her that The Ridings was just about the lousiest school in the U.K. for any child with brains, but the loyalty prevented her from questioning the choice of her parents. As long as I could remember she'd worked to disentangle herself from this loyalty/intelligence trap. She worked. She read. She asked questions. She beavered away to understand. She'd been Hannah's favourite pupil. As art hers was the only effort worthy of any consideration.

She didn't *belong* to The Ridings. That was the truth of the matter. She didn't *belong* . . . and now she'd left.

As I hauled the car out of yet another slide, I said, 'Why in hell's name had it to be Arkwright?'

It was past dawn before we got back to The Ridings. We'd been lost along by-lanes and farm roads more than once. Both of us were filthy and soaked to the skin; at various times we'd each had to push at the rear of the car, while the other revved the engine in an attempt to get forward movement.

Arkwright was still missing, everybody in the school was either up and about or out searching. And the police had been called in.

His name was Blayde, his rank was chief superintendent and from the moment Morley introduced us I disliked him. He was one of those slim, hawk-nosed men; the type who on a cinema screen can be seen standing on the bridge of a naval vessel. His eyes were of an unusually true forget-me-not blue; merciless eyes; arrogant eyes; the eyes of a man who found fault very easily.

(It may well be, of course, that I was biased. When Hannah had taken her life *that* tragedy had only called for the attendance of a uniformed sergeant and an attendant constable. But the absence of a rather silly schoolgirl apparently necessitated the presence of a uniformed chief superintendent and the usual retinue of sergeants, constables and even a duo of detectives. Howbeit, from the first I disliked the man.)

'Anything?' he asked brusquely.

'If we'd found her she'd be with us,' I said.

'Which area have you covered?'

Johnny said, 'God knows.'

I added, 'We've been lost half the time.'

'That's no way to search.'

'We're prepared to learn.'

He eyed me without humour for a moment, then said, 'You're Hemingway?'

'The headmaster's already . . .'

'I'd like a word with you.'

'A word?'

'A talk.'

'What about?'

'In private.'

I frowned, then said, 'I need a bath and a change of clothes.'

'I'll still be here.'

'Say thirty minutes?' I suggested.

'I'll still be here,' he repeated.

We used the senior prep room. A moderately large room and just the two of us; our voices sounded a little hollow and echoing in the place. I'd bathed, shaved and changed. I felt more human; more mellow; better able to cope with this stern-faced man whose manner – whose very presence – seemed to antagonise me. We stood as we talked. Strictly speaking, we lounged; I leaned against the warmth of one of the radiators, while Blayde rested his backside on the edge of one of the tables.

Blayde didn't waste time on preliminaries.

He said, 'A week ago – a week ago today – your wife committed suicide.'

'She gassed herself,' I agreed quietly.

'Why?'

'There was an inquest,' I reminded him.

'Not a satisfactory inquest.'

'The coroner seemed satisfied.'

'*I* wasn't satisfied.'

'That's unfortunate . . . for you,' I said bluntly.

'Hemingway.' He didn't raise his voice, but there was warning in every vowel. 'We're here to talk about two things. The unexplained suicide of your wife. And why a perfectly normal schoolgirl should walk out into weather like it was last night.'

'Is there a connection?' I asked.

'I think it likely.'

'I can see no connection,' I grunted.

'Unlike you, I have a suspicious mind.'

'The job, I suppose,' I commented.

He ignored the remark and said, 'Let's talk about your wife.'

'I find it a painful subject.'

'I find it a very *interesting* subject.'

'Death?' My lip curled. 'Self-destruction? Interesting?'

'From a professional point of view.'

'Perhaps it *wasn't* suicide,' I mocked.

His eyes became fractionally even more arrogant as he countered, 'Please don't think I've dismissed *that* possibility.'

'She gassed herself,' I said flatly.

'Why?'

'I don't know.'

'Suicides usually give a reason. Tell a reason. Hint at a reason. Leave a note *giving* the reason.'

'Always?'

'Far more often than not.'

I said, 'Your sergeant seemed satisfied.'

'That's his job.'

'What?'

'To give the *appearance* of satisfaction.'

'Meaning he wasn't?'

'Meaning he collected the evidence, presented it to the coroner and accepted the coroner's verdict, then went home to bed.'

'Very objective,' I murmured.

'That, too, goes with the job.'

'But you?' I cocked an eyebrow.

'I'm not a sergeant, and now there's this missing schoolgirl.'

'And you think there's a connection?'

'I do.' He nodded then suddenly – without warning – he snapped, 'Why *did* your wife gas herself, Hemingway?'

It almost unbalanced me, but I caught myself in time and said, 'I don't know.'

'Another woman?'

'No, certainly not.'

'Another man? A guilty conscience?'

'That's an offensive question.'

'Answer it.'

'No. No other man.'

'You sound sure.'

'I *am* sure.'

'Money problems?'

'No.'

'Bedroom problems?'

'Chief Superintendent, I have no intention of . . .'

'I have *every* intention of staying here until you answer the question. Man and wife. Had you bedroom problems?'

'No, damn you.' I spat the words at him. 'We were "compatible" is, I think, the polite, legal way of putting it.'

I doubt if he even noticed my anger.

He stared at my face, then said, 'That's the whole field, Hemingway.'

'What?'

'The reasons why people kill themselves.'

'Oh!'

'There are variations on those reasons, of course. But basically that's the lot.'

'They don't apply,' I said bluntly.

'Again, you sound surprisingly sure.'

'I *am* sure.'

'Therefore?'

'Therefore . . . what?' I fenced.

'For God's sake, man. Your wife killed herself. That's not normal. All suicides have a reason . . . or *think* they have a reason. Your wife wasn't unique. You'd no "problems". Therefore, you were close to each other. Therefore, if anybody can make an educated guess, that person is you.'

It seemed that this questioning had done a complete U-turn; that the concern of this uniformed inquisitor was centred around an incident which had happened a week before when it should be concentrating itself upon the missing schoolgirl.

I made no attempt to hide my annoyance as I said, 'Look, the death of my wife has nothing to do with . . .'

'An educated guess,' he interrupted.

'She was . . .' I waved a hand impatiently. Disgustedly.

'Yes?'

'Chief Superintendent,' I said wearily. 'What sort of schooling did you have as a child?'

'Elementary. Grammar.'

'You were lucky,' I said sourly.

'Why?'

'This place . . .' Again I waved a hand. 'At a guess Borstal institutions are educationally superior.'

He smiled a tight, humourless smile.

I said, 'You don't believe that?'

'I have eyes,' he said quietly.

I nodded and sighed, then said, 'I think that's why she killed herself.'

'As a . . . protest?'

'No.'

'In that case, I'm not with you.'

'The establishment creates the inmates,' I said. 'It's as simple as that. Prisons create criminals.'

'They're *already* criminals. Otherwise they wouldn't be there.'

'I think you know what I mean.'

He said, 'Let's assume I don't.'

'All right,' I agreed, 'men are already criminals before they enter a prison. The same applies here. The type of girl. From the type of family. They *start* that way . . . we merely cultivate them. Our job is to emphasise all the faults.'

'Very cynical,' he murmured.

'There are schools,' I insisted. 'Schools, like this school. Far better schools than this will ever be. And from those schools pupils go on to university, but *despite* those schools, never *because* of them. These places? They're the festering underside of the education system.'

'The public school system,' he said.

'No!' I was suddenly very annoyed with this thick-headed policeman. '*Not* the public school system. The public schools – the *real* public schools – Eton, Harrow, Rugby, Roedean, The Mount, Benenden – those places are the genuine public schools. Those sort of places. *These* sort of places? These are the parasites of the system. These are *private* schools . . . masquerading as public schools. Schools like this, schools like The Ridings, the only thing *they* teach is snobbery and ignorance.'

'My word!' He raised an eyebrow. 'Such strength of feeling.'

'I live with it,' I growled.

'And your wife?'

I took a deep breath, then said, 'The educated guess. I don't think she could take it. I don't think the sheer hypocrisy was something she could tolerate. She wanted out.'

He nodded slowly, as if understanding, then murmured, 'Hence the art appreciation class.'

'That?' My mouth twisted.

'As I hear it in effect you called them killers.'

'That's strong,' I objected.

'But . . . wrong?'

'Exaggerated.'

'Assuming . . .' he mused. 'Assuming one pupil in that class. Just one. Assuming she had feelings. Real feelings. Deep feelings. Assuming she accepted the implied accusation.'

'Daisy Arkwright?'

'Make that assumption,' he suggested.

'I'll accept the possibility,' I said quietly.

'And if – when we find her – she's dead? Dead from exposure?'

Very deliberately I said, 'If she's dead – *if* she's dead – she is no more dead than my wife.'

'And that comforts you?'

'It doesn't distress me.'

He stared at me for all of five seconds, then said, 'You've a strange conscience, Hemingway, a very strange conscience.'

She was not dead, of course. But by the same token I suppose it would be only fair to say that she was not wholly alive. The weather eased towards noon and by early afternoon a police helicopter was quartering the area, and there she was . . . crouched behind the meagre shelter of an isolated plough shed more than a mile from the nearest road.

She was rushed to the nearest hospital suffering (or so we were informed) from a combination of shock and exposure.

The panic caused by her stupidity quietened and, as he left the school, Blayde smiled at me sourly and asked, 'Disappointed?'

'No.' I returned the smile. 'Almost satisfied.'

Then, it being Saturday, there was a relaxation and some of us (myself included) returned to our beds in order to catch up with lost sleep.

That evening, and for the first time since I'd been at The Ridings, Morley was missing at dinner in the refectory. He and his wife (it seemed) were eating in the privacy of their own quarters. I was curious, I asked and it was hinted that the press coverage of Arkwright's escapade had affected him more than I might have thought.

I ate my meal in silence and for the first time contemplated what might be called 'the power of the press'. Without doubt, the newspapermen would look upon Arkwright's absconding as an item worth recording. That, at least, in the local newspapers, and, as I was well aware, a little judicious 'puffing' on the part of some local reporter could, quite easily, result in a paragraph (and of course payment for that paragraph) in one of the nationals. And, it being Saturday, that might mean a paragraph in one of the Sunday scandal rags. The possibility intrigued me. The phrase 'investigative journalism' found its way into my mind. Dedicated newspapermen. An editor fighting for increased circulation. A reading public anxious to be fed little-known facts about . . . about *anything*. It had toppled a president from his throne. It had exposed corruption in public office. What, then, could it do with The Ridings and schools like The Ridings?

I smiled to myself as I ended the meal. A very contented smile.

And Johnny's voice said, 'Feel like a run out to see how she is?'

'What?' I halted my flow of thought.

'The Arkwright kid,' said Johnny.

'It – er . . .' The notion had not crossed my mind and I needed a moment or two to decide.

'It's not far.' He was obviously moderately keen on the idea. He added, 'We can use Bertha.'

'Why not?' I decided.

'It'll buck her up a bit.'

That I doubted, but I kept my doubts to myself. I stood up from the table and within fifteen minutes we were driving towards the hospital to which Arkwright had been taken.

The journey was barely twenty miles and throughout it we talked little. In the main it was empty conversation and in the silences I reviewed this turn of events. Hannah's death was still too recent for it not to have an effect upon my thinking. The wording of the suicide note was a constant reminder of what I had promised as the soil had hit the coffin.

To kill a man. Specifically, to kill Morley.

I found it strange – disquieting – this seesaw of emotions. At that moment, had I the means, had Morley been present, I think I *could* have killed him. At that moment; throughout the journey to the hospital. It was as if my anger – my oath of revenge – had fattened upon the partial success as far as the sixth form was concerned. I *could* do it . . . that was what a tiny pea of memory insisted. The memory of that consuming rage as I'd stared down at Hannah's coffin. I *could* have committed murder.

I tried to be objective; as objective as an emotion as subjective as personal hatred would allow me to be. I tried to stand aside. To examine with as much clinical objectivity as possible, and what little I discovered frightened me.

Inside – festering away in some dark recess of the brain – there seems to be a residue of savage malice. Something left over from the Dark Ages . . . something left over from the period when man was an untamed animal with its own peculiar blood lust. Something which made man 'king' of the animal world; something which, today, might be the hidden drive behind limitless ambition; something which centuries of 'civilisation' has merely iced over. Why else the death camps of Nazi Germany? Why else the not-much-less disgusting abominations which make up the weft of twentieth-century life? This blood lust – this secret ocean of malice – would seem to have gusher-like moments of eruption. Moments when that thin icing of 'civilisation' fractures . . . and until the fracture heals the hatred remains uncontrolled. It may settle, but there is a weakness in the crust and unless that weakness mends completely spurts of hatred continue to periodically swamp the mind.

A terrifying thought?

But why else this seesawing of my loathing for Morley? Why else *everything*? Calm thought insisted that, whatever I did to Morley, whatever I did to the sixth formers, would have no effect . . . Hannah would still be in her grave. Thus, calm thought. Civilised thought. But civilised thought was possible only at certain times . . . when the gushers of hatred were inactive.

It had once been a 'cottage hospital'. In size it was not much bigger than one of those rambling, Victorian mansions built by men of means, but no taste; it was, in fact, much smaller than The Ridings. From the list of brightly painted signs facing us as we entered, it boasted four wards, an X-ray department and a physiotherapy unit; obviously there was more to the place than that, but those were the rooms to which the general public were expected to find their own way. It was a very homely place. Very comfy. The impression was that if one *had* to be ill this was a nice place in which to undergo treatment.

There was no mention on the notice board of private wards, but they were there. Daisy Arkwright occupied one.

A small, single-bed room. Again cosy and comfortable. A window, large enough to give plenty of light, and now curtained and adding to the snugness. A switched-off TV set in one corner. What looked to be a multi-stationed radio extension, complete with headphones, above the bed.

And, of course, Daisy Arkwright.

Johnny had tapped on the door and a man's voice had called us to enter. And there alongside the bed – relaxing in a small cane armchair – was the elderly man (the man whose name I knew to be also Arkwright) staring at the door from behind a lowered newspaper.

Johnny entered first and the girl's eyes crinkled at the corners as she smiled a welcome. Then she saw me and the smile melted, and the eyes widened a little.

The elderly man stood up from the chair and dropped the newspaper on to the bed.

Johnny held out his hand and said, 'Stirk, Johnny Stirk. I'm one of the masters at the school. We thought we'd drive over . . . check that she was in good hands.'

The elderly man said, 'James Arkwright. I'm Daisy's uncle. Her father's my younger brother.' He grinned and added, 'By a good few years.'

They shook hands, then Johnny half-turned and said, 'This is Mr Hemingway. Tony Hemingway. He's another master.'

Arkwright dropped his hand; a deliberate gesture of non-friendship.

In a gentle but unemotional voice he said, 'Uhu . . . I've heard of Mr Hemingway.'

That Middle Eastern saying, 'The enemy of my enemy is my friend, but the friend of my enemy is my enemy', it summed it up completely. Arkwright had been prepared to welcome Johnny as a kind-hearted master visiting a pupil, but at the mention of my name Arkwright's warmth of welcome vanished. For the sake of the girl there was token pretence, but it was a cold formal pretence.

Johnny moved nearer to the bed, smiled and said, 'Well, thawed out?'

'Yes, sir.' She returned a timid smile.

She was a dumpy girl. Short for her years and with puppy-fat still on her frame. She had a button nose and wide solemn eyes in which timidity seemed to have taken up permanent residence.

'A silly thing to do, Daisy,' murmured Johnny.

'Yes, sir.'

'Unless,' growled Arkwright, 'she was driven to it.'

'Uncle!'

'Was she?' Arkwright ignored the girl's plea and spoke directly at me.

'Were you?' I passed the question on to the girl.

Before she could speak Arkwright said, '*You* answer.'

I glanced at the girl. She looked terrified.

I remained calm – possibly a little contemptuous – and I said, 'I say "No", but obviously that's not an answer you'll accept.'

'Not at face value.'

'Mr Arkwright . . .' began Johnny.

'You keep out of this. You've saved me a journey. I was coming to The Ridings to see this man.'

'Me?' I pretended surprise.

'Something about driving your wife to suicide.'

'She gassed herself,' I said flatly.

'Because of Daisy?'

'Something.'

'An accusation.'

'No.' I shook my head.

'An *implied* accusation.'

'Not even that.'

'Daisy doesn't lie,' he said harshly. 'Not to me. Ever.'

'You *did*!' There was a sob in the girl's voice. 'You – you called us morons. You said we'd – we'd . . .'

She broke down and snivelled; a great boo-hooing of personal *weltschmerz*. I might have pitied her had it not been for the degree of scorn I had for her and her classmates.

As it was her sniffling brought the hint of a derisive smile to my lips.

'You think it funny?' asked Arkwright dangerously.

'No . . . pathetic.'

'Tony!' Johnny made a movement as if to place himself between the older man and myself. He said, 'Take it easy, Tony.'

'She tried to kill herself,' whispered Arkwright.

'I doubt that,' I mocked. 'There are quicker ways. Surer ways.'

Then he hit me. Flush in the mouth with a hard clenched fist. I'd been half-expecting it, nevertheless it caught me unawares and I staggered, then sprawled. For a comparatively old man he was very fit, the punch carried more power than might have been expected.

I tasted blood from my split lips and began to push myself upright.

'Don't,' he warned. 'If you stand up, I'll knock you down again.' Then without taking his eyes from me, 'Get him out of here, Stirk. You, too. And tell that damned headmaster there's one pupil he won't be seeing again . . . although he *might* be hearing from my solicitor.'

We shouted at each other on our return journey to The Ridings. A certain amount of volume was necessary owing to the 'open-air' construction of Bertha, but it was more than that. Johnny was outraged. Probably even disgusted. He was certainly angry and in all honesty I couldn't blame him too much.

I, on the other hand, was determined to justify my attitude. I therefore dabbed at my bleeding lips and shouted back.

'Dammit, Tony, it wasn't *her* fault,' he bawled.

'You read the note.'

'But not *her*. Not Arkwright.'

'She's a sixth former.'

'She's different.'

'The hell she's different.'

'She's different,' he shouted.

'She's dumber, that's all.'

'Tony.' He screwed his eyes against the headlights on an oncoming vehicle. 'Tony, this thing's getting out of hand.'

'What thing?'

'You know damn well what I mean.'

'The sixth-form bitches? Morley?'

'They aren't *all* bitches.'

'Hannah thought so.'

'You think she'd like what you've done?'

'Don't you?'

'She'd hate you for it,' he bawled.

'No, she'd approve.'

'She wasn't that sort.'

'No?'

'She was your wife, Tony. You should know her better than that.'

'I know what they drove her to.'

'So?'

'That's all I need to know.'

'You earned yourself a smack in the mouth tonight.'

'It was worth it.'

'Would *she* have thought so?'

'Johnny, for God's sake . . .'

'How many more smacks in the mouth?'

'I don't give a damn.'

'*She* would.'

I shouted, 'I thought you were my friend.'

'That's why.'

'What?'

'Against Morley . . . sure. This other thing . . . I don't agree with it.'

'Why not?'

'It's not a vendetta, Tony.'
'What else is it?'
'Against Morley, perhaps.'
'Against the whole damn school.'
'Tony, you can't fight the world.'
'No? Just watch my dust, mate.'

That was the general tone of our shouting match. Johnny was worried; he was my friend, he thought I was doing the wrong thing and was building trouble up for myself, therefore he was worried. That's what friends are for . . . to worry, among other things. To offer what they think is good advice; to shout that advice at you if necessary.

Johnny shouted. I shouted back. But in the end we agreed to *dis*agree.

The next day (Sunday) I went back to the grave. It seemed the right thing to do. I didn't call on her parents; indeed, I timed my visit to the mound of earth carefully – late afternoon as dusk was creeping in from the surrounding hills – knowing that Harry and Sarah would have been and gone by the time I arrived.

I had to convince myself that it had all happened only four days before. Four days since the coffin had been lowered . . . and (God help me!) I was already beginning to forget. The colour of her eyes. The curve of her smile. The richness of her voice. Even the controlled passion of her love-making. Everything! The memories no longer had sharp edges. They were still there, but they were hazing over.

I stood alone in the biting wind, looked down at the piled earth and spoke to her. Talked to her.

I said, 'They'll know. I'll *make* them know. Soon. Those who put you here will wish they were here with you. I swear.'

Johnny had said it wasn't a vendetta.

Poor old Johnny. How wrong could a man be?

She knew – *I* knew – that's *exactly* what it was.

The Fall of the Sixth Domino

Saturday, February 11th. Some Saturday! Cooley watched its dawn streak the horizon from the doorless entrance of a broken-down plough shed . . . and thought 'Some Saturday!' The rest of mankind would be going to football matches, going to race meetings, going to dog tracks; maybe trotting off for a few jars at the local this evening, maybe taking the old lady upstairs for a weekly kiss-and-cuddle, maybe paying the earth to watch how some red-hot Yankee cops wrecked motor cars . . . maybe even staying at home and watching TV (and *other* Yankee cops wrecking *other* motor cars).

The world was in a rut.

Big deal! It was a very nice rut; a very comfortable rut; a rut he wanted to return to as soon as possible.

Him?

Well, for a kick-off, that damn plough shed had been one hell of a place in which to spend the night . . . what had been *left* of the night after he'd dumped the Capri at a public car park at Beechwood Brook, then trudged country lanes before stumbling his way across weather-heavy fields until he'd found the place.

Cooley was no countryman. He didn't know it was a plough shed. If he thought about it at all it was to wonder why some lunatic had built a one-roomed hovel miles from anywhere and, having built the bloody thing, why he'd left it to fall down. He didn't know why. He didn't want to know why. Hicks were idiots . . . that was explanation enough.

Meanwhile . . .

Okay, he was safe; according to the *Yorkshire Evening Post* he was safe. The cops had dropped a clanger. Some other goon was 'helping with enquiries' – had probably been charged and slung in a police cell by this time – but, y'know. Better to be safe than sorry.

Madge would be worrying.

Funny that. No, not 'funny' . . . *nice*. One of those things a man does just once in his life. If he's lucky, that is. Find a woman who takes everything – warts and all – and never complains. Like Madge. Somebody to whom tranquillity was a way of life but, at the same time, somebody who cared. Somebody who (maybe) would have liked to change you, but somebody who having tried but failed accepted things and didn't complain.

Inside he'd met some fellow-cons. Men working a fair-to-middling stretch; whose wives weren't a bit like Madge. Jesus! The poor bastards. Slowly – day at a time, night at a time – they'd gone round the bend. Curling up inside. Not seeing, not speaking, not hearing, then exploding. Those mad sods with wigs on their heads. They didn't *know*. Nothing! To them the cage was the punishment. Hell, the cage was sweet F.A. The cage was just strips of iron bars and granite walls. It was what was happening *outside* the cage – what *might* be happening – *that* was the punishment. It drove men crazy. Good men, and okay that wasn't a contradiction, good men, *were* inside. Proud men. Sensitive men. Men with enough imagination to make them go nuts, because of the dirty pictures they couldn't move from their minds. Men without a 'Madge'.

So Madge had to be told. She had to be contacted.

He began to trudge around the edge of the field. Towards some opening which might lead to another field . . . then to another . . . then to another until he found a road . . . until he found a telephone kiosk.

His shoes ('townie's' shoes) were already ruined. He'd ruined them reaching the plough shed. They were heavy with mud and his feet squelched inside the shoes as the water they'd already taken in turned his feet into ice-cold extremities. He shoved his hands deep into the pockets of his trousers, bent his head forward and, like forcing his way through treacle, he ploughed on looking for a gate.

That same Saturday morning Lennox and Tallboy also saw the dawn. They were in Tallboy's Rover and having 'dusted the dew off' one of the men named by Mrs Cooley as a possible source of information, they were visiting that lady's home in order to reassure the men still on watch that *they* weren't the only ones who'd missed a night's sleep.

Tallboy drove slowly. Gently. He rested one hand on the lower rim of the wheel and teased the car round corners. And he talked quietly. Coaxingly.

He said, 'Breakfast?'

'When we've seen the lads.'

'Come to our place,' invited Tallboy.

'No. There's a small . . .'

'Susan's already up and about. I gave her a ring.'

'She must *love* you.'

'She does.' Tallboy grinned. 'She's a copper's wife – a copper's daughter . . . she knows we eat when we can.'

'Thanks all the same. But . . .'

'She's making three breakfasts,' coaxed Tallboy.

'Oh!'

'Lenny, you can't go on like this.' Tallboy's voice was low and sombre. 'You're killing yourself.'

'I'm losing weight. That's supposed to be a good thing.'

'Not for the reasons *you're* losing it.'

'Chris, old son.' The elder man's voice was kindly, but shot with sorrow. 'God forbid, but supposing it had happened to Susan?'

'I dunno. I've asked myself the same question a thousand times.'

'And?'

'God knows. Maybe like you.'

Lennox smiled.

Tallboy said, 'But that doesn't make it right.'

'Okay.' The fat detective nodded ponderously. 'But I come home with you. I see two people. Married. Still in love.' He sighed, then ended, 'I can only stand so much.'

'And the way *you're* living?'

'I'm living.'

'Lenny, you're liked.' Tallboy argued as he'd never argued before. 'Dammit, you're *loved*. There's only one "Lenny" . . . if we lose him, we're sunk.'

Lennox didn't answer.

'Can't you see that?' Tallboy pressed home the point. 'The young 'uns. They use you as a yardstick. "What would Lenny do?" . . . that's what they ask themselves. All the time.'

'If they do – *if* they do – they'll come up with some funny bloody answers.'

'Lenny!' pleaded Tallboy.

'There's the car.' Lennox nodded at the windscreen. 'Pull up here. I'll check that everything's under control.'

Cooley felt the hardness in the small of his back as the voice said, 'Don't do anything daft, mister. This is a twelve-bore . . . and it's loaded.'

Cooley did all the proper things. He remained motionless. He stared ahead. He slowly raised his hands to shoulder height.

The world (he thought) had suddenly gone kinky. There was a big Shoot-Cooley campaign under way. *Everybody* was pointing guns at him. Big guns, little guns, you name it, next thing they'd be strapping him to the business end of an artillery piece.

'What y'doing here?' asked the voice. A strange voice; a man's voice, but high-pitched to the point of falsetto.

'Walking,' said Cooley. He gasped as the steel was jabbed hard into his back, then repeated, '*Walking* . . . what else?'

'Poaching.'

'Holy bloody cow! Do I look like a . . .'

'Turn round. Let's have a look at you.'

Cooley turned – slowly, carefully and with his hands still raised – and for the first time saw this latest nerk who wanted to blow holes in his hide. Nor did what he saw comfort him. This one tore wings from flies and fed what was left to spiders; it was there in his red-rimmed eyes. The eyes of a complete loonie if ever Cooley had seen one. Not too tall, but *thin*! Bone him and you could use him for boot laces. And dirty with it; what looked to be years of grime cobwebbed the creases of his hollow-cheeked face, and there was enough muck under his fingernails to grow spuds in. *And* he wore clothes no self-respecting tramp would have been seen dead in. And as for his hair! . . . it didn't need scissors, it needed a *chainsaw*.

Nevertheless, five items concentrated themselves upon Cooley's immediate attention. The wide, red-rimmed eyes. The equally menacing orbs of the double-barrelled shotgun. and the claw-like finger which rested on the first of the two triggers.

'Poaching,' squeaked the man.

'The hell I'm poaching. I wouldn't know how to poach if you offered me a . . .'

'What then, mister?'

'Walking,' insisted Cooley.

'This time?' The man tilted the twelve-bore and Cooley found himself looking squarely at the twin openings of the barrels.

'For Christ's sake! If that thing goes off.'

'What then?' insisted the man.

'I – I got lost. Last night.' Cooley moved his head in a jerk, indicating the way he'd come. 'I spent the night in a building – some sort of building back there – now look, for Christ's sake, point that gun another way.'

'Lost?'

'I was – I was taking a short cut. I thought it was a . . .'

'Where from?'

'Beechwood Brook.'

'Where to?'

'I – I – I dunno. I was lost. I didn't know where the hell . . .'

'You're a liar, mister.'

'I'm not a poacher,' groaned Cooley.

'That's what *you* say.'

'Look . . .' Cooley wanted to wave his arms, but daren't lower them. 'Look, if you're a gamekeeper, I'm sorry. I'm trespassing, okay, I'm sorry. But I'm *not* a . . .'

'Do I look like a gamekeeper, mister?' Suddenly the man seemed to explode into a fit of giggles; squealing titters, which sent invisible ants crawling up Cooley's spine. The giggling stopped as suddenly as it had started. The man repeated, 'Do I look like a gamekeeper?'

'No,' gasped Cooley. 'No, mate, you don't look at *all* like a gamekeeper.'

'What y'trying then, eh?' The man lowered the barrels of the shotgun and prodded Cooley in the chest. He might never have been amused by the suggestion that he was a gamekeeper, such was his split-second change of mood. He was now suspicious. Dangerous. Deadly. He prodded Cooley as he demanded, 'What? What? What?'

'I – I dunno . . .' Cooley took a deep breath, then said, 'Look, old son, if I've . . .'

'Don't butter up to me, mister.'

'I'm not. All I'm . . .'

'I don't like being buttered up to.'

'All right. Just let me . . .'

'I fell for that once, mister.'

'Eh?'

'They buttered up to me. I believed 'em.'

'I'm – I'm not trying to . . .'

'Then the lousebags put me away.'

'Eh?'

'Locked me away.'

'What?'

'I think you're from them.' The man craned his dirt-encrusted face forward and peered into Cooley's eyes. 'Yes,' he said. 'That's it, mister. You're from *them*.'

'Oh, my God!' groaned Cooley.

The man performed an agile, sideways skip. It brought him alongside and slightly behind Cooley. He lowered the shotgun a few more inches, then prodded Cooley in the ribs.

He squeaked, 'C'mon, mister. We'll go to *my* place. We'll find who you are. Who you *really* are.'

Lennox had weakened, and the truth was he wished he hadn't weakened. He wished he'd had the strength – the discourtesy, if you like – to refuse Tallboy's invitation to breakfast. The meal (egg, bacon, mushrooms and fried bread; hot sweet tea and thick, crisp, buttered toast) had been the best breakfast he'd eaten since . . .

Since . . .

That's what drove the knife deep. The fact that Susan Tallboy knew *exactly* how a man liked his eggs fried: runny but not gooey. *Exactly* how the bacon should be done: crisp, but not crisp enough to snap at the touch of the knife. *Exactly* how the fried bread should end up: golden brown on the outside, hot and spongy inside. *Exactly* . . . everything!

His wife – the wife with whom he'd had a running mock squabble since the day they'd married; the wife who, like himself, hadn't dared to allow her near-worship to surface, because not-far-from-ugly people aren't supposed to have life-long crushes on each other . . . *his* wife, too, had known the secret of preparing such breakfasts. And it was crazy to let eggs, bacon, fried bread and strong, sweet tea bring back the pain. Crazy! Food was food, and that's all it was. A woman (or a man, come to that) could either fry a breakfast or she *couldn't* fry a breakfast. And Susan Tallboy *could*, and it was as simple as *that*.

The hell it was!

There was nothing 'simple' about it. It was the most God-awful, complicated screw-up of his whole life. Some cat (not necessarily a Russian Blue) rubbing its friendship against the bottom of his trouser leg . . . memories. Some material, seen in a shop window, of the hue and pattern she'd favoured . . . memories. Some strange woman who carried the same Christian name . . . memories, plus an inward anger that *anybody* had the right to that name.

And now, this breakfast. And more. A childless couple; a copper and his wife . . . a working jack and his wife. That selfsame combination. That selfsame acceptance of impossible working hours by both Tallboy and his missus. Stupid. Crazy. He could count legs, he could count arms, he could count fingers, he could count heads . . . *that* was how crazy. The point came when a man could *look* for reminders and if he looked hard enough – if his imagination was allowed to run wild – anything, and everything, was a reminder.

Susan Tallboy said, 'More tea, Mr Lennox?'

'Eh?' Lennox dragged his mind from a sad past to down-to-earth present.

'Tea?' Susan held the teapot poised.

'Ta.' Lennox nodded.

As she poured Susan asked her husband, 'Any luck so far?'

Before he answered Tallboy glanced at Lennox. A tiny furrow of apprehension creased his brow.

'It's okay, son.' Lennox smiled. Another 'reminder'. '*We* didn't have secrets either.'

And now Susan frowned non-understanding.

'Y'see, pet.' Lennox looked at the woman. 'Some coppers. Some coppers' wives. They daren't tell 'em. Their womenfolk don't understand. They – er – y'know . . . gossip. Talk. Nothing deliberate. Just that they can't *not* talk. So, if he's any sense, the copper plays safe.'

'Oh!' Susan replaced the teapot on its stand and sat down again.

Tallboy said, 'Look, Lenny, if you think we should . . .'

'I'm sure you *should*.'

'What I mean is . . .'

'Chris, old son. She's a copper's daughter. *Ripley's* daughter. Remember that. A man – I knew Ripley when I was a struggling D.I. . . . he was a copper and a half. She was weaned on bobbying. She's the safest of the three of us.'

For a moment (as she, too, remembered) a sadness touched Susan's eyes, then she said, 'I was thinking about Mrs Cooley.'

Both men waited.

Susan continued, 'She thinks he's injured. Thinks he might be dead.'

'Not dead,' murmured Tallboy.

'She doesn't *know*.'

'Come to that,' said Lennox slowly, '*we* don't know, but I take your point, my pet.'

'It's cruel,' insisted Susan.

'Necessary,' said Tallboy.

'Why necessary?' she demanded.

'Because . . .'

'Aye.' Lennox broke in on Tallboy's answer. '*Why* is it necessary?'

'It was your idea,' said Tallboy.

'The trouble with old age and poverty.' Lennox's mouth bent into a wry smile. 'It breeds lousy ideas.'

Tallboy said, 'She wouldn't have talked otherwise.'

'But *after* she'd talked?'

'Do *I* tell her?' asked Tallboy heavily.

'No. I'm the one.'

'Look, I'm not trying to duck a . . .'

'I know you're not.' Again Lennox interrupted. 'But, y'know, if she *has* to thread somebody through the mangle, it'll be as well if it's the right man.'

There was a silence in which they sipped tea and allowed the recent breakfasts to settle. Tallboy smoked a cigarette. Lennox lived with the same old memories which by this time had become a part of his waking life. Susan watched the changed face of the elder man with concern and something not too far removed from affection.

Then like the opening of a door it was 'bobby talk'.

'What have we got so far?' asked Lennox.

'M.O. His trade mark. No dabs . . . they weren't expected. A description of his car . . . it's a Capri and it's been circulated. Two decent footprints . . . one outside the window, another from the mud-marks on the floorboards. Archie Hall was set up for the fence. And, of course, we've alerted all divisions . . . all neighbouring forces. That's about all for the moment. The lads are out digging. Somebody should know *something*.'

'He's a one-man band,' observed Lennox.

'He has to be *somewhere*. If he tries for home he's nabbed. If he tries for Hall's place . . . same thing. And we've a man at Hall's telephone.'

'And if he telephones his wife?'

'This isn't America.' Tallboy sounded disappointed with that fact. 'We can't get taps for the asking.'

'So . . .' mused Lennox. 'She might already know.'

'That he's not dead?'

'That he ain't even injured.'

Susan said, 'Mr Lennox, you agreed . . .'

'I'll tell her, old luv.' Lennox smiled reassurance. 'All

I'm doing – all we're both doing – is working out the possibilities. If she already *knows* he's alive and in working order she might try being foxy.'

'She will,' pronounced Tallboy. 'Nothing more certain.'

'In that case, there's a fifty-fifty chance she'll take us to him.'

'Hopefully.' But Tallboy didn't *sound* hopeful.

Lennox pulled a questioning face.

Tallboy growled, 'All this "shadowing", all this "tailing", it looks so bloody easy on TV.'

'Y'know . . .' Lennox shook his head slowly. As if puzzled by some unsolved mystery. 'I dunno who sets the pace, Chris. Us . . . the real bobbies. Or the television coppers. Every squad-car driver straining his braces to get into a round-the-houses chase. And the lingo. Half the time I *have* to watch the infernal programmes to know what the hell the young coppers are talking about, and by the time I've caught up they're miles ahead, and I *still* don't understand half of it.'

'You're old-fashioned,' teased Susan.

'Old-fashioned enough to want to trace Cooley,' agreed Lennox, sombrely. 'He's not a killer. Never was. The only people he's ever harmed are the insurance companies, and o' course himself and his wife. And now . . .' Lennox sighed. 'Now he has two corpses to his credit. If he'd any gumption he'd give himself up, accept a charge of murder, then wait till it's reduced to manslaughter-self-defence.'

'If it *is*,' said Tallboy.

'With a girl guide defending him,' said Lennox confidently.

Susan said, 'I hope so . . . for his wife's sake.'

'And that,' said Lennox, pushing himself upright from the table, 'is a hint, if ever I heard one. Drop me off at Cooley's place, Chris. I'll see you back in the murder room – say, an hour – fix up a motor patrol car to pick me up.' He turned to Susan Tallboy and, very solemnly, said, 'Thanks for the breakfast, lass. It's – it's . . . the best I've had for months.'

'Come again. Any time.' Her solemnity matched his and each read the thoughts of the other.

'Don't press me.' His voice was gruff. 'I might take you up on the offer.'

Gently – sincerely – she said, 'I mean it.'

Cooley, on the other hand, didn't know what it meant. Anything! The world had suddenly gone mad. As mad as the obviously certifiable lunatic who handled a twelve-bore shotgun like it was a stick of Wigan rock. The nutter was just that . . . a nutter. He was crazy. Completely and utterly crazy. He'd been 'inside'. He'd said so. The men with the white coats had once collected him and why, in hell's name, having collected him, they hadn't *kept* him was something Cooley would never understand.

Okay, some loonies were harmless. But, this one . . . this one was *dangerous*.

And now this dump. This bloody pigsty the loonie called 'home'. It wasn't even a caravan . . . not really. A box on wheels; iron-rimmed wheels, at that. A box with a poky little window, with rough-planed floorboards, planked walls and a bit of a shelf affair that made do as a bed, with a sheet of old iron in one corner and on that iron a pot-bellied, slow-combustion stove . . . and even that damn thing wasn't lit.

As for furniture. *Furniture!* If you called one broken-down chair, a tea-chest and a couple of orange crates 'furniture' – okay, it had furniture.

And the loonie was asking questions in the squeaking, crazy voice of his, and Cooley was giving the answers – as many answers as he dared to give – and the loonie wasn't believing *any* of the answers. None of 'em.

Cooley stammered, 'Look, mate – no, I don't mean *mate*, I mean just look – what is it you want? Just tell me. That's all.'

'You're from them,' squeaked the loonie.

'No! For the umpteenth time. I'm *not*.'

'You're not Crofter's man.'

'Who?'

'Not Crofter's man.'

'I – I dunno anybody called . . .'

'Crofter's a nice man,' crooned the loonie.

'Sure. Sure. One of the best,' agreed Cooley desperately. 'Now let me . . .'

'You don't *know* Crofter, mister.'

'Eh?'

'You just said.'

'Oh, bloody hell!'

'So, that proves it.'

'All right. All right.' Cooley was in a trap without an exit. He groaned, 'I don't know Crofter. But you say he's a nice man. Okay, he's a nice man. I – I wish I could meet him. Now, will you *please* . . .'

'That proves it, mister '

'What?'

'They sent you.'

'No. Nobody . . .'

'They want me inside again.'

'Nobody wants you inside. Look, on my oath . . .'

'They were round the other day. Looking for me.'

'No. No, they weren't. Nobody wants to . . .'

'You're a liar, mister.' The loonie glanced through the partly open door. Glanced at the early morning sky. 'Out there. With aeroplanes. They were looking for me.'

'Aeroplanes?'

'They were looking for me,' repeated the loonie.

'They don't – they don't . . .' stammered Cooley. 'They don't fly aeroplanes this weather. They don't . . .'

'*Your* aeroplanes, mister.'

The sudden thought, which gave birth to the accusation,

was like a detonator to the explosive instability of the sick mind. What was going to happen – what *had* to happen – flashed momentarily in the loonie's wild eyes. Cooley opened his mouth to scream, but knew he hadn't even time to force the breath past his larynx . . . and yet, conversely, everything seemed to slow down to a near-halt. Time became a stupidity; a man-made measurement, with no basis of fact. What should have taken less than a second – what did take less than a second within the nonsense of watches and clocks – stretched itself out into hours of terror and agony.

He stared at the twin mouths of the twelve-bore. He saw the claw-like fingers curl around the two triggers. He saw the pressure; the triggers move; the hammers fall. He even realised that the right hammer fell fractionally ahead of the left. He heard the noise – the prolonged roar which seemed to last forever – and then the spray of shot came from both barrels . . . and he saw that, too. He felt the shot, as it plucked at his clothes; as it penetrated to the skin; as it tore at tiny nerve-ends at his chest, and his neck, and the lower half of his face. Then came the agony; everlasting agony; agony that went on . . . and on . . . and on. As the breastbone slowly fractured, then splintered, then drove shards of its splintered pieces into the heart and the lungs. And the heart and the lungs took up the massive symphony of pain; as the tissue ripped and the muscles tore; as the vessels were sliced and the tendons were ruptured. In the neck, too. And in the area around the jaw. One gigantic, slow-motion orchestration of increasing pain.

And, after forever, as he felt himself being thrown backwards, the last thought to pass through Cooley's pulsating mind was that he was dead . . . and glad to be dead, if only to end the pain.

Tallboy saw Lennox enter the murder room and hurried across.

'Now she knows.' The fat detective sounded relieved. He said, 'Women! She's almost happy.'

'She knows he's still alive,' said Tallboy.

'I suppose.' Lennox stifled a yawn. 'She's promised to let us know if he gets in touch.'

'I'll bet.'

'I think she will,' said Lennox slowly. 'I explained the manslaughter-self-defence plea. She understands. She's gumption enough to realise his chances of pulling that plea lessen the longer he stays on the run.'

'Good.' Tallboy smiled. 'Now for the good news. We've found his car. The Capri.'

'Where?'

'Beechwood Brook.'

'For Christ's sake! That's in our own police area.'

'I've already checked.' Tallboy delivered the items in the machine-gun fashion of a trained copper who doesn't waste words. 'It wasn't there at midnight. The night-patrol constable checked at about midnight. The early-shift constable spotted it on the car park within an hour of coming on duty. The railway station . . . only one train out between those times. All passengers seen by a D.C. on duty there. Same at the bus depot. He might have flagged a lift . . . it's a possibility, but no certainty. That leaves walking, unless he's still in the town. If he's walked, he's not too far away. Road blocks are already being set up. I've fixed with Chief Superintendent Blayde for extra men to be drafted in. As near as possible, there's a police net being spread within ten miles of the car.'

'Neat.' Lennox nodded his approval.

'If he's on foot, we've a good chance.'

'If he's on foot,' said Lennox, 'he's ours . . . however many men it takes.'

SEVEN

Monday (February 6th) saw a return to near-normality.

Whether or not Arkwright contacted Morley, threatened legal action and was mollified, I don't know. Nor was I interested enough to find out. I only know that, via that academic grapevine peculiar to all such schools, by mid-afternoon everybody (masters, mistresses and pupils alike) knew that Daisy Arkwright would not be returning to The Ridings. From hospital the child was to be taken to her uncle's home and from there . . . who cared?

That day the sixth form's final lesson was English literature; a lesson which Hannah would have taken, no doubt after hours of personal 'preparation'. According to the new timetable, it was now *my* lesson. The pattern, as worked out by Hannah, should have been a third session covering the works of Wordsworth and Coleridge, but, as my appreciation of either Wordsworth *or* Coleridge was only slightly less than my knowledge of their works, any lesson covering the writings and styles of these two literary figures was out of the question. I therefore took the easy way out. I decided to concentrate upon the works of the Brontë sisters, and talk upon a 'vamp till ready' basis for the allotted period.

I reckoned without the sixth formers. In particular, I reckoned without the head girl, Miss Leah Sykes.

I had been talking for perhaps ten minutes; I had skimmed over all the hackneyed history of the three sisters, how they'd all three been born at Thornton (now part of Bradford) and, with their brother Branwell, had been allowed an almost unique freedom to explore the moors around Haworth when their eccentric clergyman father had moved to that parish.

I was saying, 'Originally, of course, they numbered five sisters. But the two eldest, Maria and Elizabeth, died. This was before . . .'

'From exposure?' The interrupting question came from Sykes.

I stared at her for a moment, then said, 'I beg your pardon?'

'The moors.' Her lip curled. Her eyes locked on to mine. 'I know the Haworth moors.'

'Indeed?' I kept my voice cool and controlled.

'They're bleak. In winter they're capable of killing people. Especially schoolgirls.'

'*Some* schoolgirls,' I corrected her.

The atmosphere in the classroom had become charged with hatred and counter-hatred. It was no longer a lesson. It was a duel between Sykes and myself, and I accepted the challenge almost eagerly.

I said, 'You must understand that these five young ladies – especially the surviving three – were strong-willed and, in their own way, quite ruthless.'

'It doesn't show in their novels,' she countered calmly.

'Emily? *Wuthering Heights*?'

'A love story . . . surely?'

'Miss Sykes,' I smiled, 'only a madwoman would fall in love with a creature like Heathcliffe.'

'*If* the heroine of *Wuthering Heights* is meant to be a self-portrait.'

'Cathy was Emily,' I said bluntly.

'Is there any proof of that?'

'Many experts agree,' I said. 'Cathy was Emily herself. Heathcliffe was her brother Branwell. The whole novel can be viewed as a veiled confession of an incestuous relationship.'

'Incest,' she murmured teasingly.

I eyed her, suspiciously, then said, 'You're trying to tell me something, Sykes.'

'Mr Hemingway,' she drawled insolently, 'our last art appreciation class was devoted to the subject of suicide and what drives people to suicide. Today's English literature class concerns itself with incest . . . almost a justification of incest.'

'Make it devil-worship, if you wish,' I snapped.

'Sir?'

'Other Brontë experts have suggested that Heathcliffe was Emily's portrayal of the devil. If, as we suggest, Cathy is Emily . . . we end up with devil-worship.'

'If as *you* suggest,' she mocked.

'As I recall,' I reminded her, 'it was you who saw fit to interrupt the lesson with a certain loaded question. A sick question.'

'Sick, sir?' Her expression was of make-believe innocence.

'Miss Arkwright,' I said gently.

'I'm sorry, sir. I don't . . .'

'Death by exposure.'

'Oh!'

'But, of course, you didn't *mean* that,' I sneered.

'My question was about the Brontë sisters. The two who died.'

'You have . . . ' I pushed back my gown, thrust my hands into the pockets of my trousers and strolled slowly backwards and forwards in front of the class as I spoke. 'All of you. You have a certain morbid fascination with the subject of death. My wife. Vincent van Gogh. Maria and Elizabeth Brontë. Miss Daisy Arkwright . . . in that she *could* have died. The subject occupies your minds far too much. I wonder why? There must be a reason. There's a reason for everything, therefore there must be a reason for this mass morbidity.

'Death, ladies, will come. At the moment you – each of you individually – nurse an unspoken belief in personal immortality. Death is a visitation which other people must suffer. Older people. Men and women not in your age group. You will live forever . . . *that* is one of the great fallacies of youth. The mind – *your* minds – cannot yet grasp the conception of everlasting nothingness.

'But consider . . . Great works – *Wuthering Heights* for example and many other literary masterpieces – spring from the certainty of death. Often death of the young. Death of the healthy. Death of characters who die when they should not have died. Without death – without the agony which accompanies death – these novels would never have been written.

'And yet you in your innocence – in your *silly* innocence – play with the concept of death, much as a kitten plays with a ball of wool. You touch it. You pat it. You prance around it. You make mock attacks on it. You *pretend* fear . . . when that fear is both real and frightening.' I paused, lowered my head for a moment in order to gather my thoughts together. Then I raised my head and continued, 'Miss Arkwright has now learned the unpleasant truth. In one night – in one terrifying night – she gained wisdom. However long she lives, she will never again view death as an abstract. As something which can be dismissed as a hobgoblin affair. She now *knows* from personal experience. The fingers have reached out to touch her, therefore she *knows*. For the rest of her life she will live with the knowledge – the fear – of what must eventually happen. Remember that, please – remember Arkwright – when you next talk so glibly of death.'

There was a silence. It would not be too melodramatic to equate that silence with the silence of a tomb. It had that sombre, heart-stopping quality. The duel had been fought, and the duel had been won. This clique of teenage tyrants were not so very indomitable after all. They could be quietened. They had an over-abundance of that imagination peculiar to their age and sex. They could be terrified – thus tamed – by mere words.

I smiled my triumph, and said, 'Shall we continue our discussion about the Brontë sisters? Unless, of course, there are any more questions . . .'

That night Johnny and I drove farther afield in order to find a new drinking haunt. This time we used my car; it was a cold, clear evening with the promise of a hard frost before midnight, and the prospect of facing such temperatures in an open sports car was something neither of us relished. We didn't even travel our usual lanes. Instead we tried a new direction and ended up at Beechwood Brook . . . specifically at the Beechwood Brook Arms.

The bar lacked the comfort – lacked the character – of our old haunt. It is possible that it might once have been a coaching inn but, if so, it had been built at a period when coaching was going out of fashion and since then it had been 'modernised' at various points in its existence . . . and none of the 'modernisations' had added to its charm. Strictly speaking, it was more of a hotel than an inn; it catered for residents and it had a restaurant. Nevertheless, the bar – although spoiled by the unnecessary addition of chrome and glass – had a certain eccentric charm; the charm of an elderly lady defying convention of age by wearing slightly outrageous clothes. We both liked the place and the lounge was large enough for us to find a quiet, alcoved corner where we could drink and talk.

We exchanged trivialities of the day and eventually I mentioned the English literature class.

'Thin ice, mate,' observed Johnny . . . and I was surprised to see the look of concern on his face.

'I think not,' I said. 'The Sykes girl brought up the subject. I merely expanded upon it.'

'Morley's after your guts,' said Johnny bluntly.

'Possibly.'

'Nothing surer. You've lost The Ridings a pupil.'

'Arkwright?'

'He won't like you for it.'

I smiled and said, 'He can hardly blame *me* if one of his charges succumbs to an attack of conscience.'

'Tony.' He tasted his drink. 'It's a damn sight more than that . . . and you know it.'

'Water under the bridge,' I murmured.

'Not if another one goes.'

'Arkwright was the one weak link. The others are made of much sterner stuff.'

'Okay.' He nodded part agreement, once more tasted his drink, then said, 'In that case . . . watch your back.'

'Schoolgirls,' I mocked.

'If that note's to be believed, they killed Hannah,' he reminded me.

This time, I tasted my drink. I almost finished it in one swallow.

I said, 'Hannah had a weakness. She could be hurt.'

'Too true.' He nodded.

'I don't have that weakness.'

'Tough guy,' he grinned.

'One doesn't have to be tough to out-face a class of girls, surely?'

'The female of the species, mate.' He finished his drink, stood up, and said, 'Down the rest. It's my call.'

I drained my glass, handed it to him and he left for the bar. And while he was away a realisation dawned upon me.

There had been an air of disapproval present. This friend of mine – and disapproval or not he *was* my friend – had something on his mind. In the car on our way to the Beechwood Brook Arms there had been long, almost sullen silences. I'd put it down to his having had a hard day. I'd seen it before, but always in the past that first taste of booze had chased the faint cobwebs of despair from his mind. But not this time. He'd tried to hide it, but without success. It was still there peeping from behind the smile, present behind the banter. Something . . . *worrying* him.

Well, it had to be brought out into the open.

Friends – genuine all-weather friends – don't mind disagreements. They can row – play the very devil with each other – and still be friends. The difference between friends and acquaintances. That was my belief. That is *still* my belief, and I make no apology for what followed.

He'd returned to the table and we'd both tasted our second drink when I said, 'Out with it, Johnny.'

'What?' The surprised look wasn't even meant to convince.

'You're upset,' I said.

'No.' He hesitated, then added, 'Not upset.'

'Something.'

'It's not important.' He tried to brush it aside.

'Something between you and me,' I insisted.

'What the hell can there be . . .'

'I don't know. That's why I'm asking.'

He scowled, rubbed his mouth with his fingers, pushed his spectacles back into position, then growled, 'Is it so obvious?'

'Fairly obvious,' I assured him.

'Damn!' For some reason he seemed angry with himself.

'Out with it,' I encouraged.

'That – er – that note,' he said awkwardly.

'Hannah's note?'

'I . . . I think I can remember the wording.'

'That's not necessary.'

I took out my wallet, removed the suicide note and handed it to him.

As he read it he spoke the words aloud. Quietly. Slowly. Musingly.

'Tony, darling, I'm sorry. The sixth form, and Morley. I really can't take any more. Forgive me, darling.' He paused, stared at the note for a few moments in silence, then as he handed it back he said, 'Why didn't you give it to the police?'

'It's private.' I re-folded the note and slipped it back into its envelope before returning it to my wallet. 'I don't like policemen poking their noses into my personal life.'

'*Your* personal life?' The question was lead-heavy with meaning I couldn't understand.

'You don't agree?' I made it a counter-question.

'Why is she "sorry"?'

'She says. Morley and the sixth form.'

'Could mean that,' he admitted slowly.

'What else?'

'She's saying "sorry" to *you*, Tony. Why?'

'For – er . . .' I moved my hands. 'For the inconvenience.'

'Inconvenience?' There was sadness in the question.

'Of the suicide. She . . .'

'Not the sorrow? Not the heartbreak?'

'Certainly. That too. But . . .'

'But as far as you're concerned that's secondary?'

'Careful, Johnny,' I warned gently.

'No, no.' He shook his head, then tasted his beer. 'You asked . . . remember?'

'All I'm saying is . . .'

'You insisted, mate.' He pushed his spectacles back into position. 'I've given that note – the wording of the note – a lot of thought. And I knew Hannah.'

'And?'

'We're boozing buddies . . . right?'

'Right,' I agreed.

'Just about every night?'

'Often enough.'

'Every night, mate, as near as dammit.'

'As near as dammit,' I nodded.

'Now . . . I'm single. Fancy free. That sort of thing.'

'Look,' I began, 'if you're suggesting . . .'

'They're not suggestions, Tony. They're not even thoughts. It's just a *possibility* . . . that's all.'

The hypothesis was a simple one, although it took Johnny almost thirty minutes to stammer it forth. I was a drinker – indeed, we were both drinkers – and, while not being alcoholics, we were (perhaps) dependent upon our intake of beer and spirits. Our nightly – almost every night – visit to a public house had of necessity left Hannah very much on her own. Forsaken, perhaps? That I doubted, but for the sake of the proposition, I was prepared to accept the possibility. Unloved? That I was *not* prepared to accept. The depth of the relationship between Hannah and myself had been deeper than mere carnality. The expression 'soul-mates' sprang to mind and I used that expression.

'I'm not talking about sex,' said Johnny sadly.

'What else?' My patience was wearing dangerously thin.

'Neglected?' he suggested.

'Our marriage wasn't a cell. We loved . . . we didn't possess.'

'Each with a degree of personal freedom?'

'The good way. The civilised way.'

'Where was her "freedom"?' he asked gently.

'For God's sake! She could have . . .'

'Ah, but *did* she?'

'She had a choice. She knew she had that choice. She . . .'

'Tony,' he said, gently, 'she was teetotal. Or almost. She didn't like pubs. She wasn't gregarious. She . . .'

'There are other things.'

'Such as?'

'Music. She liked good music. She could have . . .'

'Where in hell can you find good music in these parts?'

'There was no reason why she couldn't have gone to Leeds.

To York. Orchestral concerts. Chamber music. She could have . . .'

'Alone?' he murmured.

'I don't particularly like that sort of stuff,' I growled.

As he finished his drink he said, 'Nor do any of the others, mate. The male and female slobs employed by Morley. Ever thought of that? They each know their own subject – and maybe a smattering of some other subject, like you and English Lit. – but they're not . . . "cultivated" is a stupid word, but it's what I mean. The Ridings is a dump, Tony. Morley isn't fit to be in the teaching profession, much less a headmaster. It follows. Decent teachers – civilised teachers – don't stay. The rest of us – those of us who *do* stay – are the dross. That's us, mate. The throw-outs. The skid-row types of the whole bloody system. You, me . . . the whole Ridings crowd. But Hannah *wasn't*. She was a one-off job and there was no way out. That note. She was "sorry". For what? Because she couldn't take any more? Could be. But any more of what? Morley? The sixth form? But also you, me . . . the whole rotten bunch of us? She didn't put it into words. That wasn't her way. But maybe that's what she *meant*.'

I stood up, took the empty glasses to the bar and left them to be re-filled while I visited the toilet. I had to walk through the lounge and, as I did so, I saw the woman. She was relaxing in an armchair, smoking a cigarette, sipping coffee and talking to a man.

I thought I knew the woman . . . was almost sure I'd seen her somewhere. Not old enough to be one of the parents. Possibly one of the pupil's older sisters. It was possible. She had that air of self-assurance. That 'superior' expression I'd come to hate. The man, too. His was no off-the-peg dinner-suit; he was of the moneyed class and it showed even in the way he lounged as he exchanged conversation with the woman.

I knew her – had seen her somewhere before – but couldn't place her . . . not that it mattered a damn.

All in all that Monday evening could not be called a success. We were still friends when we arrived back at The Ridings, but as far as I was concerned our friendship had been pushed to near breaking-point.

I had asked for the truth . . . or, to be more precise, the truth as Johnny saw it. I'd done rather more than ask. I'd insisted. And to his credit Johnny had been loth to open up his heart. It may well be that his reluctance to voice his opinions was what kept our friendship in one piece. In fairness a man cannot demand the truth then criticise that truth when he hears it.

Nevertheless . . .

I lay in bed, stared into the darkness and mulled over what had been said. What had been implied. What had been *meant*.

The proposition was that I (as much as any other person) had been responsible for Hannah taking her life. Me! Her husband who had counted her as the most precious person alive . . . and *I'd* been partly responsible for her suicide.

The idea was ludicrous.

The truth was that we had each claimed – and rightly claimed – a modicum of freedom. Neither of us had 'clung'. That had been the understanding; the firm and agreed understanding even before we'd married. There had been nothing demanding about our love for each other. Nothing suffocating. Our respective imperfections had been willingly accepted and neither of us had taken up the impossible task of 'altering' the other. I drank a little, indeed I drank more than a little. But drink was a minor vice, and I had always been able to hold my liquor. Never (however much I might have had to drink) had I made an exhibition of myself. A little garrulous, perhaps. A little loquacious. But I never argued foolishly. I never sought a deliberate quarrel. Indeed, more often than not, some slight over-consumption of liquor had the opposite effect. I became a better companion. I was more relaxed. I was more amiable. While never the life and soul of any party (that wasn't my nature) I could, with the help of a few drinks, certainly help a gathering of friends along. I could chat more freely. I could laugh more readily. I could discard certain built-in inhibitions.

I was, if anything, a *better* husband.

Hannah on the other hand . . .

Her puritanical upbringing prevented her from ever *really* enjoying life. She had a reserve – a timidity – which precluded her from any of the slightly more boisterous forms of enjoyment. Her fawn-like shyness was part of her charm. One of the reasons I loved her. One of the reasons I . . .

No!

The startling realisation that I was thinking in the wrong tense – in the present tense and not in that past – pulled me up short. I *had* loved her. She *had* had a fawn-like timidity.

Now (present tense) she was nothing . . . *now* she no longer existed.

I reached out a hand and in the darkness felt for and found cigarettes and lighter on the bedside table. I lighted a cigarette and tried to comfort myself with propositions, which over the years I'd listened to . . . and scorned.

'No person is completely dead whilever there is one person alive who can remember that person.'

But tell that to the mourner as he (or she) walks away from the grave. Tell it to the parents who have lost their child. Tell it to the wife whose husband has just met a violent death in a road accident. 'Completely dead.' But death is not a quantitative thing. Death is absolute. Death is either 'complete' . . . or it isn't there. The proposition is ridiculous; as ridiculous as the suggestion that black is merely a dark shade of white.

'The human being is not a chemical accident; its soul is to its body what its mind is to its brain. Therefore, when the body dies, the soul lives on.'

Not a chemical accident? What then about the unfortunates deformed at birth? A biological accident . . . a form of *chemical* accident? An 'unsuccessful' accident? Therefore, why isn't a normal birth a 'successful' accident? If you have one, you must have both. The choice is not there . . . it *is* or it *isn't*. Always!

And as for the mind/soul argument. Does the mind, too, live on? Are the great thoughts – the great propositions – of mankind floating around in some unseen void? Thoughts minus brains? Thoughts which have been expressed, but which now have no home? Nobody seriously postulates *that* theory. But (again) there is no choice. It is both or neither. No 'released' minds – no 'released' thoughts . . . ergo no 'released' souls.

I wonder. Does any religion – does any blind belief – ever *really* help? Perhaps, but not for me. Not that night.

The threads tangled themselves into an impossible knot and, after it all, I reached only one firm but sad conclusion. Hannah had not had a happy life and perhaps Johnny was right . . . perhaps some of her unhappiness had been *my* fault.

It was not a pleasant thought with which to squash out the cigarette, settle down into the bedclothes and seek sleep.

For two days life at The Ridings plodded its dreary course. On the Tuesday Johnny was fully occupied supervising prep and checking that the girls climbed the stairs to the dormitories at the correct time. On the Wednesday there was what was euphemistically called a 'staff meeting'; a get-together of all free members of the teaching staff at which Morley pontificated and laid down more petty rules and regulations.

On the Thursday it was my turn for prep supervision and its attendant chores.

That was Thursday, February 9th.

It was just after ten-thirty when I called in at the staff lounge and helped myself to a last cup of lukewarm coffee dregs from the urn. Most of them – including Johnny – had already turned in. For perhaps ten minutes or so I relaxed in an armchair, sipped the disgusting liquid I'd drawn from the urn and flipped through the pages of an out-of-date issue of *Yorkshire Life*; glancing at the usual pictures of weddings, functions and fêtes which form the bulk of the illustrations in these county magazines. The normal set-pieces, and as always my mind soured a little as I saw the grinning and grimacing features of the well-to-do and the would-be-well-to-do caught in the act of empty enjoyment.

I tossed the magazine on to one of the tables, pushed myself from the armchair, returned my empty cup to its place alongside the urn, wished the few remaining members of staff a meaningless 'Good night', then climbed the stairs to the flat.

I opened the door of the flat, switched on the light, then closed the door in one practised continual movement . . . and *then* I saw Sykes.

Leah Sykes. Until that moment she'd been a schoolgirl; a seventeen-year-old pupil and head girl at a very crummy scholastic establishment known as The Ridings. That's what she *still* was, but she was also something more. Something much more. She was also a temptress and, moreover, she knew how to play the part. She was relaxed in the rocking-chair – Hannah's favourite chair – rocking gently to and fro and watching me from behind mockingly half-lowered lids. She wore pyjamas – thin, skin-hugging pyjamas – and a first glance was enough to see that that was *all* she wore. A pair of mules were on the carpet . . . as if they'd been kicked aside. Her dressing-gown, too, was on the carpet; crumpled, with one sleeve badly torn at the shoulder.

For what was no more than five seconds – but a never-ending five seconds – we stared at each other. Her mouth curved into a sardonic smile . . . and I *knew*. Only a complete fool wouldn't have known. The scene was perfect. I was the only character that had been missing. And now I *wasn't* missing.

I felt my throat contract and with my hand still on the door handle I waited.

'You asked me to come,' she purred.

I didn't answer. I didn't even move.

She said, 'At prep. I asked about Gauguin . . . Van Gogh's friend. I asked about him. I have witnesses. Two girls from the sixth form. They heard you suggest that I visit you here after dorm.'

'You're a liar,' I croaked.

'I have witnesses,' she smiled.

I moistened my lips and said, 'Get out of this room, Sykes. Get back to the dormitory where you belong.'

'Mr Hemingway.' She smiled tauntingly. 'Come away from that door. It's too late . . . *far* too late. Come away from that door. Let's discuss things.'

'What sort of things?'

'Gauguin.' She chuckled. 'We can *start* with Gauguin. It might be interesting. You have a flair for introducing side-issues . . . don't you?'

Slowly – with great reluctance – I uncurled my fingers from the door handle and moved farther into the room.

'Sit down, Mr Hemingway,' she mocked.

I lowered myself into the chair opposite her. I tried to keep my gaze fixed upon her face, but the truth was it was an effort; there was a vibrancy – an animal urgency – which denied any attempt at ignoring the fact that beneath the thin sheath of those pyjamas was a young body goading me to commit indiscretions.

'This.' She gave a short laugh, as if at a private joke, then raised a hand to the neckline of the pyjama jacket. 'It isn't very strong material . . . and I can scream *very* loudly.'

'Rape,' I said hoarsely.

'*Attempted* rape,' she corrected me.

'All right.' I struggled to collect my spinning thoughts. 'What is it you want?'

'Don't be impatient, Mr Hemingway.'

'You must want something. You must have *something* in mind.'

'We don't like being accused of murder,' she said solemnly.

'We?'

'The sixth form.'

'*Has* somebody accused you of murder?' I parried.

'Of your wife's death. The same thing.'

'Has somebody accused you of *that*?'

'The art appreciation lesson. We all knew exactly what you meant.'

'You must have guilty consciences.'

'Careful.' Again she moved a hand to the neckline of her pyjamas.

'Why?' I was gradually getting the measure of things. 'You're going to tear that jacket. You're going to scream the place down. Why should I be careful? What good will it do me?'

'Suicide. Madness. Death. Daisy Arkwright.' She itemised each very slowly.

'You *have* guilty consciences,' I mocked gently.

'You're finished, Hemingway.'

'*Mister* Hemingway.'

'We've declared war on you.'

' "We"?'

'The sixth form.'

'Excluding Daisy Arkwright . . . of course.'

'She was soft.'

'But . . . the rest of you?'

She smiled. Such a knowledgeable smile. Such an assured smile.

'Did you love your wife?' she asked gently.

'I don't see what the devil that has to do . . .'

'*Did* you?'

'Since you ask . . . yes.'

'She didn't think so.'

'What?' I stared. The conversation – if it *was* a conversation – had taken an unexpected turn.

'She was miserable.'

'Look, I don't see what the hell . . .'

'She told us so.'

She was lying. She *had* to be lying. She was playing with me like a cat teasing a trapped mouse. It was her perverted idea of 'fun'. It was . . .

'Not in as many words. Hints. Warnings . . . about how to take care when *we* chose husbands.'

'You're a lying bitch,' I breathed.

'Not in as many words,' she repeated. 'I think she even sought advice – some sort of advice – from Morley. *That* thick-headed oaf!'

'Sykes, I'm warning you,' I whispered hoarsely. 'If you so much as . . .'

Suddenly she seemed to lose her temper and snapped, 'The whole school knew. Everybody! And you have the gall to suggest that *we* drove her to suicide. Of the whole staff she was the only one we respected. The rest of you? God! You make me sick.'

I was shaken. Badly shaken. Accepting the fact that she was a vindictive little cow – accepting the fact that, to use her own words, the sixth form had 'declared war' on me – accepting all these things . . . *why*? What was the point of lying? Where was the object of spewing out untruths concerning the reason for Hannah's suicide?

She saw my expression. The disgust – probably the agony – on my face. She was shocked. Genuinely amazed. God knows what she *expected*; what reaction she was waiting for after sitting there and mouthing what we both knew to be black lies. Whatever it was – whatever she'd been expecting – she was obviously startled by the manner in which I showed my outrage. Just for a moment – for no more than a moment – I saw puzzlement cloud her eyes. Then she was back on course . . . knowing (or thinking) she had me in a cleft stick.

'There's a cop-out,' she said flatly.

I waited.

'You'll have pen and paper here somewhere.'

I nodded.

'An apology,' she said. 'Addressed to the sixth form in general. To Daisy Arkwright in particular.'

'What sort of an apology?' I croaked.

'About the art appreciation class. About the things you brought up during the Brontë lesson. About what you've been . . . and what you still *are*.'

'And then you hold it over me,' I sneered.

'No. We pin it to the notice board tomorrow morning.'

We stared at each other for a moment. We both saw mutual hatred and anger; contempt and disgust.

I took a deep breath and began, 'If you seriously think . . .'

'And what happens if he doesn't?'

Johnny's voice came from the doorway. We both turned and saw Johnny and Miss Lowther standing there. How long they'd been there – how much they'd heard – I didn't know and it didn't matter. I felt almost dizzy with relief.

Johnny said, 'Do you still go through the "attempted rape" routine?'

Miss Lowther gasped, 'You – you *wicked* girl.'

And never did anybody look more deflated – more terrified – than Miss Leah Sykes. She gaped like a stranded fish and her face was ashen.

Johnny spoke directly to me. He offered explanations. 'I saw her leave the dormitory. Heard the whispering and laughing from the other girls. I saw she was making for your flat. Something – y'know . . . *something*. I thought we'd better have a woman present.'

'You heard?' I asked.

'Most of it.' He nodded. 'We couldn't head you off before you got here. But we heard most of it.'

'Thanks.'

Miss Lowther stared at the frightened Sykes and repeated, 'You wicked, *wicked* girl.'

'Right.' I stood up from the chair. I was trembling with rage and I passed messages to Johnny with my eyes. I moved over to where Sykes was sitting and growled, 'Now it's *my* turn.'

Miss Lowther made as if to intervene, but Johnny put out a hand and held her arm.

I stood over Sykes and snarled, 'I think the exercise under discussion was rape. Am I right?' She didn't answer, so I clasped her face with the heel of my hand under the chin and thumb and fingers gripping each cheek. I tilted her head back until I was staring into her terrified eyes and repeated, '*Am I right?*'

'Sir, I . . .' She ran out of words.

'Rape.' I savoured the word quite deliberately. 'Such a simple accusation. So easy to make . . . so difficult to disprove. Rape. Or attempted rape. But now the boot's on the other foot.' I tilted her head more and, with my free hand, caught the neckline of her pyjama jacket. Beneath my hand I could feel the young body cringe away . . . and yet in some strange way almost present itself for violation. Miss Lowther gasped some sort of inane remark, but I wasn't listening to – I wasn't interested in – Miss Lowther. Just this young bitch who'd been so damn sure of herself only a few moments before; who'd used her sex, and the most damningly easy accusation her sex could make, as a vehicle for blackmail. In a very soft, very cold voice, I said, 'Would you *like* to be raped, Sykes? Is that what you *really* want? I can oblige . . . if that's what you're after. And now *I* have witnesses. Not cringing sixth formers. A master and a mistress . . . both of whom will swear I *didn't* rape you. Swear that I didn't even touch you. Swear that you weren't even *here*. So . . . if it's rape you want.' I tightened my grip on the pyjama jacket, then whispered, 'Or was there something about a letter? An apology? Tell me . . . can we do a deal?'

What would have happened had not Johnny and Miss Lowther been present I would not like to guess. Perhaps I might have held myself in check. Perhaps not. It is a purely academic question, but nevertheless an *interesting* question. Sykes certainly thought she knew the answer. It was there in the blind panic of her expression . . . and not for one moment did she give even passing thought to either Johnny *or* Miss Lowther.

On reflection I think Miss Lowther saved her.

She almost shouted, 'Mr Hemingway. Don't you *dare*!'

I released my hand from the pyjama jacket and at the same time relaxed my grip on the girl's face with a throwaway motion of disgust. Her head snapped sideways, and I could see the scarlet marks of my thumb and fingers on the waxen cheeks.

I snapped, 'Get out of here. Go back to your precious classmates. And tell them, if it's war you want consider it declared.'

She ran from the room. Johnny and Miss Lowther stepped aside to let her pass.

Then Miss Lowther said, 'Mr Hemingway, I don't think you should have . . .'

'What?' I almost snarled.

'What you did. Done and said what you did.'

'You saw what her game was.'

'Nevertheless, I think . . .'

'Forget it Miss Lowther,' I said harshly. 'I owe you thanks for being here . . . and thank you. Now take her dressing-gown and her slippers and call the episode closed.'

'I really think Mr Morley should be . . .'

'The hell with Mr Morley. The episode's closed. Finished. What can Morley do that hasn't already been done? She's been frightened out of her wits. That's enough.'

Reluctantly – very reluctantly it seemed – Lowther nodded agreement, collected the dressing-gown and slippers, then left. Johnny closed the door, walked to the rocking-chair vacated by Sykes and sat down.

It was closing up to midnight and we'd emptied a few cans of beer between us. Johnny was still in the rocking-chair . . . and he was still a frightened man.

For the umpteenth time he said, 'You were lucky, Tony.'

'Agreed.'

'If I hadn't spotted her.'

'It could have been awkward.'

'Mate . . . you could have ended up in jail.'

'I doubt it.' And I meant what I said.

'They were prepared to commit perjury. Not just Sykes. The whole bloody sixth form.'

I smiled and tasted beer straight from the can, then said, 'They'd have broken, Johnny. Under police questioning – under cross-examination, in court – at least one of them would have broken.'

'You have faith, my friend,' he sighed solemnly.

'More than you . . . obviously.'

Then he touched the raw spot. I'd been expecting it, but even so when it came I felt the anger rise a little.

He said, 'That explanation she gave.'
'You heard it.'
'Sure . . . and Miss Lowther.'
'They had to *have* an excuse.'
'Yeah . . . I suppose.'
'A very empty excuse.' I could feel my voice becoming a little more brittle.
'Yeah.' It was a noise. It meant absolutely nothing.
'*You* don't think there was any truth in it?' I made it a direct challenge.
Instead of answering he tasted his beer, paused a few moments, then said, 'Tony, they're dangerous.'
'Sixth-form schoolgirls,' I scoffed . . . and perhaps I had already forgotten the Sykes episode.
'Mate.' Johnny shook his head sadly. He pushed his spectacles back into position, then repeated, 'Mate.'
'They want war. They shall have war.'
'War,' he sighed, 'equates with casualties. People – sometimes innocent people – get hurt.'

The Fall of the Seventh Domino

Tallboy said, 'We can't be one hundred per cent sure.'
'It's tight,' said Blayde shortly.
'How tight?' asked Lennox.
Blayde said, 'Road blocks. Patrol cars keeping their eyes open. Leave cancelled, duties re-scheduled. We've a ten-mile perimeter round the town . . . *that* tight. Men posted at strategic points with binoculars. The chopper's on stand-by.'
Lennox nodded his satisfaction.
Satisfaction? Oh, aye . . . *satisfaction*. Up to a point. But beyond that point. For the last few months Lennox had had a lot of time for self-examination. Too much bloody time! Self-examination and watching the love of his life die in prolonged agony. It had been a little like putting your heart

through a paper-shredder . . . *that* painful. Nobody's fault, of course. Nothing was *ever* anybody's fault. Kismet . . . that was the fancy name for it. Fate. Well, screw fate, for a start. That lass of his had done nobody any harm. Ever. In all her life. Not one bad thing, so where was the justice?

For himself? He'd put some right bent bastards behind bars in his time. Some real beauts. And yet looking back – looking back as he'd sat alongside the bed of his dying wife – he'd realised he wasn't too proud of what he'd done. Every time – every blasted time! – when the man wearing the wig had pronounced sentence he, Lennox, had felt an empty feeling in the guts. A feeling of ineptitude. A deep-rooted feeling that this wasn't the answer . . . or, if you like, the *wrong* answer. The wrong way of doing things; like sweeping muck under a carpet and calling the room 'clean'. Bloody barmy. Because – all right, His Nibs had a rough time behind bars . . . but no rougher than his wife and kids were having. And *they* hadn't done a damn thing.

Added to which . . .

Prison just wasn't the answer. For every hook it straightened out, it made a dozen more bent than they'd been before they went inside. Sod the statistics. Every working jack knew the score; knew it better than any sociologist, or any other bloody 'ologist'. Prison was an academy; a university where aspiring criminals were taught by experts and came out with an invisible degree in lawlessness. So, there *had* to be another way. A better way. Jesus wept, we could land on the moon, we could boomerang around Mars, we could blow the whole world sky-high at the press of a button . . . but we still caged men away like animals, but unlike animals we expected them to come out 'tamed' when we opened the cage door. We were mad. The whole chuffing world was mad. And he Lennox was . . .

'If he's spent the night in the open we'll need a blowlamp to thaw him out.'

Blayde's sardonic remark broke in on Lennox's musings.

'Unless he's found shelter,' observed Tallboy.

Lennox said, 'Let's hope the stupid clown *has* found shelter.'

Blayde sniffed expressively. Very obviously, Blayde couldn't have cared less had Cooley been quick-frozen into deep-freeze fodder.

The three officers were gathered around Blayde's car in one of the municipal car parks on the outskirts of Beechwood Brook. It was the 'waiting game' period which, on every major crime enquiry, sharpens tempers and sours dispositions. Everything that could be done *had* been done. The trap was set and ready to be sprung. All it lacked was the quarry. It was early afternoon, on Saturday, February 11th, with a biting wind from the north-east and promise of another hard frost come nightfall. And they were waiting; waiting within hearing distance of the radio in Blayde's car, and hoping that Cooley was somewhere within the police net.

Apropos something to say, Blayde growled, 'Two Saturdays on the trot.'

'What?' asked Lennox.

'Farting around, searching open country this weather. Last week it was that brainless schoolkid.'

'Oh, aye.' Lennox nodded. 'Arkwright. I saw the report.'

'From The Ridings.'

'Much of a school?' Lennox wasn't really interested . . . why should he have been? It was just something with which to break the monotony of silence.

'Fishy,' said Blayde shortly.

'Oh, aye?'

'More of an institution than a school. I've seen more comfortable detention centres.'

Tallboy chipped in, 'That's what you pay for.'

'What?' Lennox turned his head.

'Education in spartan surroundings. It makes for character building . . . so they tell me.'

'I must have missed summat.'

Blayde said, 'Not with those bloody teachers.'

'Uhu?' Again, Lennox switched his attention.

'The kid – Arkwright – swears one of the masters accused 'em of driving his wife to suicide.'

'Did she?' asked Lennox with slight interest.

'Saturday . . . the Saturday before.' Blayde frowned at the sudden realisation. 'Everything happens on a Saturday at that bloody place. She gassed herself.'

'Because of the kids?'

'That's what Hemingway says.'

'Hemingway?'

'One of the masters . . . husband of the dead woman.'

'A hell of an accusation,' said Lennox.

'Straight up-and-down?' asked Tallboy.

'What?'

'The gassing job?'

'Tallboy.' Blayde cocked an eyebrow. 'I didn't arrive with the morning milk.'

'No. I'm not suggesting . . .'

'The hell you're not. Sudden death. Treat it as possible murder till you're satisfied it's *not*. I know the rule book, too. Take my word for it . . . it was suicide.'

'Sorry,' grinned Tallboy.

Lennox mused, 'But a hell of an accusation to make . . . eh?'

Blayde said, 'Hemingway's a nutter.'

'The master? The woman's husband?'

'They're *all* nutters,' pronounced Blayde. 'The headmaster Morley . . . the lot of 'em. *I'd* commit suicide if I had to live with that lot.'

The loonie squeaked, 'You're not Crofter's man, mister. *They* sent you. They want me inside again. Think I don't know? Think I'm *that* daft?'

He didn't seem to realise that nobody could hear him. That the thing in the corner, punched against the blood-splashed shot-pocked boards, wasn't a man any more. That the chest had gone and the head and neck were scarlet cavities from which gore still spilled to add to the spreading pool on the floor.

Therefore he continued to twitter, 'So, now you know . . . don't you, mister? Now you *know*. Ned's not as daft as they make out. Eh? Eh? Ned knows 'em. Ned can recognise 'em. Aeroplanes. Motor cars. It makes no difference . . . see? Ned can always tell. You. Hiding there all night. Trying to catch people out. But not Ned, mister. Ned's not going back inside. Not nohow. Not back into that place. You tell 'em, mister. When you get back, you tell 'em. Just leave me alone . . . eh? Just stay away from my place. That's all, mister. My place. Crofter's place. Don't you come here any more . . . see? That's all. Just don't come here any more.'

Towards the end his tirade tapered off to a muttering whimpering, as he turned his back on the mangled corpse, shuffled down the wooden steps from the door of the cabin-like structure and returned to the open air.

He took fresh cartridges from the pocket of his wretched coat, broke the shotgun and re-loaded. Then in a half-crouch he stalked his way through the covering of snow alongside the hedgerows.

There was fear – a mad, unreasoning fear – in his every movement. His eyes were never still; they seemed to have a crazy life of their own; searching for something – searching the dull, grey sky, peeping through gaps in the leafless hedges, glancing back whence he'd come – everlastingly on the look-out for some terrible thing which haunted the muddle of his ailing mind. The weather seemed unable to touch him. Inside the battered boots and holed socks, his feet squelched in the ice-cold soak from the near-bog of snow-saturated earth. The steady, freezing wind caught his dank, filthy hair and, like greased whiplashes, drove it across his face, but he seemed not even to notice. His progress never varied; a slow-paced stalk with the twelve-bore at the ready and the fingers clawed around the triggers.

Madness and terror. He epitomised the two emotions. He mumbled to himself as he walked; meaningless words mouthed at little more than a whisper. Seeking . . . seeking . . . not knowing *what* he was seeking. Not knowing, but fearful that he might find it.

Lennox leaned with his back against the rear door of the car and wondered about poor old Cooley. He felt pity. A bloke with a bit of a kink, that's all. A thief – a breaker – but a thief without brains. He'd found a gimmick – the contact-adhesive trick – and he'd thought he'd conquered the world. He hadn't even the gumption to realise that *that* was his trademark. Like a signature tune – like a catch-phrase – as peculiar to him as *that*. And the contents of his bowels near the point of entry, that too. Not like some – making their filth and emptying their bladders *inside* the house – Cooley always relieved himself *outside*. Another catch-phrase. Another signature tune. Who the hell couldn't feel some measure of pity for a poor bastard as dumb as *that*?

And now Cooley was a killer. Some day soon he'd stand in a dock and some bewigged prosecuting barrister, who couldn't even *conceive* the thought-process of men like Cooley, would systematically paint him as black as a tar-baby and twelve ordinary people would listen and believe . . . and a judge would put the poor devil away for anything up to twelve/fifteen years. The self-defence–manslaughter charge? Aye, well, Cooley *had* broken into the house in the first place and, even though Page *had* been shooting bullets at him, to spear a man to death, then bash his girl friend's skull in, made very grisly listening. It *had* to be a long stretch.

Lennox said, 'What was Page like?'

'Rich and randy,' said Blayde.

'Why the hell . . . ?' began Lennox, then closed his mouth without voicing his thoughts.

Tallboy glanced at his watch and said, 'We'd better strike oil before it's dark. Otherwise . . .'

'He has to eat,' growled Blayde.

'There'll be a temptation to starve till the light goes.'

'Do the farmers all know?' asked Lennox.

Blayde said, 'They've been warned. And the pubs. And the cafés.'

'Assuming,' mused Tallboy, 'he's spent the night in the open.'

'That's why we're waiting,' countered Blayde.

'Some shelter,' continued Tallboy.

'We've checked just about every barn. Just about every outbuilding in the area.'

'He'd find *some* shelter,' insisted Tallboy. 'Somewhere.'

Blayde grunted.

'Something,' said Tallboy. 'Something we've missed.'

Blayde scowled, then said, 'There's the old plough shed. Where that kid Arkwright spent the night.'

'Checked?' asked Lennox.

'No. Come to think of it . . . no.' Blayde frowned at his own forgetfulness.

'Should do,' remarked Lennox mildly.

'I'll get the local man.' Blayde opened the front door of the car and reached inside for the microphone. 'Out there – back o' nowhere – there could be quite a few places not marked on a map.'

Deep inside himself, Jack Warton wept. No tears reached the surface. The heartbreak didn't show itself in his expression; he stared ahead, stone-faced, as the car swallowed the road leading back to the farm. He sat bolt upright in the front passenger-seat as his younger daughter Julie drove. The harsh Northern pride forbad him to give even so much as a hint of the turmoil which raged within him; a terrible pride – a killing pride – which through the centuries had earned him and his kind the undeserved reputation for cruelty.

And yet, although he fought it with the not inconsiderable power of his will, he was unable to prevent at least part of the agony from riding his voice. The tone was lower than usual. The words more carefully enunciated, to iron out any possible catch or sob. And the pauses between each sentence . . . long pauses, as he thought out each combination of words in order that he might not stumble.

He said, 'She didn't deserve it. Whatever she was, she didn't deserve *that*.'

Julie Warton murmured, 'No, Father.'

Julie Warton, too, was having difficulty with her retrospections. Angela – her sister – but what *should* a woman think when her sister has been battered to death? Shock? Of course, the circumstances were shocking, therefore she was shocked. Sorrow? Yes, that too. But sorrow was a quantitative thing. To be 'sorry': for precious milk spilled from a knocked-down pail because of the kick from a cantankerous cow? For a dog she'd loved since it was a puppy – one of the finest sheep-workers in the north – but because it had been gradually blinded by the backlash of the ling-heather of The Tops on to its face it had had to be put down? For the death of a mother who, through no fault of her own, had been forced into the refuge of a self-made shell; a shell which she had never left, in case she might be hurt once more? For a marriage that never was, and never could be, because an elder sister had coaxed a future husband into her bed as a demonstration of her own sexual prowess? For the death of that same elder sister, whatever the circumstances of that death? For *any* woman – family, friend or stranger – whose life has ended in the gory smashing in of her skull? What *was* sorrow? What did it really mean to be 'sorry'? And could genuine sorrow ever mix with that nagging, almost pleasurable, feeling of 'just retribution'?

Warton said, 'You'll come back home, Julie?'

'I'll – I'll have to think about it.'

'I'd like it.'

'Perhaps. Don't ask for a decision just now.'

'Think about it,' growled Warton softly.

Julie hesitated, then, in a gentle voice, said, 'Andrew?'

'I've asked the police to notify him.'

'Shouldn't – er – shouldn't *you*?'

'What?'

'Shouldn't *you* have telephoned him . . . or something?'

'They'll tell him better than I can.'

Julie said, 'I think *you* should have told him.'

'Andrew doesn't count.'

There were, perhaps, another couple of miles of silence. Julie forced herself to concentrate upon driving; fought to clear her mind of wrong thoughts; worked deliberately to 'remember' the few good times she and her murdered sister had enjoyed together. The effort saddened her. They added to less than a dozen . . . and none within the last ten years.

Warton said, 'Why didn't you let me know, Julie?'

'What?'

'That she was with you.'

'She *wasn't* with me. She left. I thought she was going to Andrew's.'

'She came to you. In the first place.'

'Yes.'

'Why didn't you let me know?'

'Father,' she said slowly, '*you* turned her out.'

'I worried.'

'Like hell you worried!' It was a sudden blaze-up of anger. 'You've never worried about *anybody*. Angie. Andrew. Mother. Me. All your life . . . you've worried about *nobody*.'

'As bad as that?' muttered Warton.

Julie quietened her temper, then murmured, 'Sometimes.'

'My God.' Warton pinched the bridge of his nose as if he had been touched by a sudden headache. He sighed, then said, 'It needs summat – summat like this – then you get at the truth.'

'Who's perfect?' Julie tried to retreat from the hurt she knew she'd inflicted.

'Aye.' Warton nodded slowly.

'I . . . I'll not be coming back,' said Julie in a low voice.

'No.' Warton seemed to accept the decision without feeling.

'I'm sorry.'

'It's your decision, lass.'

'It's – er – it's no good sitting on it for days. Perhaps weeks. You should know . . . *now*.'

'Aye.'

'I'm sorry,' repeated Julie.

'No.' There was gruff, north-country bloody-mindedness in the soft, harsh words. 'Never be sorry, lass. Never . . . about owt. Your own tram-track, see? Bugger the others . . . whoever they are. Your way. Not *their* way. You'll live longer . . . cry less.'

'Like Angie,' said Julie in a whisper.

The stable had that tangy, sweaty smell beloved of horsemen the world over. The palm of Billy Edwards's right hand followed the path of the curry-comb as he gently groomed the mare's flanks. Occasionally one of the muscles gave a twitch of pleasure as the animal responded to the youth's touch.

And, as he worked, Edwards crooned comforting affection.

The words – the tone – which, though rare, gives final proof of the complete empathy between animal and man.

'Easy, Lady, old luv. Easy. You're almost better. That old foot of yours won't be long now. Come spring, you'll be there, showing the others the way. As good as new. Easy, old luv. I'm not going to hurt you. Just clean you up. Make you shine. Make you beautiful, old girl . . .'

'How is she?' The man called Preston asked the question from the stable door.

'About better, sir.' Billy Edwards straightened, patted the horse's side and eased his way from the stall. 'Another week . . . thereabouts. Then I reckon we can take her for a quiet canter.'

'Aye.' Preston nodded dour agreement.

'Sir.' Billy Edwards frowned his worry. 'About Miss Angela.'

'None o' your business, lad.'

'Yes, sir.' The youth swallowed, then blurted, 'I reckon it's my fault, sir.'

'Don't be daft.'

'The row, between her and the gaffer.'

'It was coming,' said Preston flatly.

'Yes, sir. But if I hadn't called her . . .'

'Billy.' Preston's voice softened slightly. 'You've a way with horses, especially Lady . . . be thankful.'

'It's – it's the gaffer,' muttered the youth. 'When he gets back, he'll . . .'

'What?'

'He'll hand me my cards.'

'Why the devil should he do *that*?'

'Mr Preston.' The youth worked hard to put his thoughts – his fears – into words. 'It was – y'know – what I called her. I shouldn't have. I know I shouldn't have. And that's what started it. And now . . . He'll blame me. Who else can he blame?'

'Lady?' suggested Preston straight-faced. 'Lady threw her.'

'He can't blame Lady! It wasn't Lady's fault. *She* didn't . . .'

'The motorist?'

'What motorist?' The youth's eyes showed puzzlement.

'The one driving the car that made Lady shy.'

'Do we know who the . . .'

'The bloke who *made* the car? The bloke who sold the car to the motorist? God . . . because he made it snow at the wrong time?'

The youth remained silent.

Preston's face relaxed into a rare smile as he said, 'The blame only goes so far back, lad, see? After that it starts being barmy. What's happened to Miss Angela was her own fault. Not yours. Not even the gaffer's. You'll not get your cards. I know Mr Warton better than you do. So, just get on with your work. And stop worrying about nowt.'

'Where?' asked Blayde.

Braithwaite, the patrol constable responsible for the Lower Tops beat, waved a hand in the general direction of what looked to be an endless succession of snow-crowned fields.

He said, 'Out that way. Three fields, maybe four, then it's tucked away beyond Friar's Coppice.'

'No way in?' asked Tallboy.

'On foot,' said Braithwaite.

Lennox muttered, 'This was a brilliant bloody idea.'

Blayde (whose 'idea' it had been) tried to pass some of the heat on to the patrol constable.

He said, 'There must be a nearer way.'

'No, sir.'

'The hell! That schoolkid . . .'

'She crossed the fields. One field leads to another. This is as near as you can get by road.'

'D'you ever visit the place?' asked Blayde nastily. 'Check it?'

'About once a month.'

'I wouldn't call that "often" . . . would you?'

Braithwaite let the criticism slide past without, apparently, even noticing it. Braithwaite was long in the tooth and wise in the ways of top brass; he'd been Lower Tops bobby when Blayde had taken over the chief superintendentship; he'd even been Lower Tops bobby when Blayde's predecessor, the legendary Ripley, had first moved into the division. He'd seen 'em come. He'd seen 'em go. Three more years and it was pension time and until that golden day he could stand there and take whatever a whole army of 'Blaydes' cared to throw at him. After that he could tell 'em to go screw themselves, in batches of ten!

'No easy way?' murmured Lennox more in hope than anticipation.

'No, sir.'

'So, it's shanks.'

'Gumboots?' suggested Tallboy tentatively.

Blayde said, 'Not unless you have a few pairs in your hip pocket.'

'C'mon.' Lennox shoved his hands deep into the pockets of his mac. As he waddled towards the gate he said, 'Mush!'

Lennox had taken the immediate heat out of the situation, nevertheless Blayde's expression showed zero amusement. Tallboy shrugged philosophically, and followed the stout detective chief superintendent. Braithwaite followed Tallboy, and Blayde took up the rear.

Beyond the gate, Lennox paused and said, 'You'd better come up front, Braithwaite. You know the way.'

And, Indian-file fashion, they followed the local constable alongside hedges, over stiles and through more gates. Always at least ankle deep in surface-frozen snow. Often brushing more snow from the branches of the leafless hedgerows.

Gradually becoming colder, wetter and (as far as Blayde was concerned) more ill-tempered.

About ten yards from what would have been the final gate – with the plough shed in sight at the far corner of the next field – Braithwaite stopped at a gap in the hedge.

He pointed a gloved finger and said, 'Somebody's been through here.'

Tallboy pushed his way to the front, examined the impressions in the snow, then straightened and said, 'Cooley.'

'Straight from *The Boy Scout's Manual of Woodcraft*,' mocked Blayde.

'No.' Tallboy smiled. 'Straight from the plaster-cast taken outside Page's place. That left shoe. There was a distinct V-mark at the side of the heel. It's *there* if you look closely enough.'

Blayde bent, then straightened. He nodded. Satisfied.

'Sorry,' he said.

'He climbed the gate.' Again Braithwaite pointed. 'The snow's dislodged.'

'Gently,' warned Lennox in a low voice. 'If he's still in there.' He paused, then said, 'Blayde. Take Braithwaite. Through the hedge, round the back . . . come at it from the other side. I'll wait here with Tallboy. When we see you're in position, we'll move in together. Left and right.'

Blayde nodded, then forced his way through the gap in the hedge. Braithwaite followed.

Miss Leah Sykes conspired with her friend, the deputy head girl. They were alone in the deserted gym, surrounded by the paraphernalia of 'keep fit' junk, but they kept their voices low.

Sykes was saying, 'He *must* do something.'

'Knowing Morley . . .' The deputy head girl didn't sound too sure.

'If he doesn't,' pronounced Sykes, 'I bring the press in.'

'How on earth . . .'

'An anonymous telephone call, duckie. Names, dates and Hannah gassing herself. They'll bite.'

'Leah, I'm not too happy about . . .'

'For God's sake!' Sykes's impatience was no mock affair. 'I want Hemingway. *I* want Hemingway. After Thursday night's snarl-up – after the way he treated me – *I* want him. And don't forget Hannah. It's what he deserves. It's what they both deserve . . . what they *all* deserve.'

'Leah.' The deputy head girl's expression showed increased anxiety. 'We've the others to think about.'

'What others?'

'The other girls. The other . . .'

'You want to cop out, duckie?' Sykes's lip curled. 'Go ahead. I don't need you. I don't need anybody.'

'I know, but . . .'

'*Do* you want to cop out?'

'No. Of course not. But . . .'

'All right, then. Remember Hannah. Remember that silly goose Arkwright. Those are enough reasons. Hemingway thinks he's good. Hemingway, Stirk, Morley . . . they *all* think they're good. But this is where we knock them *all* from their precious perches.'

Blayde waved them to a halt as they reached the gate. Then, via an exaggerated pantomime, he beckoned them to move away from the hedge – away from the footprints – and farther into the field.

'I suppose he knows what he's doing,' grumbled Lennox.

'Something they can see, we can't,' said Tallboy.

'Aye.'

They hoisted themselves over the gate, then, as directed, moved away from the hedge. Blayde and Braithwaite came towards them and they, too, moved into the field. All four moved cautiously and, other than a glance at the ground to ensure a reasonable foothold, all four kept their eyes on the opening to the ancient plough shed.

Lennox muttered, 'You're the young 'un, Chris. If he makes a bolt I'll dive for the hedge – try to head him off – after that it's up to you.'

Tallboy grunted a soft reply.

But there was no need for any heading-off or any diving for the hedge. The four officers joined forces opposite the entrance to the shed and, as they did so, Blayde shook his head meaningly.

'Flown?' asked Tallboy.

Blayde glanced to where he and Braithwaite had been standing and said, 'Footprints leading away. The V-mark's in the heel.'

'Damn!'

'Check the shed . . . just in case,' said Lennox.

They checked and the evidence was there to see. The cigarette ends. A mass of footprints in the muddy floor; including four perfect impressions of a left shoe with a V-mark in the heel. Even the sign of urinating against one of the crumbling walls.

'He had a cold night,' observed Lennox.

'He's walking.' Blayde sounded satisfied. 'He's inside the net. That's the main thing.'

Tallboy said, 'So, all we do is follow the spoor.'

'Real Fenimore Cooper stuff,' said Blayde sardonically. 'Makes a pleasant change from house-to-house time-wasting.'

'Not forgetting the chilblains.'

Lennox said, 'Let's find the poor bugger before he freezes to death.'

Braithwaite remained silent . . . but looked vaguely worried.

The footprints were easy enough to follow. Most of them were mere drag-marks in the snow alongside the hedgerow, but here and there the heel-print with the V-mark satisfied them that they were following the route Cooley had taken.

After almost twenty minutes of trudging they reached one of the occasional gaps in the hedges which separated the fields, and Cooley's footprints were joined by other marks in the snow. An undefined pressing down as two sets of footprints met; a meeting and a certain amount of turning and shuffling.

Then *two* sets of footprints led away from the gap in the hedge.

'A meeting,' mused Tallboy.

Blayde said, 'A funny place for a rendezvous . . . unless Cooley knows these fields better than most.'

Braithwaite muttered. 'Daft Ned.'

'Who?' Blayde asked the question.

'Daft Ned,' repeated Braithwaite sadly. 'That's who it'll be.'

'Who's Daft Ned?'

'I dunno his other name,' said Braithwaite awkwardly. 'Just that Crofter lets him stay on his land.'

'Crofter?'

'The bloke who farms most of these fields.'

'Tell me . . .' said Blayde gently. 'Tell me all about this Daft Ned character.'

'He's – er . . .' Braithwaite cleared his throat. 'He's a bit soft in the head.'

'How soft?'

'He's been inside . . . a couple or three times.'

'Harmless?'

'I – er – I wouldn't be too sure,' muttered Braithwaite.

'Meaning, he's *not* harmless?'

'He . . .' Braithwaite waved his arms a little. 'Crofter uses him as a buckshee gamekeeper . . . sort of.'

'Sort of?'

'Doesn't – doesn't pay him. Just lets him park his van on the land and scare away the poachers.'

'Scare away the poachers?'

Braithwaite nodded miserably.

'How?'

'Sir?'

'Just *how* does this Daft Ned character scare away poachers?'

'He – er – he chases 'em off the land.'

'Braithwaite,' said Blayde patiently, 'don't arse me around. You know – *I* know – poachers aren't the easiest people in the world to frighten. And – now you mention it – I can't remember anybody being nicked for poaching in these parts . . . which is a little strange.'

Braithwaite remained silent and looked unhappy.

In a more kindly voice Lennox said, 'Summat's worrying you, old son.'

'Yes, sir.' Braithwaite nodded.

'This Daft Ned chap?'

'Yes, sir.' Once more Braithwaite nodded.

Lennox said, 'We've all chanced our arm. We've all come unstuck. It happens . . . all the time. And *when* we've come unstuck . . . that's when the going gets rough.'

'Yes, sir.'

'So . . .' Lennox glanced first at Blayde then at Tallboy. 'Between us four, eh?'

And thus encouraged Braithwaite told the story.

Daft Ned; the only name he'd ever been known by. Stories galore; obviously fifty per cent of them sheer moonshine. But the other fifty per cent? Not a man to tangle with; more of an animal than a man; befuddled to such a degree that he truly didn't know right from wrong.

He'd been around in Ripley's time and Ripley – being Ripley – had taken things day at a time and (thank God) nothing too dramatic had happened. A handful of unwary poachers running for their lives, with the odd lead-shot pellet embedded in their backside. Fortunately – *very* fortunately – Daft Ned hadn't too much of an idea of range as far as twelve-bore shotguns were concerned.

He'd been 'inside' . . . loony-bins, not prisons. Prison wasn't the place for men like Daft Ned. But (it happens sometimes) while inside – while under treatment – he'd been normal . . . well, more or less. To Braithwaite's certain knowledge he'd been inside twice . . . maybe three times. And each time the quacks had solemnly decided that Daft Ned *wasn't* daft, after all. A six-month stay . . . thereabouts. E.S.T., tranquillisers – the whole shooting match – and then a clean bill of health. That's how much the quacks knew! That's how daft the nut doctors were. Okay, maybe they *were* pushed for beds, but each time they opened the gates and let Ned loose he'd been a slightly bigger problem.

The object was to get him out of circulation, right? To park the poor sod somewhere where he couldn't do much harm. Where he was *away* from people. So when Crofter had come up with the idea of buying one of those old-fashioned, iron-wheeled caravan things used by local councils when they had a hunk of road-work under way – sort of temporary homes for watchmen to live and kip in – and park this hut-on-wheels contraption out of harm's way in a coppice way and gone to hell from the nearest road . . . what else but a good idea? Ned didn't have anybody. No family, or if he *had* nobody knew of 'em. Just Crofter. And Ned *loved* Crofter. Maybe something to do with dignity. Some sort of dignity. The dignity of a man whose brain only fired on one cylinder.

Crofter? Well, now, Crofter was a do-gooder. In a big way. A great fighter for the underdog. Excuses? Crofter could think up excuses for just about everything – up to and including mugging and suchlike – except trespass and poaching. A kink . . . y'know how everybody has some sort of kink. Crofter's kink was trespassing. Everything else was fine. But not that. And Daft Ned somehow knew about this kink of Crofter's. Instinct, maybe. But for whatever reason . . .

'And he has a gun?'

Blayde asked the question as they plodded their way along the peripheries of fields; through gates; over stiled fences. As they talked – as Braithwaite told his story – they followed the marks in the snow made by the two sets of footprints. They no longer examined the footprints; they were happy to ensure that no one set of marks branched away from the general disturbance of the snow's surface.

Braithwaite said, 'He has a gun, sir. A twin-barrelled twelve-bore.'

'Who the hell gave him that?'

'Crofter, sir, from what I hear. To keep the vermin down. And to shoot for his own pot.'

'A nutter with a twelve-bore,' growled Blayde.

Tallboy said, 'Constable, why the devil have you kept this situation under wraps for so long?'

'I haven't.' Braithwaite's tone was full of disgust as he added, 'But that's what I'm going to be accused of.'

'You say you haven't,' said Lennox. 'You have a reason, presumably?'

Braithwaite said, 'Chief Superintendent Ripley knew.'

'*I* didn't damn well know,' snarled Blayde.

'If Mr Ripley didn't tell you, sir, that's not . . .'

'All right.' Blayde accepted the argument with ill grace. 'But you're no grass-green recruit.'

'No, sir.'

'It must be obvious – must have been obvious for years – that a man like this Daft Ned type shouldn't be allowed to roam at large with a gun in his fist. A twelve-bore. Christ, that's more lethal than a . . .'

And so it went on. Four grown men – four coppers –

ploughing their way through varying depths of snow, slush and mud; arguing and counter-arguing; blaming and refusing to accept the blame; cut off from the machine of which they were a part and, if the truth be told, each feeling that faint prickling of the nape hairs – that instinctive near-knowledge born of years of law-enforcement – which warned them of something terribly wrong.

They talked as they worked their way towards their destination. Their talk was never-ending. It would be wrong to even suggest that they were afraid . . . and yet their talk was on a par with children whistling in the dark.

The man they called Daft Ned forced his way through the branches and rustling leaves of a high copper-beech hedge. No normal man would have even tried to force a way through such a barrier, but to this man normality was something beyond his ken. He bent forward and shouldered his way through head first, and the hedge fought back and left his face slashed and bleeding.

Beyond the hedge he stopped . . . and realised he was *still* lost.

He had left what the naturalists – what the ornithologists – might have called his 'territory'. The fields – the few thousand acres – farmed by his friend Crofter. Those he knew; every tree, every rise and fall of the land, the run of every rabbit, the favourite evening perch of every pheasant. He knew which stretch of land favoured which crops. He knew in which hollowed oak the solitary red squirrel nested in hard weather. He knew which trees the grey squirrels stripped of bark. He knew the sets of the badgers, the forms of the hares, the lairs of the foxes. No man (not even Crofter) knew that 'territory' like *he* knew it.

And now he was lost.

He dodged away from the beech hedge and pushed his way

through a small forest of laurel and when he'd cleared the laurel . . .

'The Place'!

Not *the* place; not the place where they'd kept him locked away; where men and women in white coats had tortured him with needles and electrical wires; where his daily companions had been wild-eyed and staring – not knowing that they were mad – not knowing that *he* was the only sane person in a tight little world. Not *that* place. But a similar place. Another place. Equally hateful. Equally terrifying.

He dodged back into the laurels and the shivering took over. The shivering and the whimpering and the muttering of meaningless words. These places . . . they were everywhere. Waiting for him. Eager to trap him – cage him – destroy him.

Which meant . . .

For the sake of his own freedom he had to destroy them. Kill them. Smash them . . . otherwise they'd grow and multiply and, eventually, smash *him*.

Gradually, the trembling eased. He crouched within the laurel forest, and slowly his sick mind worked out a means by which he might destroy this place . . . his enemy.

They found the van, they found the body and at that point all bickering ceased. All passing of blame was forgotten.

Braithwaite took a deep breath and whispered, 'Christ Almighty!'

Tallboy stooped to get a clearer view of the left shoe, then straightened and said, 'Cooley,' in a flat unemotional voice.

Certain it is that better, and more accurate, identification was impossible until fingerprints were taken. The chest, the neck and the lower half of the face were little more than minced flesh and bone; what had once been the jaw hung by a single tendon from one cheek; the slashed and mutilated windpipe showed white and shiny within a cave of congealing blood.

Lennox glanced at his watch and said, 'The dogs . . . and before it gets dark.'

'I'll go,' volunteered Blayde. 'I'll get things moving.'

'The chopper?' suggested Tallboy.

Lennox said, 'If they can get a damn dog into the thing. If not a Land-Rover – summat like that – something capable of taking these fields without getting bogged down.'

'I'm on my way.'

Blayde hurried from the van and began a steady jog-trot across the fields towards the distant car.

Lennox said, 'Stay here, Constable.'

'Yes, sir.'

'Inside or outside – it's up to you – but don't try any heroics. He's armed and if he comes back we don't want any more bodies.' Lennox turned to Tallboy and continued, 'We'd better follow the tracks. It's better than standing here waiting for the dogs.'

'Sir.' Braithwaite spoke.

'Aye?'

'You, too, sir,' said Braithwaite solemnly. 'Don't *you* forget he's armed . . . and mad.'

EIGHT

Friday (Friday, February 10th) was a normal sort of day; normal, that is, for an establishment like The Ridings. Hectic in so far as staff and pupils alike were hounded from pillar to post by a never-ending ringing of bells, but that *was* normal. My outrage at the previous night's attempt to intimidate me quietened a little. I had no doubt that Sykes had learned a lesson; that she would not again attempt moral blackmail in this so-called 'war' which had been declared between the sixth form and myself.

Fortunately – probably fortunately for my own peace of mind, and certainly fortunately for the undoubted embarrassment it would have caused Sykes – the sixth form was not included in my lessons on that day. I was able to encourage the younger pupils to daub and scrawl and in one session attempt to guide them through the clever, but intricate, speculations of Wells's short stories contained in *The Country of the Blind*.

And yet . . .

The memory of Leah Sykes refused to leave me. Leah Sykes, no child but a seventeen-year-old woman, in gossamer-thin pyjamas. With all the taunting mockery of a practised harlot. Conscious of what she had to offer, and also conscious of what men – men stronger and more worldly-wise than myself – had sacrificed for the taste of what she possessed.

Dangerous. But if dangerous . . . wise. It followed. Without wisdom (of a sort) she would not have been dangerous. Stupid, perhaps. Possibly even reckless. But not *dangerous*. Her wisdom had made her dangerous.

But if she *was* wise?

That stupid, pointless question. 'Did you love your wife?' Did I love Hannah? *Did I love Hannah?* The most stupid – the most pointless . . . and yet the person who had asked the question possessed wisdom! And (and although I loathed the little bitch, this much I had to concede) the question had been asked in all seriousness. Not flippantly. Not goadingly. Not mockingly. It had been asked as of a friend . . . 'Did you love my friend?'

And the other remarks. Equally solemnly spoken. Equally serious. Each (or so it seemed with hindsight) a probe; a probe to reach the truth before the business of moral blackmail was embarked upon.

'She was miserable.'

'Warnings about how to take care when we chose husbands.'

'I think she sought advice – some sort of advice – from Morley.'

The truth?

The truth is I love art; I love beauty; I love perfection. To some degree, all other things bore me. Mathematics, logic, philosophy . . . I don't understand them, I don't *want* to understand them. To me the heart – not the brain – is the seat of understanding. If it moves the heart, if it stirs the emotions then, by definition – by *my* definition – it succeeds. That two and two make four is of no importance whatever compared with the perfect curl of a dying leaf. A knowledge of the complexities of an atom is a useless nonsense when set alongside the heart-stopping splendour of a seascape, that split-second when the sun dips below the horizon. In music Brahms and Wagner can touch me to tears, but Bach and Britten leave me unmoved. People – people who profess to know me – have called me a 'romantic' (in the true sense of that word) and I have seen fit to deny that description. I 'feel' rather than think. My *forte* – if, indeed, I have one

– is that I am receptive, albeit only to things and persons with whom I have an affinity.

I stress these things – these strengths, these weaknesses – in an attempt to explain my complete lack of understanding of any motive or reason for the remarks made by Sykes the previous evening. I couldn't *understand*. However objective I tried to be – however I worked to push aside my personal dislike of the girl – there remained the utter *stupidity* of what she had said.

'Did you love your wife?'

Damnation, I *married* her. I shared my life with her. I had no secrets from her. She knew my every thought, my every mood, my every dream. Of *course* I loved her . . . and it was an unforgivable impudence on the part of a teenager even to ask such a question.

'She was miserable.'

Hannah? Miserable? Again, the gall of a seventeen-year-old to make such an assessment! Hannah had been a naturally quiet person. Withdrawn. An introvert. A solitary, unpretentious person; a person who, unlike myself, rarely (if ever) exhibited any outward show of emotion. Therefore, how did Sykes know whether she was or was not miserable?

'Warnings about how to take care when we chose husbands.'

That so much could be read into so little! It was possible – I was prepared to accept the possibility – that Hannah might have made some passing remark to that effect. It would not have been unlike her; to give an obvious warning to a class of girls on the brink of womanhood. A passing remark . . . no more. But with impressionable girls such an innocent piece of throw-away advice could be expanded and magnified until . . . My God, it was almost beyond belief.

'I think she sought advice from Morley.'

That, of course, proved everything. That *proved* Sykes to be a liar. Hannah's scorn – her utter contempt – for Morley matched my own. To even suggest that she might approach Morley for advice on *anything* – much less marital advice – was a form of lunacy.

It was possible, therefore, to dismiss the accusations made by Sykes the previous night as the mouthings of a seventeen-year-old girl with an over-active imagination. That's all they were . . . that's all they *could* be. It needed no logic, in the true sense of that term. It needed no philosophy. It merely required that I place those utterances alongside what I knew to be the truth, and their emptiness became obvious.

It pleased me to prove their falsity . . . even to myself.

And yet . . .

The fact is, a person says something and if you take the words at their immediate face value there remains a nagging doubt. And that the doubt is foundless makes it no less real. And as always that doubt – that *ridiculous* doubt – lodged at the back of my mind and refused to be dismissed. Even though I knew the reason for this illogical doubt – that at the beginning of my thought process I had credited Sykes with wisdom when, in fact, it had been schoolgirl cunning – even then that doubt (which in effect was something less than a doubt) remained.

That night at the Beechwood Brook Hotel there was much talk of a double murder in the district. A local celebrity – a man named Page who, from what we heard said, had been more than moderately wealthy – had been butchered along with his mistress at his home on the outskirts of the town.

As he returned to our corner table with his round of drinks, Johnny said, 'It's really got them going, mate.'

'What?'

'This murder. A lance and battle-axe job from what they say at the bar.'

'Sounds more like a joust.' I smiled as I tasted my new

drink. 'Some people . . .' I made a face instead of ending the sentence.

'I wonder.' Johnny resumed his seat and he, too, tasted his beer.

'What?'

'Murder. Maybe we all have a breaking-point.'

I said, 'Some people are born to be murdered.'

'Think so?'

It was a pure arguing point. I'd heard the proposition at some time in the past. It had seemed then (as, indeed, it seemed now) a somewhat wild and over-simplification of cause and effect, but it was worthy of alcoholic discussion.

About two drinks later we'd reached the subject of the previous night: Leah Sykes and her visit to my room. The conversational progression had been smooth and natural but once we touched that subject I felt an unease in Johnny's manner.

I said, 'The subject scares you. Why?'

'They have little to lose.' He pushed his spectacles back into the bridge of his nose. He added, 'Less than we have.'

'We?'

'I'm in it, Tony,' he sighed. 'That's what worries me. After last night . . . it's both of us.'

'All *three* of us,' I smiled.

'Who?'

'Miss Lowther. She was . . .'

'Forget Miss Lowther. She just happened to be handy.'

'Johnny, I don't see why the hell . . .'

'We're drinking buddies, mate.' He smiled sadly. 'Academics – okay pseudo-academics – who booze a lot. That's us. Comic-postcard types.'

'We like each other's company. Is that a crime?'

'No.' The smile became a little more twisted. 'It's not a crime. But – y'know – it gives the little bitches a double target.'

'At you, through me? At me, through you?'

'Something like that.'

'You worry too much.'

'I worry,' he agreed. 'Too much? Let's keep our fingers crossed and hope so.'

Perhaps it was this murder thing everybody was talking about. For whatever reason, Johnny was a somewhat dismal drinking companion that evening. The usual banter – the usual 'in' jokes – did not bespatter the conversation. And as always the less we talked, the more we drank and when Johnny steered Bertha towards her home garage his driving tended towards alcoholic recklessness.

The next morning (Saturday, February 11th) I had a bad mouth and a throbbing head. A gargle, followed by a hot-and-cold shower, cleared away much of the aftermath of the night before and when I went downstairs for breakfast I was (more or less) normal. As was my practice, I called in at the entrance hall to check with my letter-rack before I went for the meal. There was nothing for me, but Johnny was there looking very worried and (or so it seemed) merely hanging around.

'Slightly too much last night,' I remarked.

'Tony.' He caught my arm. 'Is there . . . ? I mean, have you been down before?'

'Here? For my letters?'

He nodded.

'No,' I said. 'The usual thing. I collect any . . .'

'Damn!'

'Something wrong?' I asked.

'No – er . . . no.' And the emphasised negative certainly meant an affirmative. 'It's just that . . . I was expecting a – a letter.'

'The post these days,' I murmured.

'Not – not exactly a letter. More of a package.'

'In that case . . .'

'A – a newspaper. It should be here. It's never been late before.'

I said, 'It'll be here Monday. Tuesday. Someday next week.'

'I just thought . . .' He shook his head slowly. 'Y'know, it might have ended up in with somebody else's mail . . . that they might bring it back.'

'If it has, they will,' I smiled.

As I wandered towards the refectory for breakfast, I pondered upon the wasted talents of a man like Johnny Stirk. He tended towards self-effacement but, little though I knew about the subject, even I was conscious of his passion for his test-tubes and what he was pleased to call his 'firework displays'. Science – science in all its various branches – fascinated him. I recalled how he had once spent a whole evening trying to explain to me the basics of the Theory of Relativity and had been almost angry at my inability to either understand or be concerned that I *didn't* understand. Such a man at a good school would have been a jewel – witness his present agitation at the non-arrival of some scientific magazine he apparently expected – but at The Ridings . . .

God!

Not for the first time I marvelled that we – that any of the teaching staff – tolerated the sheer wastage of what had taken us a small lifetime to learn.

Later that morning I drove to Harrogate; to one of the smaller galleries where an exhibition of Surrealism prints was being shown. It was more of a chore than a pleasure. This multi-marriage of Cubism, Dada, Collage and Constructivism – the so-called Surrealism school – was something I had long tried to understand. I had always failed and that Saturday I failed again. How art can be removed from pictorial reason remains for me a mystery. But as an art master my conscience insisted that I examine the prints with as open a mind as possible in one more attempt to enter into that fantasy dream world of Ernst and Klee, of Picabia and Dali.

Honesty insists that I admit to enjoying a late lunch more than I enjoyed the exhibition. This realisation annoyed me. It was a very irrational annoyance; it was, I think, born of the argument which insisted that as an art master I should at least *understand* every aspect of my chosen profession.

I was in a black mood as I drove back to The Ridings.

Muriel, the maid, met me as I entered the tiled-floored entrance hall and she gave the message that Morley wished to see me in his office.

'Soon,' I grunted.

'He said it was urgent, sir.'

'Did he?'

'*Very* urgent.'

I muttered, 'Everything's "urgent" with that man,' but with my mac still folded over my arm I hurried to see what the latest 'urgency' was.

Johnny was in Morley's office. The impression was that he'd been there for some time. He was in one of the wing-chairs, he was pale-faced, he seemed to be trembling slightly and he gave the impression that at any moment he might break into tears.

Morley sat behind his desk and wore an expression of thunderous outrage.

As I closed the office door he snapped, 'At last!'

'I beg your pardon?' I stared, glanced at Johnny, then returned my attention to Morley.

'We've been waiting for more than an hour, Hemingway.'

'For me?'

'For you.' Morley nodded.

'For what?' I asked tersely.

'Shall we say . . . for this?' He pushed a recently unfolded publication towards me with the tip of a forefinger. He made it look as if he was touching dirt, and that he would require to scrub the finger clean at the first opportunity. He added, 'Or for some form of explanation?'

I walked to the desk, picked up the publication and saw it to be a copy of the *Gay News*. Having seen what it was, I dropped it back on to the desk.

I stared at Morley, then said, 'An obvious question springs to mind. Why me?'

'I am a fair-minded man,' he said pompously.

'Good. In that case, tell me what you want.'

'An explanation. An excuse, perhaps.'

'For what?'

'That.' He pointed the forefinger at the offending journal. 'You know what it is, of course.'

'I've heard of it.'

'Read it?'

'No . . . why should I?'

From behind me, Johnny groaned, 'I'm sorry, Tony. God . . . I'm so *sorry*.'

'Your friend Stirk is sorry,' mocked Morley.

I turned my back on the pompous fool and spoke directly to Johnny.

I said, 'Are you – er – gay, Johnny?'

He nodded.

'This morning something was missing from your post. This *Gay News* thing?'

'I – I arrange for it to be sent,' he whispered.

I turned to face Morley and sneered, 'And, of course, it ended up in some other person's letter slot . . . by mistake. Some shocked little schoolgirl. Shall we say . . . Sykes?'

'Sykes merely did her duty,' said Morley.

'Of course.' I walked to an empty wing-chair, sat down, draped my mac across one knee, then said, 'So, back to that original and obvious question . . . why *me*?'

'Homosexuals require a partner.'

'And I've been nominated?'

'Rather more than "nominated".' His mouth twisted. 'This – er – this great friendship you have with Stirk. Unnatural, wouldn't you say?'

'We drink together,' I said flatly.

'And more.'

Strangely my anger was not a boiling, erupting thing. Instead, it was cold. Permafrost cold; hard and unyielding. Somehow I knew that this was the final clash between Morley and myself; that for all practical purposes Johnny and I were finished at The Ridings. The fact is, it was a relief. No more idiot ideas thought up by Morley in an attempt to impress wealthy parents. No more addle-brained daughters to be taken by the hand and guided through basics any ten-year-old child should know. Freedom. Freedom to think . . . and above all else, freedom to speak and freedom to express an opinion.

I said, 'Morley, you're a fool.'

'Insults won't . . .'

'I'm not insulting you. I'm stating a fact. That Sykes bitch has you by the nose and she's leading you up her own chosen path, and you haven't even the brains to know it.'

'It was her duty to bring to my notice . . .'

'It was *not* her duty to filch that publication from Johnny's letter-rack. Tampering with Her Majesty's mail. That's the official description . . . and it's illegal.'

'She found it in her . . .'

'The hell she "found" it! She sought it. Deliberately.'

'She must have known where to look,' he sneered.

'Probably.'

'In that case . . .'

'In that case it makes Johnny a reader of the *Gay News*. Not a thing more.'

'Hemingway, he's already admitted . . .'

'In that case *he*'s a fool. For myself – and as far as you're concerned – I wouldn't admit to having two arms and two legs.'

From his chair Johnny moaned, 'Tony, I'm sorry. I should have told you. I should have ...'

'Shut up,' I snapped. Then I continued my attack on Morley. I said, 'Thursday night. Up in the flat. Sykes tried to ...'

'I know.' Morley nodded slowly. 'Stirk's told me all about it. I must presume she had had some sort of encouragement.'

I said, 'You really are an unmitigated fool, Morley. Miss Lowther was there, too. She heard what was said. She came with ...'

'I've questioned Miss Lowther,' he interrupted softly.

'In that case ...'

'She gives it as her considered opinion that, had *she* not been present, you would have committed a sexual assault upon the girl Sykes. That even with her there you threatened such an assault.'

'Oh, my God!' I raised my eyes to the ceiling in disgust.

Johnny breathed, 'He has us, Tony. It's no good . . .'

'Like hell he has us!' I stabbed a finger at the smirking Morley and snapped, 'You – you brainless idiot – you should make up your mind. Am I a queer or am I *not* a queer? Am I capable of raping a schoolgirl or am I *not* capable of raping a schoolgirl? Homosexual or heterosexual? Which?'

Morley drawled, 'Hemingway, I may not be an expert on matters of perversion, but – er – bisexuality?'

It stopped me in my tirade.

He allowed a smile to touch his lips and said, 'What little I know of sexual psychology. But . . . being attracted by members of *both* sexes?'

'You're mad,' I whispered.

'Not unknown,' he murmured.

'Yes. Unknown ... as far as *I'm* concerned.'

He hesitated then, very deliberately – very solemnly as if aiming each word at an exposed nerve-end – he said, 'Your wife didn't think so.'

I gazed at him. I disbelieved him . . . utterly and absolutely.

With equal care – with equal deliberation – he said, 'She sought advice. From me. I understand that – in a more roundabout way – she sought advice from members of the sixth form.'

'You're a damn liar,' I croaked.

'No.' He shook his head. 'That you see fit to dismiss the truth does not destroy the truth, Hemingway.' He paused, then asked, 'Why do you think she committed suicide?'

'You.' I suddenly realised that my finger was still pointing at him. I dropped my hand and said, 'You . . . you bastard. And the foul-minded little cows from the sixth form. They're all . . .'

'Tony!' It wasn't quite a scream. Not quite a scream. And yet it had the hysterical quality of a scream. High-pitched and terrified. A voice almost out of control. A voice carrying far more torment than it could ever hold. I turned and saw Johnny sitting bolt upright in the chair. White-faced, wild-eyed and with his hands gripping then releasing the arms of the chair in a steady rhythmic fight to stave off complete collapse. From the back of his throat he rasped. 'Listen to me, Tony. Listen to me. Not him. Not Morley. To *me* . . . because I wouldn't lie to you.'

I nodded. I listened. I believed . . . and my world fell about around my ears.

That Hannah – *my* Hannah – should have carried such a burden of secret doubt. That in desperation she should have gone to Morley for guidance . . . shared her anguish with Sykes, and other chosen members of the sixth form.

All true. All true.

That – because of what she'd done, because of the questions she'd asked – I had become the most hated person in The Ridings. That my loathing of the sixth formers, and my loathing of Morley, had been nothing – *nothing!* – when placed alongside their loathing of me. That even Johnny had known about this hatred and counter-hatred – and the reason for it – but other than veiled hints hadn't dared to tell me.

All true. All true.

That this foul and festering suspicion – this evil possibility – had grown and magnified until it had assumed the proportions of a certainty. And with the certainty had come the shame. The shame of being my wife. The shame of sharing the secret. The shame of . . . everything. Too much shame to live with.

All true. All true.

All true . . . all true . . . all true . . .

A question. Where does misery end? Where does self-pity take over? Somewhere within that maelstrom of emotion – somewhere within that mind-tearing vortex – misery becomes so great that the sufferer *must* spare some pity for himself. But where?

In the privacy of the flat, I sat on the edge of the bed – still holding my mac folded over one arm – and I fought and slashed away at the whirling thoughts and memories.

I was (I told myself) an academic. I had a disciplined mind. I could (I insisted) stand aside and be objective. This madness – and it *was* a madness – could be tamed. Cause and effect . . . that's all it was. Cause and effect. Viewed calmly, unreason did not exist, reason if sought could be found. The black areas, the grey areas . . . they could be separated and, once separated, they could be understood.

Everybody had been so wrong – so monumentally wrong – and nobody more wrong than myself.

That note. The suicide note. I read it again. I can't

remember taking it from my pocket, but suddenly it was there in my hands and once more I read it.

Words. That's all. Words dragged from a mind demented by shame. Meaningless words, or if not meaningless, only able to suggest a *wrong* meaning. The sixth form? Morley? They had shared her secret and in allowing them to share her secret she had – or so she'd thought – disgraced *me*. She was sorry. She begged forgiveness. But . . . for what? For seeking guidance and, in seeking guidance, playing traitor . . . or so she'd thought.

Then Johnny was with me . . .

Odd. I hadn't noticed his arrival. Just the slight movement of the bed and I'd turned my head . . . and he was there alongside me. Tears flooding down his cheeks. More miserable – more helpless – than any man I'd seen in my life.

'Not your fault,' I muttered.

He nodded, then dropped his face into the cupped palms of his hands and the sobs ripped through his body.

'Not *your* fault,' I repeated hoarsely.

I placed my arm across his shoulders and he came to me like a broken-hearted child, buried his face into my shoulder and wept, while I stroked his hair in an attempt to comfort him.

How long?

Minutes? Hours? A question beyond answer . . . just that gradually I became aware of noise. A lot of noise. The noise of a great commotion . . .

The Fall of the Eighth Domino

The man they called Daft Ned saw the car arrive. He watched from the cover of the laurels and saw Hemingway drive to the rear of 'The Place'. Moving with the agility of those things of nature which he understood so well, he dodged through the evergreens and saw Hemingway leave the garages.

Garages. Motor cars. He hated motor cars; boxes on wheels; prisons on wheels, in which they confined a man until he could be delivered to . . . 'The Place'.

To destroy this hateful building. A huge thing. A massive thing of stone and timber, but to *destroy* it! To revenge himself upon one, as retribution for what he had suffered in another. What matter? They were all the same. All of a kind. All evil and deserving of destruction.

Ah, but how?

Motor cars. Of course . . . *motor cars*.

His thin voice piped a chuckle of glee as the realisation entered his crazy reasoning. Fire! Fire could level a forest . . . he'd seen it with his own eyes. Up on the High Tops where the heather was spongy and thick – indestructible – but not by fire. He'd seen great black scars where the fire had destroyed even the heather. Anything! It could destroy anything. And it was good to watch; the flames, the smoke, the explosion of sparks, when something collapsed into the burning centre. Good to watch. Exciting. And it destroyed. It destroyed *everything*.

And garages meant motor cars. And motor cars meant petrol. And petrol meant to kill this, 'The Place'.

Tallboy said, 'He's making for the school.'

'Which school?'

Lennox's breath rasped at the back of his throat as he asked the question. He was an unfit man carrying a lot of weight but, despite this, he'd refused any suggestion from the younger Tallboy that they ease their pace as they followed the tracks in the snow.

'The Ridings . . . a place for young ladies.'

'That's *all* we bloody need,' gasped Lennox.

Nevertheless, they leaned their bodies forward a little

more, pumped their arms a little faster and increased their stride.

This was bobbying; an aspect of bobbying never touched upon at any police college, because this brand of bobbying was beyond simulation. It's common name was 'experience' and it couldn't be found within the covers of any textbook. It couldn't even be taught. It came with age, it came with worry, it came with an increasing awareness of responsibility . . . and sometimes, despite these things, it didn't come at all. Rank had damn all to do with it. Nor, come to that, had I.Q. levels. It was (as it were) a cup into which might be caught and retained the essence of all past incidents and some men (and some women) had that cup . . . and some hadn't.

Tallboy's cup was not yet as full as that carried by Lennox, therefore Tallboy's concentration was centred upon the quarry. To reach this man they called Daft Ned before the shotgun could leave another tattered corpse; before a crazy man could reach a school filled with kids and teenagers; before more murders or maiming were committed.

But Lennox . . .

Lennox also looked ahead. He, too, kept the capture of the madman in the forefront of his mind, but in addition he looked both behind and farther ahead. Constable Braithwaite . . . an unarmed police officer alone and, supposing Daft Ned had doubled back on his tracks and by this time was making for the hut he called home, what then? Or, come to that, Blayde . . . again an unarmed copper with a homicidal maniac on the loose – and supposing *he* bumped into this Daft Ned character? They – Lennox and Tallboy – were comparatively safe. They were where Daft Ned had *been*. But where was he *now*? Pointing a gun at Braithwaite? Pointing a gun at Blayde? Or, perhaps, pointing a gun at some schoolgirl?

And supposing he was already at this school . . . what then?

Not a siege. Nobody can play siege games with a madman.

Something sudden. Something unexpected. Something . . .

Assuming they were in time.

'How much farther to this damn school?' gasped Lennox.

'Not much more than half a mile.'

'Chris.' Lennox fought for breath. 'D'you ever pray?'

'I am now,' panted Tallboy.

'Hard, old son. As hard as you ever have. That we get there in time.'

At The Ridings it was Saturday afternoon prep period; a weekly ritual which gathered the pupils into their various prep rooms under the supervision of those of the teaching staff on duty, while the menials prepared the Saturday dinner, flicked the last of the dust from the furniture or busied themselves checking that the dormitories and cloakrooms were ready for the evening inspection.

Those not thus employed were either in the staff lounge or relaxing in their own bedrooms.

With the exception of Sunday mornings (when pupils and teaching staff were required to attend the local church more than five miles away for Communion) this late Saturday afternoon period was the quietest time of the week. In summer, when the sun blazed down from a cloudless sky, an occasional figure might have been seen strolling across the sheep-cropped grass alongside the playing fields, but in February? Those who had the freedom to relax stayed indoors and gave thanks for the invention of central heating.

Which, in turn, meant that nobody saw the figure dart from the shelter of the laurels, scurry along the side of the ivy-covered boundary wall and duck into the row of garages which had been converted from what had once been stables.

Lennox, quite sincerely, thought he was running himself to death. His breathing was laboured to a degree which made it painful each time he inhaled; his lungs were demanding far more oxygen than he was able to gulp in and, consequently, his exhalations were short-lived jerky raspings of used air through his opened mouth. And it was a vicious circle; the demand of his lungs for more oxygen denied him the time needed to empty his lungs in order to *take in* more oxygen . . . which in turn made matters worse. He'd already ripped his tie loose, but he still felt to be choking and the agony in his chest increased with every stride.

His legs, too. They ached with the strain of stumbling forward through the snow and mud at a non-stop, never-slowing pace. His head throbbed and, occasionally, a whirl of grey swam before his vision and he had to concentrate upon the shoulders of Tallboy in order to prevent himself from staggering around in a zizag drunken path.

And yet . . .

He was running himself to death, but it didn't matter. One part of his mind busied itself with possible problems when (*if!*) they caught up with the man called Daft Ned. But another part of his mind seemed to settle down – as if in the comfort of cushions – and view the possibility of death as rather a nice thing. A state of affairs to be applauded. Almost a relief.

These last few months he'd tasted loneliness. A strange and terrible rootlessness. Previously a man of great good humour, of almost limitless compassion, he was now choked by a never-ending sense of depression. Something which couldn't be shrugged off. A black, almost suicidal mood, which despite the top-dressing of verbal normality under which he fought to hide it remained part of him.

Therefore, if he *was* running himself to death . . .

Ahead of him Tallboy gasped, 'There. That's the boundary fence of the school.'

But Lennox was unable to answer.

The maths master slipped out of the middle-school prep

room, took two or three steps towards the staff toilets, then stopped. His nose twitched and a puzzled frown lined his forehead.

He muttered, 'What on earth . . . Petrol!'

He quickened his stride and made towards the side door – towards where the smell of petrol seemed strongest – and, as he turned a corner, he saw the tramplike figure moving crabwise around a bend in the stairs. A strange figure. Something from that last second before awakening from a nightmare. A crooked caricature of a man, bent under the weight of two jerry-cans – one in each hand – with a shotgun tucked awkwardly under one arm.

And the petrol was everywhere. It had soaked into the carpet and squelched underfoot. It ran along the polished surface of the stairs; dripping down from one step to the next. It had even been splashed on to the walls.

The maths master gasped, 'Oh, my God!' then turned and raced towards the main entrance hall.

Behind him he heard the clatter of an empty jerry-can, as it was thrown aside and tumbled down the stairs.

The maths master yelled as he ran and doors opened and pupils and staff stared. He reached the entrance hall dived for the glass-fronted fire alarm button and, as he punched a fist through the glass, a great roar of flame seemed to start from somewhere over his head, raced to ground level, then licked along the corridor from the side stairs.

Then all hell was let loose . . .

'Great hell, he's fired the place!'

They were in the grounds, within shouting distance of the building itself, when the school itself seemed to explode. Three first-floor windows spewed their glass and frames outwards and from the openings in the stonework globules of flame mushroomed, then steadied themselves into a hungry licking and blackening of the side of the building.

Tallboy yelled the words, then sprinted for the shallow steps leading to the main entrance. Lennox tottered after him, like a man sick to the point of collapse.

Tallboy reached the entrance as pupils and staff surged out of the building. He bulled his way up the steps and through the door saw a gowned man nursing a bleeding fist and grabbed him by the elbow.

'Where is he?' snapped Tallboy.

'Who?' The maths master was dazed. He stared uncomprehendingly, and held his injured hand to his body.

'This fire,' bawled Tallboy. 'Who started it?'

'Who – who are you? What . . .'

'Police. *Who started this damn fire?*'

'He's – he's upstairs. He's . . .'

'Fire service, ambulance and police.'

'Eh?'

'For Christ's sake! Pull yourself together. 999, *now*. All the services, as soon as possible.'

'It's – it's Mr Morley's respon . . .'

'It's *your* responsibility,' shouted Tallboy. He was suddenly caught by the edge of the tide of people rushing for the door. He dragged himself clear, caught the maths master by the lapels and slammed him against the wall. From a distance of not more than twelve inches, he roared, 'Grab yourself. You're a grown man. Get that telephone call made. Now . . . where upstairs?'

'Where? What . . .'

'The man, you blithering idiot. The man who set fire to this place.'

'Up-upstairs.' The maths master pointed to the sweeping main staircase. 'Up there. He'll – he'll be towards the back. I saw him . . .'

'Thanks.'

'Chris.'

Tallboy stopped his dash for the stairs before it had

started. He turned at the sound of his name and saw Lennox leaning with his back to the wall, gulping air and struggling to regain some sort of control over his limbs.

'Lenny, you shouldn't be . . .'

Lennox seemed to gather every last gram of his remaining strength, pushed himself from the wall and, in a single movement, pivoted on the ball of one foot and scythed his extended arm. The forearm caught Tallboy flush in the mouth and sent him spinning to the tiled floor.

'Sit on him.' Lennox panted the words to the dumbfounded maths master. 'Anything . . . just keep him here. He has a good lass for a wife.'

Then – and still at a staggering run – Lennox headed for the main staircase.

Lucidity. Sanity. An awareness of *in*sanity. That, too, is part of being mad. To surface for a few minutes – and no longer than minutes – and be a part of the normal world, but for those few minutes, to *know*.

The truly damned are thus tormented. For great stretches of their life they live with ghosts and mirages of their own making and, throughout those stretches, they are if not happy, at least unaware. But then – periodically – they are allowed a glimpse. Some damaged pawl of their brain comes into play and, until it once more slips from its place, they are sane and because they are sane they are aware of their usual state of madness.

The man they called Daft Ned gazed around him and winced as the heat from nearby blazing bedclothes wafted in his direction. He felt the warming steel of the shotgun barrels against his hands. He was surrounded by fire – fire and smoke – and his temporarily sane mind back-tracked from the fire, to the reason for the fire, to the reason for running and, finally, to a mutilated body which he'd left sprawling in the hut in which he lived.

And, as if questioning some dark angel into whose care he had committed his conscience, he said, 'Why? In God's name *why*? What makes me so sick? What makes me do these things?'

'Ned.'

He turned and saw Lennox standing inside the dormitory, framed against the newly ignited door-surround. The fat detective's clothes smouldered where the fire had touched them, and a smear of soot marked one of the loose-skinned cheeks.

'I . . .' Ned swallowed then, almost choking on his self-disgust, he said, 'I did this.'

'Aye.' Lennox nodded solemnly. 'We know.'

'There's – there's a man . . .' Ned moved the shotgun in a hopeless, helpless gesture.

'We know that, too,' said Lennox sombrely.

'Why?' Ned's face twisted as the pain of realisation hit home.

'I think you know the answer, old son.'

'It's – it's not . . .' He was unable to find the right words.

'I know. It's not you. Not the real "you".'

'It isn't . . . I swear.'

Lennox stepped closer.

'I swear,' repeated Ned.

'Time was . . .' Lennox sighed. 'I wouldn't have believed you.'

'But now?' There was pleading in the question.

'Now.' Lennox nodded slowly.

'Who – who are you?'

'Police. Lennox. Detective Superintendent Lennox.' The stout man paused, then said, 'I'm sorry, old son.'

'Them,' said Ned sadly.

'I reckon you could call us that,' agreed Lennox

The scene was, perhaps, beyond the comprehension of any normal man. Around them mattresses and bedclothes burned and smouldered. The window drapes had long been ashes. The superficial blaze from the ignited petrol had quietened to a lesser, but gradually increasing, fire as the woodwork caught alight. The smoke caught at their throats and prickled their eyes. Sweat from the slow build-up of heat shone on the skin of their faces.

And yet there seemed to be no immediate hurry. There was a gentle but mutual disregard of whatever danger they were in.

Lennox put out a hand and took the shotgun. Ned made no attempt to prevent the move.

Ned said, 'They'll put me away again.' He made it a statement, not a question.

'I reckon,' agreed Lennox gently.

'In a madhouse?'

Lennox nodded.

'Not . . . *me*.' Ned scowled concentration as he dropped his chin on to his chest. He muttered, 'Sir . . . I like dogs. All animals. But I like dogs.'

'Cats for me,' said Lennox quietly. 'My missus liked cats.'

'Mad dogs.' He raised his eyes and stammered. 'Y'know . . .'

'Aye.' It was gentle, understanding agreement.

'Them places . . .' Ned searched for a sane argument. 'They – they don't *cure* you. Quieten you . . . that's all. And – and electric shocks. That makes you forget. For a while. Some of the things. Then – then you remember . . . and you *know*.'

'Steady, old son,' murmured Lennox.

'You – you know what you *are*,' continued Ned. 'Then they need drugs to make you forget. So . . . you go nowhere.'

'They try,' said Lennox.

'This.' Ned glanced at the build-up of flames which surrounded them. 'I do things like this. I kill people. Just . . . people.'

'They'll cure you.' But it was what it sounded like. An empty promise.

'But – but not to dogs.' There was a terrible, cold sanity in the words. 'They don't put mad dogs together. That's cruel. They'd – they'd kill each other. Make each other *more* mad. Like people. They don't kill each other – they're not allowed – but the other thing.'

'Son, I'm sorry,' sighed Lennox.

Ned looked the stout detective in the eyes and very calmly said, 'Leave me here . . . please.'

Lennox shook his head.

'If . . .' Ned took a deep breath. 'If I was a dog.'

'I know,' sympathised Lennox.

'*Then* you'd leave me here.'

'No.'

'But quicker.'

'Quicker,' agreed Lennox hoarsely.

'I wish . . .' The two men looked at each other. They spoke to each other with their eyes. Pleading and understanding. Affirming and appreciating. Then Ned said, 'Sir, if I'm to be mad – and I know I *am* to be mad – I wish I was a dog.'

Then he turned his back on Lennox and his narrow shoulders squared and the long, dank hair dropped below his collar as he held his head in a last gesture of pride.

Lennox's face was quite expressionless as he thumbed back the hammers of the twelve-bore. As his fingers curled around the triggers. As he raised the gun until the twin muzzles rested at the nape of Ned's neck.

'LENNY!'

But Tallboy's scream was almost lost in the roar of the explosion and the headless corpse pitched forward and sprawled across one of the burning beds.

'Lenny . . . for Christ's sake!'

Lennox turned, smiled sadly, then held out the shotgun.

'What the hell?' Tallboy took the gun. It was an automatic

gesture. It meant nothing . . . a trained copper going through the required movements. He gaped at Lennox and gasped, 'Lenny – in God's name . . . it wasn't even self-defence.'

'It wasn't meant to be,' said Lennox gently.

'In that case, why the . . . ?'

'Murder,' said Lennox. 'Leave him for some fireman to find, Chris. We'll get out of here . . . then you can do what you have to do. To you it's murder. It *has* to be.'

'And to *you*?'

'He loved dogs.' Lennox smiled. 'And . . . my wife loved cats. Just the three of us. *We* understand.'

NINE

I could still fix the day and the date. I could fix the time to within a few minutes and I could fix the place.

But on that Saturday – mid-afternoon on Saturday, February 18th, three weeks almost to the hour since Hannah had killed herself – the anger and the stupidity, the urge for revenge and the immediate heartbreak, had melted with the [illegible]ow of that blizzard-swept day when they lowered the coffin.

It was not yet spring. Not by a long way. And the hills [illegible] the Nidd Valley still funnelled a biting wind across the [illegible]metery slope.

And yet . . .

The mound of earth had settled. Soon there would be a [illegible]adstone and a surround, and her name etched out in gold [illegible]af. Then the bird-droppings. Then (perhaps) a gradual [illegible]ing of the stone and the surround as 'dust' really *did* return to 'dust'. And after that – when her parents had joined her in the earth . . . what then?

The Nidd would still be there. And the valley; the slopes, the dry-stone walls, perhaps even the chapel.

And as for Hannah. A mere name. Then, not even that, because eternity is all-devouring. She'd be no less dead and no more dead. Her gesture – the taking of her own life – a pointless stupidity.

Harry's voice said, 'At least *she's* at rest.'

I turned. I hadn't heard him arrive; this tall sombre man; this father-in-law of mine.

He said, 'It's a habit. I usually take a walk . . . to talk to her.' He paused, then said, 'I read about the school.'

'It's finished,' I said bluntly. 'Bad publicity. The fire. The policeman who murdered the fire-raiser. Other things. Very bad publicity. And Morley was a fool . . . he was grossly under-insured.'

'Nobody was killed . . . fortunately.'

'Only the man who fired the place.'

'I'm glad.' He glanced at the mound of earth. 'I'm glad she was out of it in time.'

We stared at the grave in silence for a moment, then, for no obvious reason, I said, 'I – er – I was ready to kill Morley.'

'Morley?' He sounded startled.

'Things I thought,' I said vaguely.

He looked at me, and said, 'She wrote. Morley was friend.'

'It's possible,' I muttered.

'Tony . . .' He seemed to have difficulty in finding the words. He rubbed his jaw and said, 'Her mother – y'k she doesn't understand things.'

'She doesn't like me.' I said what *he* wanted to sa

'It boils down to that.' Then, almost apologetically. 'F can't help what they are.'

'No.'

His eyes moved to the grave once more and he murmured, 'Poor Hannah.'

I tried to explain. I said, 'It wasn't her fault. It wasn't *anybody's* fault. Nobody knew . . . even *I* didn't know.'

Still staring at the grave he said, 'I think *I* knew,' and it was a soft, sad statement.

I left him there. Parting words would have been a little silly; we weren't going to see each other again and we both knew it. I climbed the slope, past the chapel and to the road where Johnny was waiting in Bertha.

Some day – somewhere – some school is going to need a B.A. and a B.Sc . . . somewhere.